CW01186000

DEAD END

BARBARA BIERACH

authorHOUSE

AuthorHouse™ UK
1663 Liberty Drive
Bloomington, IN 47403 USA
www.authorhouse.co.uk
Phone: UK TFN: 0800 0148641 (Toll Free inside the UK)
UK Local: (02) 0369 56322 (+44 20 3695 6322 from outside the UK)

© 2023 Barbara Bierach. All rights reserved.

No part of this book may be reproduced, stored in a retrieval system, or transmitted by any means without the written permission of the author.

Published by AuthorHouse 09/06/2023

ISBN: 979-8-8230-8420-8 (sc)
ISBN: 979-8-8230-8421-5 (hc)
ISBN: 979-8-8230-8419-2 (e)

Cover illustration: Holger Windfuhr
Literary agent: Velmont Media

Print information available on the last page.

Any people depicted in stock imagery provided by Getty Images are models, and such images are being used for illustrative purposes only. Certain stock imagery © Getty Images.

This book is printed on acid-free paper.

Because of the dynamic nature of the Internet, any web addresses or links contained in this book may have changed since publication and may no longer be valid. The views expressed in this work are solely those of the author and do not necessarily reflect the views of the publisher, and the publisher hereby disclaims any responsibility for them.

In memoriam of Audrey and Timothy,
One a born mother, the other a born storyteller.

"We ought to have as great a regard for religion as we can, so as to keep it out of as many things as possible."

Sean O´Casey: "The Plough and the Stars"

CHAPTER 1
The Barn

October 1964

She squinted. With craned neck she searched the bales of hay stacked high up to the barn ceiling. "Dixie, where are you?" In the dim light the cats were gliding by like shadows. Only Ginger, a fiery red, fat tomcat, didn't bother to hide, but stayed perched serenely up in the beams. With green eyes he stared down on her, almost mocking.

"You can laugh!", she called up to him, "there's no danger to you, even though you keep making the new kittens!". No sign of Dixie though, maybe she'd ducked into the stables to birth and hide her babies. The cat knew from sad experience that it would lose its kittens if the humans found them.

Her thick unruly copper-coloured hair elaborately twisted into a bun low at the nape of her neck. The hair clips constantly threatened to jump out and release its wild splendour. Knowing her mother was resentful of this unladylike hair, she nervously tucked a cheeky strand behind her ear.

It was Saturday, but she was wearing her best dress, which was usually reserved for going to church on Sundays. Visitors were due today and her mother had insisted that she'd dress up. But because the yard was a muddy puddle from the autumn rains, her slender legs under the wide-hanging petticoats stuck in her old, green, dirt-smeared wellingtons.

Before afternoon tea she had rushed from the big house to the barn to look for her beloved, heavily pregnant Dixie. Darn it! She really couldn't see much in the twilight. Cautiously she climbed a ladder leaning against the intermediate beam of the hay shed and beckoned:

"Dixie, Dixie, Dixie... Where are you, my little one?" Still, she wasn't sure if she even wanted to find Dixie and her babies. If she did, she would have to pack the little bodies in an old hessian sack, together with a heavy stone and throw the package into the sea from the pier. The thought made her shudder.

In the dim late afternoon light, she didn't notice that the barn door was pushed open a little further. Hence, she didn't notice him until he stood at the bottom rung of the ladder, staring up at her legs. She felt his gaze though, looked down and involuntarily gathered her skirt to protect the vista of her legs.

"Hello. I didn't know you were here already!"

"Well, don't you want to come down? Tea will surely be served soon."

He deepens his voice on purpose, she thought. To appear more honest, serious and older. Small wonder in his job! Determined, she turned back to the ladder and descended into the barn. Standing in front of him, his already extending belly in the black shirt was only inches away from her chest. He was ten years older than her and a good head taller.

When her eyes met his, she saw that strange smile in them, the one that he seemed to reserve for her whenever he came for a visit. As if he knew something about her that she herself hadn't even found out yet. She stepped back to avoid his breath. The proximity to that man felt uncomfortable. She was about to turn back to the house, when he came even closer and pushed her hard in the chest. The girl staggered backwards and landed on a bale of hay that one of the farmhands must have pulled down for the evening feed of the cattle. Before she could catch herself, he was already on top of her, one hand under her skirt, his breath hot on the back of her neck.

"No, please don't!" she whispered, as he yanked her knickers off her buttocks.

"You say no? To me?" He was almost laughing.

She pressed her legs together and considered screaming. But whom would they believe? Wouldn't they all think she had hit on him and then got scared when things got serious? He made the decision for her:

"If you let out a peep, I'll tell the whole village how you threw yourself at me, you wee bitch!" All she saw then were her mother's accusing eyes.

As his abdomen punched rhythmically into hers, she stared at the barn ceiling, into the twilight. God is up there, they said, she thought, why doesn't he prevent something like this? But there was only the cat up there.

Now he grunted like the boar in the pigsty when he mounted the sows. She felt nauseous. Outside, a crow was screaming like it was fighting for its life. It will be dark soon. It's tea time, they must be waiting for him in the house!

When he was done, he got up, grabbed a loose bundle of hay, wiped himself off, and pulled up his pants. His rubbed his mouth roughly with the back of his hand, as if to get rid of something disgusting:

"No one will believe you. But if you do say a word, I'll make you and your life utterly miserable!' Then he left, after all, he was expected for tea over at the house.

When she sat up, blood ran down her chin and down the inside of her thigh, she had bitten her lower lip.

Ginger was still sitting on his beam. Grinning.

CHAPTER 2

Armstrong House

March 2005

Emma Woods stood at her kitchen window, staring out at the early morning rain. Almost seven thirty, but still not quite light. Across the street in Doorly Park, the terraced houses were narrow, row by row, each door painted a different colour. A rainbow of good cheer, but the sky above was still like molten lead, raining grey threads. Another dark, damp day. Winter just didn't want to end at all in the Irish Northwest this year.

There were already some lights appearing in the windows: Sligo was preparing for another working day. Emma's kettle was steaming, the water for her tea would soon be boiling. And I always thought the weather in New York was lousy – blizzards in winter and hot and humid in summer – but I didn't know Sligo then. Her face broke into a half-grin as she thought back to her childhood in the East End. She still had harboured illusions then, and not just about the weather! Returning to the present and her sober white kitchen, she turned to wet the tea and Stevie said:

"What's there to smile about this morning?" He was 15, and usually only grunted in front of his mother. She probably should be grateful for a sentence uttered voluntarily, especially if it was said before breakfast, even if it came across as subtly aggressive,

"I was just thinking about how stupid I was as a teenager." Emma's words weren't quite out yet when Stevie's face darkened. Oh shit, Emma thought. Now he probably thinks that I'm making fun of him and his adolescent moods! Yet she had been quite honest and had dispensed with her usual irony. But too late, Stevie had already retreated behind his grumpy-leave-me-alone face.

The separation from his father Paul had happened a long time ago, but Steve never completely forgave his mother for destroying his idyllic childhood world. Or that at least what he thought it was. He got up from the table, his chair scraping against the dark blue linoleum and turned to leave:
"I'm going to dad's after school. At least he comes home at a normal time."
Full of regret, Emma looked at her child's broadening back, somehow she still couldn't get used to the fact that her baby was almost a man now. And like one, he wanted the undivided attention of the most important woman in his life to date. But Emma couldn't give that to her son. After all, she'd finally made it into the Irish Police's criminal investigation unit, of the Garda Síochana, three years ago. From the Local Detective Unit in Sligo she now worked on all the serious crimes in the county.

To rise to the heart of the local police force had taken long enough. Like all Irish police officers, she had attended the training college in Templemore and had learned her trade from scratch, but still her colleagues treated her with a seemingly ineradicable distrust. She was and remained "the outsider" because she was born in Ireland as a child of Irish parents, but had grown up in the USA. It wasn't until she was 20 that she returned to Ireland with Sligo-born Paul. She'd met him at the Irish Pub on Maiden Lane in downtown New York City, where she was waitressing on Friday nights. He manned the bar there and, with his thick accent, was the token Irishman in an otherwise all-American place.

Still, even more than 15 years in the old homeland didn't count for much in the eyes of her colleagues. If they didn't know someone from the cradle, the Irish were inherently suspicious – especially in the countryside – and County Sligo was one of the most sparsely populated corners of the Irish Republic, even of Europe. Most colleagues found Emma "somehow American", which for many was a capital offence – even though Emma could now speak almost as broad a dialect as the fattest potato farmer in the district.

Only because they could not ignore her performance, she was reluctantly accepted. But for all her success, Emma remained difficult to read for most of her colleagues. Her appearance didn't help her either: Emma was tall, blessed with long legs and dark blonde curls and, above all, was still slim. She was better looking than the average woman her age, more ambitious and obviously not trying to please people with an endless stream of chitchat was only half the of the problem. From the point of view of her peers and the majority of people in Sligo, as a Protestant, she belonged to the wrong religion – and to top that off she had overly liberal views. Separated from her husband… single mother… You just didn't get that with proper Irish folks in Sligo.

Paul, on the other hand, remained everyone's best friend despite the divorce, and nobody wanted to hear about his binge drinking and the aggressions Emma had suffered during their marriage. Allegedly, Emma, his ambitious, "American" wife, who was never seen at church, was to blame for the failure of their union. Neither was Paul seen at the altar, by the way, but for him it was accepted. He was busy, after all. Or something.

To this day Emma had only a handful of friends in Sligo, but Paul's Seeds & Household Store on Finisklin Road was always crowded, although many customers obviously just came in to chat with him. He regularly locked up this shop at five o'clock and returned to his flat near Sligo General Hospital, not far from the Grammar School where Stevie attended, while Emma often sat in the Pearse Road police station until late and wrote reports. So it was hardly surprising that Stevie enjoyed spending late afternoons with his jovial dad...

The ringing of the phone snapped Emma out of her motherly self-doubts. The display said 'pain in the butt' – hence it was Aidan O'Leary, her always cheerful partner.

"What's up?"

"Good morning to you too, my dear!" Emma could almost see his wide grin in front of her. But before she could continue, Aidan's voice came out of the phone again: "Armstrong House on John Street. Call from an hysterical cleaning lady. A body, she claims."

By the time Emma pulled up on John Street in her beat-up, sky-blue Peugeot, forensics had already arrived and Aidan was leaning by the front door, chewing on an unlit cigarette, obviously trying to stay out of the technicians' way. He was Emma's opposite in everything – on the shorter side, edgy with curly black hair, dark eyes and a dazzlingly cheeky grin. To make matters worse, he was almost always in a good mood, not even Sligo's rain could change that.

Emma got out of the car, fumbled in the back seat for her umbrella, and then struggled with the opening mechanism. While she was collecting her gear, Aidan was pushing off the wall. He straightened, and sauntered towards her. Why did the guy look so damn good? A police officer didn't have to have model qualities!

"Fecking thing's stuck again!" Emma growled, shaking her umbrella as if she wanted to force it to stop resisting an arrest.

"Oh boss, that mood again this morning?" Aidan teased. "Bad dreams?"

Emma, who was half a head taller than Aidan, straightened up and stared at him wordlessly.

"So – what do we have here?" Aidan fumbled a pad out of the pocket of his worn dark blue jacket and answered his question himself:

"Reverend Dean Charles Armstrong. Not young, not pretty either, looks like a strangulation." Then his tone switched from official to private, and Aidan, grinning, pointed his chewed up fag towards the sky:

"Apparently his reverence has an appointment with his boss! One of your club, well, that's going to be fun!"

"Oh, just leave me alone with religion. I can't stand this Irish obsession with it!"

"Well, you'll have no choice but to deal with it. The dead reverend was Dean of Elphin and Ardagh. Don't you know who this is? You're a Prod – don't you recognise your own people?" Aidan's eyes flashed mischievously again, knowing full well that Emma would rather go to the dentist than into a church.

"What did you say, what's the man's name?

"Charles Armstrong – spelled the same as this house."

"Oh my goodness, a local boy. The gaff is probably even named after him – or after his ancestors," said Emma, letting her gaze wander over the stately building. Next to the narrow-breasted neighbouring houses – only two windows and a door wide – Armstrong House, which was set back from the street and was six windows wide, looked downright noble. The middle part presented in beautiful old Irish stone, flanked on both sides in bright ochre walls. What do the Armstrongs want with so many rooms? Emma wondered, most Irish people lived in small houses.

"Well, let's get to it then!"

At the end of a dark corridor, an oak door led into a surprisingly large study. This would have been a nice room, Emma thought, if the furniture hadn't been so dark and heavy. Two deep leather armchairs, those typical English ones with the buttons in the leather, Chippendale? Side tables, a floor lamp. Two of the four walls were adorned with bookshelves up to the ceiling, plus sliding ladders to get to the top. Overall, the room felt more like one in an English gentlemen's club than the office of an Irish parson – if it wasn't for the heavy cross on the third wall. In the fourth was the door.

An elderly male sat in one of the deep winged chairs, a rather battered abomination made from brown leather. Blueish, his tongue hung out of his mouth, glasses askew, his eyes bulging, his still thick, reddish-grey hair tousled. A kind of bruise circled his thick neck above the even thicker belly like a blue necklace, obviously caused by a cord or a noose. The man had been garrotted or strangled, probably from behind. His head was overstretched backwards, resting on the upholstery of the armchair, the standing lamp next to it still shining, probably since yesterday evening. A signet ring stuck on his pinky. Two glasses with red wine rims stood on the side table, a bottle of Bordeaux next to them still half full. This dead man, an ordinary pastor, whom had he annoyed so badly that their rage would last long enough to tighten the garrotte until his life was gone?

Emma was taking in the situation when the pathologist came back from his coffee break, wearing the typical full-body protective suit of forensic scientists.

"Ah, Emma, good morning."

"Good morning, Doctor McManus. Do you have anything for me yet?"

McManus was a slight male in his 50s, looking even more petite than he naturally was in his white outfit.

"Looks like a strangulation. I can't say much more yet."

"Time of death?"

"More details after the autopsy. Probably between 5:30 and 9pm last night." With his chin he indicated towards the reading lamp next to the armchair. "Must have been at least late afternoon, the light was already on."

With a curt "thank you, Doc," Emma turned to Aidan.

"Signs of a break-in?"

"No, the forensics team didn't find anything of the sort. The victim must have let his attacker or attackers into the house himself."

"Right. And what is that?"

Aidan's gaze followed Emma's to the desk in the room. The drawers were wide open, papers, brochures, bills, pens and files were lying around in wild abandon. "That doesn't quite go with the order in the rest of the room, does it?"

"The desk has apparently been searched, yes. We don't know yet if anything is missing."

"Who found him?" Emma asked. "And where is the wife? The man was married." Obviously, Aidan hadn't yet noticed the modest thin gold ring on Armstrong's left ring finger.

"The neighbour found him, a Mrs. Higgins, who apparently comes regularly to clean."

"And where is that lady now?"

"In the kitchen."

When Emma and Aidan entered the kitchen, Mrs. Higgins was sitting at the kitchen table drinking tea with a female patrol officer.

"... it had to end like this," said Mrs Higgins before she fell silent in the face of Garda in plain clothes. The officer in uniform nodded and withdrew.

"Good morning. I'm Inspector Emma Woods and this is my colleague Sergeant Aidan O'Leary. What had to end like this?"

Mrs. Higgins's rosy cheeks became even redder at these words until they almost matched those of the little rose pattern on her apron. She was rotund and so small that her little feet almost didn't reach from the chair to the kitchen floor. She hadn't strangled a heavy guy like Armstrong. Not even from behind.

"I come to clean, Fridays, ever since the reverend and his wife came back from the missions."

"The missions?" Emma asked.

"The reverend was a missionary with the Chinese and such, with the pagans. Came back home ten years ago. A very great man, the Reverend."

"And you found him this morning?"

"Yes, as I said, I came over to clean, I only live a few houses down the road. I also have a key, the Reverend trusts me, he always says 'Dear Mrs. Higgins, I trust you, you have such honest eyes'... But I didn't need to use the key, the door was open this morning."

"The door was open?"

"No, not like this. It was latched. But it wasn't locked. That's unusual, the reverend always locks everything up at night like he's afraid of a visit from the auld devil himself." Mrs. Higgins looked very pleased with her analysis.

"So first things first," Aidan chimed in, "exactly when did you get here this morning? And did you touch anything?"

"Just before seven, the Armstrongs get up early, as do I!"

"Speaking of the Armstrongs – where is Mrs. Armstrong?" Emma asked.

"In Belfast. With her sister. For shopping, I think."

Emma gave Aidan an almost imperceptible nod to communicate a work order to him: Find the lady! Order her back for an interview!

Aidan continued the questioning, "So the door wasn't locked, and then you came in."

"Yes, I called out for the Reverend, but got no answer. Then I went into the kitchen and, as always, put on the kettle. After all, people need a cup of tea before work can begin."

"And then?"

"Well now, that's when I realized something wasn't right."

"Okay," said Aidan, smiling his most seductive smile, causing Mrs. Higgins to turn pink again. Emma rolled her eyes at Aidan using his dimples like a service weapon.

"Yes, the Reverend was obviously not up yet. Because normally, when I come in the morning, there will already be a mess in the kitchen. Coffee grains, crumbs and such. Out foreign, the Reverend had taken to drinking coffee, but I don't know, I don't like the dark brew..."

"And then?" Emma interrupted, growing impatient.

"Yes, then I went upstairs to the bedroom to see if everything was all right with the reverend. Knocked, but nobody answered. Then I pushed the door handle and saw: The bed is untouched! At first I thought he must be next door..."

"Like next door? Next door in another room?"

'No, next door at Mrs. Morrow's. But a good Christian person shouldn't speak ill of the dead ... and certainly not about the Reverend." This time, Mrs Higgins paled:

"But don't say anything to Mrs Armstrong, will you? Please, garda."

"Who is Mrs. Morrow?"

"That's the neighbour on the other side. She's half the reverend's age and always here, especially when the reverend's wife isn't around and her own husband is at work," Mrs. Higgins' pink mouth gushed. "The reverend and her were obviously good friends, but I would not trust her as far as I could throw her, if you know what I mean."

Meanwhile, Emma had resigned herself to her fate and remained patient:

"No, I don't know what you mean". This time Aidan rolled his eyes.

"When I went back down, I saw a light in the study, the door was half open. And that's where I went in, and there were two wine glasses on the table and stuff. Yes, and there was the Reverend." Mrs. Higgins began to sob.

"Why do you think Mrs Morrow was here? Have you observed anything that makes you think that?"

"No, I'm just saying... She was here all the time."

"Apart from the tea things, did you touch anything else here in the kitchen this morning?", asked Aidan.

"Just the phone to call the guards."

"You really think that was a frustrated lover or a cuckolded husband?" Aidan asked as they stood outside in the rain again. The air was so humid he had trouble lighting his cigarette. Emma didn't even bother to fight the rebellious umbrella again. Let it rain.

"The old man was at least 70. Still a lover at that age? And then he's a clergyman? I am not sure."

"Armstrong is 75, says Higgins. Not sure the reverend would have let a playmate's angry husband in. The door was unlocked, according to Higgins. But otherwise he always secured the house like he was protecting the gold stores of the Central Bank. Have you seen the security locks on the windows? They are state of the art. The man must have been scared of something," said Emma.

Aidan looked back at the house and nodded thoughtfully.

Then Emma's cell phone rang.

"Yes sir, immediately, no problem, sir."

Aidan knew from Emma's tone that it was their boss, Superintendent Liam Murray.

"Well, did the old man summon you for a report?"

'Yes," said Emma curtly, putting the phone away, imitating their boss: "...important man in Sligo. Sensitive case. Don't upset the church... blah blah blah, you know him!"

"Oh dear, the upset could interfere with Murray's playing golf. Or maybe there's a pal of Armstrong's in his club, or the mutts get diarrhoea when someone dies..."

Emma grinned. Murray loved to play golf and when he wasn't swinging a golf club he was busy with his Irish Setters. He wasn't averse to whiskey either. A brilliant investigator with a superb reputation in Phoenix Park, the Gardai headquarters in Dublin, he had transferred back to his old home town of Sligo in his mid-50s in order to devote himself to his golf balls, dogs and liquor bottles in peace and quiet. Any disturbance by criminals he took as personal insult.

"I'll go to the office and hold Murray's hand," Emma said. "You go to see Mrs. Morrow and ask her about dear Charles. We're going to need her fingerprints too, and her husband's. The ones from Mrs Higgins . When you're done with that..."

"... I also ask the other neighbours if they have seen or heard anything. Sure, of course."

"Exactly. And when you're done with that, we need to find the lady of the house. Mrs Armstrong is supposed to be in Belfast. Shopping with her sister."

"Aye, aye, boss!"

February 2004

"Violet!", and then "Violet!" again. Catherine was serving breakfast at the Oak Gardens nursing home in Manchester when she heard Margaret call out. Most of the old people here had dementia and just dozed all day – a result of all the medication. They were supposed to take away the Alzheimer patients' agitation, but they also robbed them of all other emotions. Well, maybe that's a good thing, Catherine thought, as she often did in one of those moments when she couldn't bear her job. She, who had always wished for a real family could not understand that so many people simply dropped off their loved ones somewhere and then never showed up again. She didn't want to imagine what was going on with the elderly: Alone in a strange environment that they have to experience anew every day because their short-term memory had given up and they couldn't remember exactly where they were. Oak Gardens was a good house, specializing in dementia and really trying to make the old folks' last few years as comfortable as possible. Still, the penetrating smell of food, room deodorant, disinfectants, depression and urine in her workplace frazzled Catherine's nerves.

She pushed open the door to Margaret's room, the tiny little old lady was like a ray of hope. Already washed and dressed, she was sitting on her bed like a wrinkled old doll. On her bedside table were the photos of her grandchildren. Judging by the landscapes, a girl was growing up somewhere near the Alps and two blonde boys in Australia – or at least the photos were taken in a petting zoo that featured kangaroos. A few old pictures in black and white were from somewhere in the Irish countryside and from another time. Margaret was completely confused, but at least she still talked to Catherine occasionally, even if it was often just silly stuff.

"Good morning Margaret!"

"Violet!", came the echoed back. Violet was Margaret's favourite word at the moment, she repeated it 100 times a day. The brains of many people with dementia seemed to get bogged down with certain terms or names. Mad King George of England is said to have cried out "Peacock!" in his fits of madness. "Peacock!" The only strange thing was that Margaret always said Violet when Catherine came in to her, it was almost as if Margaret was calling her by that name. Margaret looked her in the eye expectantly.

'I want to go home, Violet, to Linborough House. To Linborough, to Mother'.

"Yes, Margaret, but first it's breakfast." Catherine placed her tray on Margaret's table. "I have delicious tea for you and toast with honey, you like that so much!" Now she just had to get the old lady down from her high hospital bed and make sit down at the small table in her room. At last the two sat facing each other and Catherine poured Margaret tea, with three lumps of sugar, as usual. Margaret looked like a tiny bird and ate little accordingly. But anything sweet still seemed to give her pleasure. Just as Catherine was spreading honey on the almost-cold toast, Margaret reached up and grasped Catherine's thick copper braid. She stroked the hair and said almost tenderly: "Oh, Violet!"

March 2005

Holding a coffee mug in each hand, Emma wondered why every police station in the world had the same bad coffee. At least every station she had ever worked for. You bring perfectly good coffee and first-class milk into a station and yet, as if by magic, this nasty black liquid came out of the machine.

The sign on her boss's door read "Superintendent Liam ray". Liam Murray's "Mur" had been scraped off by some prankster years ago.

"Sir, please open the door, I've got my hands full," Emma called. "Sir!"

Emma's co-worker Patrick McNulty walked by – Catholic to the core and one of Emma's favourite enemies. Short, doughy, with watery blue eyes, colourless hair thinning at the front.

"Well, look who's trying to wind some brownie points with the boss with cheap coffee? Enjoy!"

"Oh, Paddy, that sentence says more about your mindset than about mine. I don't have to suck up here, my work speaks for itself. Which you obviously can't say about yourself. I'm just being nice, but that's something you probably can't imagine."

The door opened abruptly. Murray stood in the scratched frame, glasses pushed high on his bald forehead, spit-coloured eyes blinking short-sightedly.

"What can McNulty not imagine?"

"Patrick McNulty can't imagine anything," said Emma and, carrying the coffee mugs, pushed past her boss into his office. "I'm supposed to be reporting on the Armstrong case and thought I'd bring some coffee. It tastes awful, but at least it's warm on this nasty morning."

McNulty shrugged, said "Morning, boss," and pulled away, Murray slamming the door shut.

"Well Emma, let's get started then. What happened at Armstrong House?"

"Why is the gaff called Armstrong House?"

'Well, that's no coincidence, when Charles Armstrong became Dean at St. John's Cathedral he had the half-ruined vicarage restored. It was pretty run down and needed either demolition or renovation. He somehow raised the money for it, and in gratitude the community renamed it Armstrong House. Nobody could have known that he would claim it after his retirement as his new home. I don't know who authorized that in the Church of Ireland, old Armstrong seems well connected, though." Murray took a sip from his coffee mug and grimaced.

"Was well connected, now he only has traces of a wire around his neck."

"Well, I have heard you crack more tasteful jokes, Em. But seriously: strangled?"

"Looks like it. Autopsy is not yet available."

"And what else?"

"The door wasn't locked, although the man was otherwise very security-conscious," according to the cleaning lady who found him. And she's right, there are proper locks on all the windows, too. The desk was ransacked, but we don't yet know what's missing. Aidan is trying to track down the victim's wife, who is said to be shopping with her sister in Belfast. The cleaning lady's chatter suggests that Armstrong might have had an affair with a neighbour. We're also investigating that, but I don't really believe in a jealousy drama."

"So, so old Armstrong's flesh was weak..."

"That's what it sounds like, but I'm still not sure where the gossip ends and reality begins."

"Well, find out. That's what you get paid for. But be mindful, nothing sordid about a so-called girlfriend gets through to the press. It would be a feast for the town gossips and a disaster for the Church if a churchman in Sligo couldn't keep it in his pants. And then to top it all gets killed for it. I don't need a scandal! Otherwise, I want to be in the loop at all times, after all, Armstrong wasn't a nobody in the community. Tomorrow at eleven we'll meet here at headquarters, then I want to know what's going on. Bring Aidan!" And after a tiny pause: "Oh, and take that coffee away with you, or are you trying to to kill me too?"

A listless Emma wandered back to her office. It barely held two battered desks end to end, plus an office chair on each side, and a filing cabinet on either side. The visitor's chair was an old, rickety swivel chair, which would have passed as antique at the time of President Kennedy's assassination, and which squeaked its torment with every movement. A half-dead yucca palm stood on the windowsill with an unclear diagnosis: was it so sad because the sun just never shone in Sligo? That was Aidan's theory, as he was from Cork, which was said to be so much warmer than the Northwest – or was it because Aidan watered the thing way too much – that was Emma's opinion, who never watered any plants herself. Mainly because she didn't have any plants. You shouldn't lock up living things, she thought, and potted plants were one of those. Green things belong outside in the meadows or forests and should take care of themselves, was her opinion, all these decorative vegetables simply had no place in the house.

On Emma's side, the room was chaotic. The drawers in the filing cabinet stood open because they were jammed and wouldn't close now anyway due to all the files spilling out. Her desk was a jumble of old newspapers, printouts of reports that were overdue but only half-finished, interspersed with more or less empty coffee mugs. The wall behind her was decorated with Stevie's drawings. They were many years old, but Emma couldn't part with them and dragged them from office to office.

With her right forearm, Emma carelessly pushed aside the stacks of paper to make room for the newest coffee mug in her collection. Her back started acting up. She couldn't bear standing for long periods of time, nor, by the way, sitting for any length of time. In fact, her back couldn't take much at all. So she swallowed two painkillers on an empty stomach, knowing full well that it would do her as much good as a kick in the stomach.

When there was a knock on the half-open door she made the medication disappear in the paper chaos. It was Miles Munroe, a little pointy-nosed man and the forensics chief whom almost everyone but Emma just called the lab rat.

"Em, do you have a minute?"

"For you always, Miles. Come in! Do you have anything on the Armstrong case yet?"

"Not much, I'm afraid." The visitor's chair whined audibly as Miles settled into it.

"Or not much more than I'm sure you saw for yourself on the scene. There are no signs of a break-in, Armstrong must have let his killer into the house himself. In the office, the desk, glasses, wine bottle and surfaces appear to have been wiped down, we only found a single partial fingerprint next to an electrical power point. We're going to chase that through the system now to see if anything comes up. And we still have to match it with the prints from the cleaning lady and some visitors, maybe it's from a family member or something..."

"Aidan is getting fingerprints from the cleaning lady and the neighbours. For matching. Found anything interesting on the desk?"

"Just the usual paperwork. Notes, letters, bills and so on."

Emma's cell phone rang – Stevie. Because the boy had to put up with so much due to Emma working constantly, weekend shifts or otherwise accumulated overtime, she had made it a habit to always answer the phone when her son wanted something from her.

"Miles, this is my son, I just gotta..."

By the time Emma had finished talking to Stevie, Miles had left. She hadn't even heard him leave, despite the protests from the visitor's chair. Stevie wanted to spend the night with his father today: "You're always in the office until late anyway". Emma could picture him, cell phone to ear, long dark hair falling across his face. It was Friday and Emma was actually thinking of a cosy evening watching TV with her son and having take away pizza. Still, she agreed – so she could stay in the office and finally finish some of those stupid reports. With a sharp crease between her eyes, she turned on her computer.

Emma didn't look up until Aidan stomped in.

"Well, are you comfortable in your mess, Emma?" Aidan collapsed into his chair and slammed his feet on the table. "Man, what a day."

"Did you find this Morrow woman? Fingerprinted? Everything delivered to the lab?"

"Aye aye, ma'm, it's the lab rat's turn."

"Oh come on, poor Miles. Don't call him that..."

"Ah lookit! Since he has such a pointy nose and sticks it in everything to sniff around, lab rat is exactly the right name for him."

"So go on, tell me!"

"Morrow says she was home all night last night, watching TV, with her husband. He can confirm that, she says, but I haven't met him yet. We'll have to go there again tonight."

"And Mrs. Armstrong?"

"I haven't spoken to her either, the lady doesn't own a cell phone, she thinks it's newfangled nonsense. Her sister told me that when I spoke to her on the phone. Haven't told her, though, what it's about, thought we'd talk to the Missus first."

"Yes, and where is the said lady?"

"On the train, back to Sligo."

"And she doesn't know anything?"

"Nah, where from?" Aidan had to grin.

"Christ, you can't just let her run home like that and then she'll be standing in front of a police seal and won't be able to get into her own house!"

"We can pick her up from the train," Aidan said, smiling at Emma. "It arrives at 4:10 pm."

"That's in 25 minutes!"

She should have been mad at Aidan and his nonchalant handling of the situation, instead Emma was glad to turn off the computer again. After all, she hadn't become a police officer to fill in forms and file away folders. At least that's what she told herself. In fact, she was never mad at Aidan, she liked him far too much for that. Because even when push came to shove, he was loyal which was more than you could say about some other colleagues like McNulty. In the end, team spirit was more important than any rules or regulations.

Emma shivered in the spring wind. Sligo's station was a symphony in grey: grey stone building, grey platform, grey track, grey light. From the outside it looked so forbidding that many tourists mistook it for the town's old jail. Soon it was getting dark again, but at least it wasn't raining. Aidan was chewing an unlit cigarette again.

"Are you finally going to quit or not?" Emma asked, pulling the leather jacket tighter around her.

"I've already stopped. This thing isn't lit."

"Hmm. But why do you still have fags if you don't smoke anymore?"

"Oh, I've got a fishing rod too, although I haven't been to Lough Gill in years... And you still have your pills, which you say you're not taking no more."

Emma quickly changed the subject: "Aidan, you are bonkers. Seriously. She's about to get off the train... do you want to tell her here on the platform that her husband is dead? Or do we drive her home and keep her wondering why the garda are picking her up from the station? It's all shite!"

"Oh, boss, tell her right away. Anything else is worse."

"Do we know what the lady looks like?"

"No, but don't worry. I can spot a pastor's wife." Aidan grinned again, and Emma felt like Aidan looked through her. Aidan knew too well that he could tease Emma with that sort of topic. When it came to religion, she simply climbed up on every palm tree that he put in front of her. Emma would have loved to yell at him now, but first of all that wasn't professional at all and secondly the train was pulling in.

Aidan was right. Somehow, Jean Armstrong couldn't be missed. So bolt upright that she seemed taller than her maybe 165 centimetres. Grey hair carefully curled and sprayed into a helmet that miraculously withstood the winds of Ireland's Northwest. Practical shoes, a beige, single-breasted coat covering a huge balcony, strong features, filled with their own importance. Small overnight case on wheels. The only thing that didn't go with this look of a practical, responsible pillar of the Protestant community was the pink lipstick. It looked like it had been painted into her face by someone else's hand. Her sister had probably persuaded her to choose this colour when they went shopping.

"Hello, Jean Armstrong?"

"Yes, and whom do I have the pleasure of meeting, if I may ask?" came a surprisingly young and firm voice.

"I'm Inspector Emma Woods, and this is my colleague Sergeant Aidan O'Leary," Emma said, presenting her badge. "If we might have a word with you? Should we do that right here on the platform or shall we drive you home first?"

"Gardai, well, that's not good, so now is as good a time as any to tell me. So what's happened?"

"Mrs Armstrong, your husband was found dead this morning. We are very sorry for your loss."

Jean put her suitcase down, adjusted her coat and straightened up: "Charles? Found dead? Nonsense! Charles was in excellent health when I boarded the train for Belfast yesterday morning. This must all be a misunderstanding."

"I'm afraid not, Mrs. Armstrong. Your cleaning lady, Mrs. Higgins, found him in his study this morning."

Jean slumped and staggered slightly, Aidan grabbed her elbow to steady her. "Ma'am, let's take you home first, then we'll see."

Stunned, Jean allowed herself to be led to the car.

"No squad car?" she asked, seeing Emma's unimpressive Peugeot.

"No, we thought you definitely wouldn't want to be driven around the neighbourhood in the paddy wagon." Jean nodded wearily. She sat frozen like and only moved again when Aidan broke the police seal on the door of Armstrong House.

Jean, in a trance, turned on the light in the long hallway, then frowned at the grey fingerprinting powder that forensics had left everywhere.

"That was us," Aidan said apologetically, "it had to be done."

"It's okay, I understand."

Jean, still in her buttoned-up beige coat, started moving towards the study, where she stood in the doorway, surveying the room and the clutter around the desk. "Where is my husband?"

"At the morgue."

"Would you like some tea?", Jean asked.

Unusual, thought Emma. Her husband is being cut open by the pathologist and she thinks about tea.

"No thanks, not at the moment, but let's go into the kitchen to talk." The cups from breakfast were still sitting around. Mechanically, Jean put them in the sink and said: "But do please sit down."

Emma briefly and neutrally described Higgins's early morning call and the arrival of the guards.

"Your husband was strangled, Mrs Armstrong. It appears he himself let his murderer in as the door wasn't damaged in any way."

Jean dabbed at her eyes with a Kleenex.

"Mrs. Armstrong – we know you are in shock, but at first glance could you tell us if anything is missing from your husband's office?"

"I'm surprised the cross is still there. It's a valuable carving from our time in Germany."

"And otherwise?"

"I'd have to take a closer look first, but the only thing missing is the radio."

"The radio?" Emma asked.

"Yes, you know, a little transistor radio. Charles always listened to cricket and the rugby and of course the news. He played a lot of rugger as a young man, quite well actually… I don't really care for sports though…" Jean's voice trailed off.

"And that's gone?"

"Yes, that's the only thing I can say at the moment. This radio was always next to his leather armchair, on a small side table."

"Does his desk always look like this?"

"Oh no, for heaven's sake, Charles wouldn't have that. He is always very tidy. Or was very tidy…" she started choking back the tears.

"Any idea why the desk is so messed up today? Could your husband have been looking for something? Or did a burglar ransack it? Was there anything of value in it?"

"No, at most postage stamps. I have no idea what anyone was hoping to find in Charles's desk."

"Did Charles have enemies?" Emma asked.

"Enemies? Charles was far too smart for that. He avoided making enemies. But since Philip died, he hasn't had many friends either."

"Who is Philip?" Emma wanted to know.

"Philip Anderson, the bishop. His former mentor and friend, who got him into the army, back then."

'You mean the Archbishop of Armagh?" Aidan probed.

"Yes, exactly. The head of the Church of Ireland. My husband and Philip have known each other for decades."

However, Emma was interested in something else: "Army? Mrs Higgins talked about pagans and missionary work."

"Oh, that story is easier to tell than saying that Charles spent his life in the British Army as a military chaplain. We were stationed everywhere. Also in Germany for a long time. One of our daughters was born in Herford."

"How many children do you have?"

"Three, well, actually only two daughters now. My son Ron passed away from a tumour a few years ago. His father kept tearing into him, pushing him, no wonder the boy ended up getting sick... I kept begging: leave the lad alone, but it didn't help..."

Now, finally, Jean started to cry. She only played the grieving widow to conform to social conventions, Emma could tell, but the grief for her son was genuine.

"I will have to let the girls know."

"Where are your girls?"

"Jane is in Laragh, here in County Sligo. She's just renovating that old box of a house! The house has actually always been my husband's family's homestead. Alice moved to Australia. To Brisbane. Alice always has had wanderlust, no wonder, when her father dragged us halfway around the world."

"It sounds like you didn't particularly enjoy your stays abroad?"

"Enjoyed? Well, no. China was terrible. If I had known what was to come, I would never have married Charles. The dirt! Such poverty! And only green tea. It was way too hot for me in Malta, let alone China. I simply can't stand the heat. The flies, everywhere! And the winters in Germany can be terribly cold. All I really ever wanted to do was stay in Ireland and take care of my garden. But roses don't grow in extreme heat – and they don't grow in the cold either. But Charles... We always had to move somewhere else. And always taking the children with us. And I always was supposed to live in these miserable barracks. I hated that. I always wanted to live close to Belfast, my home."

Emma thought to herself: Is she serious? Belfast? In the 80s and 90s? A Protestant military chaplain in the British Army settles in Belfast? If that got out, the IRA would have had a bloody feast. You could hardly leave the house safely and had to check the car for explosives every time you did. Any day in the news you would have heard about bomb scares, murdered Royal Ulster Constabulary police officers, shot dead British soldiers and the civilian casualties of the riots. Belfast as a place of longing – I've never heard of anything so daft! Aloud she said: "Then why Sligo?"

'As I said, my husband is from Laragh, not far from here, and Charles has always determined where we live. Besides, Belfast would have been too dangerous for us."

Emma and Aidan met eyes, so they didn't have to ask. The lady wasn't completely insane after all.

"That's enough for today, Mrs. Armstrong," Emma said. "Can we call someone so you don't have to be alone tonight?"

"It's okay, I'll call the girls. Jane will be sure to come and be with me."

"Okay, we'll get in touch with your daughters, too. Just routine. We'll see each other again tomorrow – but if you can think of anything else or notice anything untoward in the house, call me anytime!" With that, she pressed her business card into Jean's hand.

It was dark outside and it was still drizzling. "Come on, I'll drive you home, Aidan."

"Oh, I was hoping we'd go to the pub later. Discuss the case? Tomorrow is Saturday..." Aidan dimples were in action again. Something began to flutter in Emma's stomach, then she thought better of it.

"No, I have to go back to the station. If I don't get back with my report by Monday, Murray will rip me a second one."

"Oh, Murray doesn't even notice if you write reports or not, he's too busy with his golf magazines. And seriously, I'll go over to the Morrows and find out where Madame was last night."

"We can talk about that tomorrow... I'll be at the station at nine, we have an appointment with Murray at eleven. He says he wants to know what's going on by then."

"Shit, another weekend gone," Aidan muttered. "I already have 150 hours of overtime this year."

"Have you ever seen a murder case after which you got the weekend off? Certainly not me."

"This job is starting to get on my nerves, I was planning to go fishing with the boys..."

"Tell me, a grieving widow looks different, doesn't she?" Emma changed the subject.

"Well, they must have been married for decades. The lady obviously had enough of her man years ago."

"Yeah, that's pretty obvious. But did she kill him? Jean would have enough strength, she is fit for her age. But why? And why now and not 20 years ago?"

"Dunno, maybe she found out about the Morrow girl next door?"

"How could she have done that? Belfast to Sligo and back is a couple of hours drive. The murder happened in the early evening..."

Aidan nodded, "Yep, her sister would have noticed a disappearance. I'll call her in the morning and get that alibi straightened out."

"Unless she is involved. So a second confirmation that Jean was in fact in Belfast and staying there would be good."

Aidan made a face. He was almost on his way the inevitable fag in the corner of his mouth, when he turned back to her and planted a smoky kiss on her cheek. Then he disappeared into the night.

Emma rummaged in her bottomless black leather bag for her car keys with a big smile.

Aidan walked down John Street until he stood in front of the Morrows' front door, painted bright blue. Downstairs a window and a door, upstairs two windows, above that the roof with a dormer – typical for lower middle class in Sligo, thought Aidan O'Leary, who himself was a proud working-class kid and knocked resolutely on the door.

He had to knock again before the door finally opened. In the frame stood a man in socks, jeans and a t-shirt. The outfit matched his beer belly. The grey hairs on his chest were thicker than those in the ring of hair around his head.

"Yeah?"

"Hello, my name is Garda Aidan O'Leary. Are you Mr. Morrow?"

"John Morrow, that's right, this is my place. What else do you lot want?"

"Charles Armstrong was found dead this morning and we're talking to all the neighbours."

"I know, you guys were already here and took fingerprints of me and me wife – to exclude us from the 'list of suspects'. I thought that was pretty outrageous ... 'list of suspects' for fucks' sake!"

"May I come in or do you want to discuss the matter here on the street?" Aidan asked.

"Come on in then. But hurry up, there's a match on tonight. Nothing's gonna mess with that."

Aidan was ushered into a narrow living room that was far too crowded. Two thickly upholstered sofas, armchairs, wall unit, giant TV. Plus pillows, candlesticks, coasters, knick-knack – the usual, Aidan thought. Working-class kids who had made it into the ranks of middle class thanks to the Celtic Tiger economic boom and were now trying to make their house look like what they suspected middle-class living looked like. He shuddered.

A blonde woman with smudged makeup sat on the sofa staring at the TV screen with the sound muted. She had obviously been crying. "My wife, Sue," Morrow said, "please have a seat," turning to Aidan – and to her: "The guards again."

Aidan introduced himself and immediately and without further ado: "Mrs. Morrow, are you friends with the Armstrongs?"

"Not with that one from Belfast", came the reply. "She thinks she's better than me. But Charles. He's nice, always has an open ear." The last comment was addressed to her husband, a more or less veiled criticism. John Morrow really didn't look like he liked listening to crying women, even when he was married to them.

"Charles Armstrong was strangled about this time last night and I would like to know where you were at that time?"

"Are you off your trolley? What do we need alibis for? We didn't do anything to the old git!" John was clearly ready for a row.

"Don't get upset. Pure routine. We're asking anyone who has had recent contact with the Armstrongs. And you had that, didn't you?" Aidan asked Sue.

She was crying again. "I still can't believe it. Charles is – was – such a good friend."

"So where were you over there last night, say, between five and nine?"

"I was at evening prayer, like, until seven... and then I was home. John came in ten minutes after me, I cooked. We always have bangers and mash on Thursday nights – one of John's favourite dishes. After that we watched the telly."

"Which church? Can anyone confirm that?"

"St John's of course, just around the corner. Just ask the Reverend Alan, I was in the third row on the left, he would have seen me." Sue gave a sniffle. How could the Garda doubt her?

"And you?" This question went to John.

"I was about my business. I own the taxi and limousine service on Bridge Street. I was there until a little before six. Afterwards here, food and television, like every evening. She already told you." His chin pointed to his wife, who ignored him.

"Can anyone confirm that?"

"My drivers, of course. The day shift ends between five and six and the night drivers take over the cars. I spoke to at least three, even longer to Troy. He was late again and I told him I'd fire him if that happened again. I'll give you his phone number, if you want it."

"What were you watching?"

"On the telly? 'Proof' of course, the best series ever produced in Ireland," said John, grinning. "I love how the show takes on these corrupt fucking papists. Boozed-up assholes, they're going to ruin this country!"

"Did you like the Reverend Armstrong?"

"No, but I'm not alone with that. No one liked him, except my dopey wife, of course. Not even his own old lady. Jean had long since seen through the fella. Always colossally holy on the front, but in reality muck behind. Missionary! Jesus, Mary and Joseph and the wee donkey! I wouldn't be surprised if they kicked that one out of China. Not even the Chinks could stand a hypocrite like that!"

Meanwhile, Sue cried softly into her snotty handkerchief.

"Was he after your wife too?"

"You bet on it!" said John. "But she didn't dare. She knows full well that I would kill her if she cuckolded me. But she's still alive, as you can see."

"You pig!" came a hiss from Sue's corner. She got up and left the room, door slamming. Aidan found himself reaffirmed in his stance that nothing comes after marriage that's worth bothering with and just stared at John in silence.

Morrow grinned: "Do you know that one? An American walks down Antrim Road in Belfast. An IRA soldier with a ski cap over his face and a weapon at the ready comes towards him and yells at him: 'Are you a Catholic or a Protestant?' The American says: 'Neither, I'm a Jew!' The IRA man yells: 'Yes, but are you a Catholic Jew or a Protestant Jew?'"

There was provocation in John's eyes, but Aidan O'Leary wasn't that easy to tease.

"Oh my goodness, that joke really has been around as long as that wee donkey you mentioned," he said dryly. "But seriously. You have an alibi for the period in question?"

John relaxed as he obviously had a worthy opponent in front of him who wasn't easily lured out of his reserve. That restraint was rare in Ireland, where men liked to jump out of their skins and into fisticuffs quickly and thoroughly.

"Listen, I didn't do anything to the old git."

Suddenly John's tone was softening: "Of course he tried to mess around with my old girl. After all, she's 30 years his junior. But probably only out of habit, 20 years ago it would have been a different story. Sue enjoyed the attention. We've been married 15 years, and God knows I'm not the romantic type. A bit of admiration from the old guy made her happy. But it's guaranteed that nothing happened, the old man was already too busy for that."

"What do you mean?"

"I saw him," says John, "the old philanderer. With a blonde who had seen better days. But after all, Charles wasn't a youngster any more either."

"Where did you see Charles Armstrong? And with whom? And when was that?" Aidan suddenly was interested.

"So I stood with my car at Knock airport, waiting for the passengers from London Stansted. I had been booked by some girl with a mighty fine English accent. Could I drive such and such a distinguished gentleman to Classiebawn Castle?"

"The one in Mullaghmore? Belongs to the English royals?"

"Yes, it did once, now belongs to some other rich faggots, but the guy I was driving didn't have that big a wallet. He came with Ryan Air on the cheap. And his luggage wasn't worth mentioning either. He only spoke posh, but I'd say he was about as noble as meself." Aidan and John both had to grin.

"But what does that have to do with Armstrong?" Aidan asked, who, at least on the job, was not a fan of the Irish tendency to tell long stories as convolutely as possible. That part of the national character must have pre-dated the invention of electricity, when you had to somehow get through the long winter nights. With telling yarns and singing. Both endlessly. As if to seal this theory, John scratched his head theatrically.

"Yes, I saw him there. With a blonde, like I said. Went up the driveway and dropped the English toff off in front of Classiebawn Castle and then decided to take the non-existent tip that cad didn't give me to the Pier Head Hotel."

'Yes, I know it. You can see the beach and the fishing boats. And the beer isn't bad either."

"Exactly. And when I come in there, I see two heads stuck together at a table. You know him, I thought. And as the two separate again, I see: That's ol' Armstrong from next door. I was surprised: At that age, in a pub. In public. The man being a pastor and everything."

Aidan couldn't believe it so he asked: "The Reverend Dean Charles Armstrong was sitting in the pub on the pier at Mullaghmore in the company of a blonde whom he apparently knew well?"

"Exactly. Knew pretty closely if you ask me. When he saw me, the two jumped quite apart. Their bad conscience hung in the room like a stench."

"So he saw you too?"

"Yes, the sight of me frightened him quite a bit. Apparently he had other plans that day, the old man, there are rooms for rent at the Pier Hotel." John smiled crookedly.

"When was that?"

"I can tell you that exactly, that was on February 14, Valentine's Day. I didn't feel like going home at all, because no matter what I think up for Sue, she's always disappointed..." A shadow flitted across John's face.

But Aidan really didn't have time for marriage counselling right now: "And who was the woman?"

"I don't know, like I said, a blonde. No spring chicken. I have never laid eyes on her since."

CHAPTER 3

The Good Heart

June 1965

She still couldn't believe it. So this was where they sent her. She remembered her mother's cold eyes and the anger on her brother's face.

"You bitch! You bring shame on us!", he had roared. "On the whole village! You probably didn't even think about my reputation or my position, you stupid whore! Can't you keep your legs together?"

Then he had slapped her. But that was almost better than her mother's cutting voice:

"Enough now! Girl, you will go and only come back when you got rid of this..." – wagging her hands in the direction of her stomach. You will be considerate of your family and do as you are told. Your brother will accompany you."

"But I didn't do anything..." she had tried to explain. But her mother had scolded her:

"Enough! I don't want to hear any of your excuses. Get out of my sight!"

Now she was standing in the meadow behind the mother and child home. Throughout the journey her brother's anger had lay between them like a dark cloud and smothered the words from her. He hadn't spoken to her much on the drive anyway. His only word had be threats:

"You've already ruined your own life, if you drag me into this and ruin my reputation and my career, too, you'll regret it!

I'll make them kick you out at home! Then you can see where you will end up!"

On arrival he had almost thrown her out of the car, same as her small bag. Such was his hurry to get rid of her. Then he had sped off without any further word.

The bees were buzzing in the waist-high grass and the blackbirds were singing as if everything was all right. But in this place, in this house, nothing was right. Every day she heard the girls scream in anguish when they went through labour without the help of a midwife or doctor, only with the assistance of the sisters in Bon Coeur. The sisterhood though did not deserve its name, because there was no question of a good heart. Not even of basic decency. Many of the young women, some of them almost children themselves, died in childbirth – the miserably large cemetery next to the small church a few hundred meters away was a silent witness to the last hours they had spent screaming. She kept hearing them wailing in the delivery room. Soon it would be her turn, and despite the warmth of the day she shivered, and wrapped her arms protectively around her bulging stomach. It wouldn't be long now.

The other girls here were in the same situation as her. Unmarried, pregnant, isolated from their families, beaten, cast out and washed up here in Bon Coeur. a home for unmarried mothers and their children. Except that this facility had nothing to do with a "home" in the true sense. The furnishings were deeply puritanical, sparse, almost as poor as the rations. And the young women had to be on their knees constantly, either to pray or to scrub the floors. Which was not so easy with their big bellies.

When another one of the newborns had died, she didn't understand what happened to their little bodies, they just disappeared. There were rumours that the sisters simply threw the "children of sin", as they called them, into the waste water tank and then tightened the lid back on. And it wasn't just the dead babies that vanished into thin air. Often a car would come, many with English license plates, and then an infant would be selected and taken across the Irish Sea for adoption. At night she would hear their mothers crying themselves to sleep. A sob escaped her throat – what was to become of her? What about the baby?

March 2005

Emma had slept badly. In her dreams men in dark robes had chased her down endless corridors, up stairs and down again. Her pursuers hadn't come any closer, but they hadn't shown any signs of relenting either. It was as if she had to walk down these corridors forever, without rest, because this evil would always be after her. Emma woke up in a sweat, her pulse racing. And the all too familiar pain welled up inside her. Where were her damn pills? She rummaged around in her night stand for her pills. Well finally! With a sip of water from the glass that always stood by her bed, she washed down two.

She felt better immediately. But she didn't have many left of the little helpers. And her GP, Dr. Egerton, was getting hesitant about the prescriptions. Emma could already hear his protests: "Emma, you've been taking this stuff for far too long! Painkillers are not lollipops! Emma, you need to reduce the dose!"

If he knew that the pathologist McManus used to give her a prescription every now and then, too, when she flirted with him a bit ... That stupid Egerton had no idea how her back felt. Her pelvis. Her legs when the pain spread downwards. The rising panic that she could no longer do her job because of the pain.

Her head was pounding. How she wished she could sleep on – deeply and dreamlessly. Instead, Aidan was on her mind. That had been happening a lot lately, and actually way too much. What do you want with a man five years your junior? And a Catholic? Why get involved with love again? The idea of starting over again is just Hollywood madness, Emma told herself. I would just be swapping one problem for another.

Good thing she hadn't gone to the pub with Aidan. Instead he had marched on to the Morrows and she had driven to the office to sit down to do her tiresome reports. When she got home around nine, the breakfast dishes in the kitchen were still untouched. Apparently Stevie hadn't bothered to come home after school, and when he eventually did, he hadn't cleaned up. He had probably rushed off to his father.

Emma had ignored the mess in the kitchen, poured herself a whiskey and collapsed onto the sofa. She let the golden liquid slosh around in her mouth for a long time. Emma loved the taste of peat fire and moor. One whiskey turned into three. Or even four. Was it Oscar Wilde who said alcohol, taken in sufficient quantities, may produce all the effects of drunkenness? In any case, Homer Simpson put it wisely, when he quipped: "alcohol is the cause of and solution to all problems". Then she must have fallen asleep with liquor in her stomach instead of dinner and woke up frozen to the bone in front of the flickering screen at half past two in the morning. Somehow she had crawled into her bed.

Now she struggled out from under the covers, traipsed into the bathroom like a sleepwalker and let the hot shower patter on her aching back. It took a while before she found the strength to throw herself into her gear.

She always wore jeans for her work. Combined with an almost inexhaustible supply of white blouses, boots and her trademark, a black leather jacket. From her point of view, an outfit in which an officer of the law was prepared for just about anything. From an overdosed junkie in a pub toilet, or a beaten housewife to a meeting with the chief of police in Dublin.

After she finished washing up in the kitchen, she left a note for Stevie: "Sorry! I'm in the office!" and put 20 euros on the table. Experience has shown that he would be hanging out with his buddies this Saturday and probably would be going back to his father's place for dinner.

At nine she was standing in the station's kitchen, waiting for the coffee maker to finish bubbling, when she heard familiar footsteps in the hallway. A moment later, Aidan's tousled curls appeared in the doorway.

Emma had to smile. What was it about this guy?

"Obviously you did go to the pub, you don't look exactly as fresh as the first morning dew."

"Oh, come on, no proper good morning and criticism instead? By the way, boss, you look like thin beer with spit yourself."

"Morning, morning, and don't be like that. Would you like some coffee?" Emma asked. Aidan didn't need to know about last night's lonely drinking on the sofa and her wild ideas in the morning. But he had already moved on to the office, leaving behind only a faint scent of aftershave and cigarette smoke.

When she put a coffee mug down in front of him a little later, he lifted his head from the daily newspaper and complained: "The beer is getting worse and worse. Ten years ago it didn't give me such a headache."

"Jaysus, that's not the beer, that's your age. Give me the newspapers. What did the scumbags dig up this time?" Without a word, Aidan handed her the two sheets. The "Irish Independent" was loud as ever with a headline: 'Man of God Murdered!' Along with an official-looking photo of Armstrong which the journalists must have gotten from the Church of Ireland. Emma skimmed the short, rather fluffy text, which revealed that the journalist had spoken to Murray, who had brushed him off. The "Irish Times" didn't know much more either, but at least they had apparently gotten Jean on the phone the evening before. Her comment was similar to Murray's: "My husband's demise is completely incomprehensible to me. He was a family man and a man of the cloth. He had no enemies!"

Well, he must have annoyed someone! Emma pursed her lips, sat down at her desk and booted up the computer. Shortly thereafter, she studied her e-mails.

"Miles obviously worked late yesterday as well. He emailed me the progress of his results." Immediately, Aidan looked a lot more awake.

"So what does the lab rat say?"

Emma took her time with her answer: "Not much. They found a partial finger print next to the power point in the victim's study. Everything else was wiped clean. But the partial impression doesn't help us. There is nothing in the system. The person who left it has not been registered anywhere."

"Well, an innocent lamb doesn't kill people. Maybe a cool pro who just doesn't make mistakes?"

Emma frowned thoughtfully: "Maybe, but a professional doesn't leave half a fingerprint either."

"Where exactly did the colleagues find it?"

"On the socket," Emma replied. "By the door, next to the chair where we found the victim. The floor lamp was plugged in right next to it. Like a double plug, you know."

"A burglar?"

"Well, I don't know. The fancy cross is still hanging there... And according to Jean, the only valuables in the mess of the desk were stamps. If this was simply a robbery, then a monstrously unsuccessful one."

"And the only thing apparently missing is a small transistor radio? Do you think this is related?" Aidan looked at her thoughtfully.

"How do you mean that? What is related to what?"

"Well, the killer grabs the radio on the table next to the victim, unplugs it, puts the cord around his neck and pulls. Then he takes the murder weapon – the radio plus power cable – put on gloves and wipe everything down. He forgot the area around the socket, though, hence the partial imprint. Then our killer left the house, pulled the door shut and disappeared into the darkness. All done."

"Yes, it could have been like that. But why did Armstrong let his enemy into the house in the first place? He must have known his attacker, maybe he even expected him. The red wine with the two glasses was certainly no coincidence."

After a few minutes of thoughtful silence, Aidan reported on the previous evening and the conversation with the Morrows.

"She was at church, he was at work, after that they were both at home. Pastor and staff can allegedly confirm the first part of the evening, for the time after that they give each other an alibi. Said they were watching "Proof" together on the telly."

"And? What do you think of the two?"

"She's slightly hysterical and was apparently trying to make her rather bored husband jealous with Armstrong. With limited success. He's a typical working-class Irish fella with a big mouth and not much behind it. He certainly doesn't think herself was involved with the old man next door. There's not much to be gained there, I don't think either of them has anything to do with it."

"And her? Definitely not Armstrong's piece on the side?"

"It sounds like she visited him regularly to whine. Yesterday she was crying and saying 'Charles is such a good listener' and so on. I can't say if there was more. But John Morrow says Armstrong was way too busy anyway." Aidan grinned.

"What's that supposed to mean?"

Aidan took a deep breath and told the whole sleazy story.

Emma couldn't believe it: "The man is a clergyman and he's meeting a lady friend at the Mullaghmore harbour pub on Valentine's Day? And his wife is at home? What a bollocks!"

Aidan just shrugged. "You know my stance towards holy matrimony. We garda wouldn't be half as busy solving murders if people just let this stupid marriage thing go..." He didn't finish the sentence and blushed.

Emma had to smile. Obviously, he had suddenly remembered that his boss was divorced and probably didn't have any glorious memories of marriage either. Sensitive as a sledge hammer. Emma ended the sentimentalities quite dryly: "Well, see to it that you get the Morrows' alibis confirmed and, ideally, Jean's as well. Why don't you call the sister in Belfast again – and also ask if there is another witness who can confirm that Jean was indeed shopping at the time in question. Maybe a sales person will remember the old girls. I'm going to investigate who was Armstrong's squeeze and who would be upset about it."

As Aidan picked up his phone, Emma's rang.

"Hey, Laura here, how are you? And more importantly, what are we doing tonight?!"

Jesus, she almost forgot. She had an appointment with Laura McDern tonight. She didn't have many girlfriends, but Laura was a loyal soul, even though Emma had stood her up many times due to work. Laura ran a law practice in Ballysadare, not far from Sligo town, and Emma appreciated her intelligence and sense of humour.

"I'm fine! But how did you know that I am in the office on a Saturday?"

„Piece of cake! I read the papers at breakfast and saw that somebody topped old Armstrong. You're in serious crimes… The rest shouldn't be hard to put together."

Laura laughed her dark laugh and Emma's heart felt warm. She replied: "Okay, Sherlock, your power of deduction is sensational. So let me know what you want to do tonight?"

'Why don't we meet at Hargadons on O'Connell? We'll have a drink in the bar and if we get hungry… They can cook there, too." Emma was fine with that, the traditional joint on O'Connell

Street was one of her favourite pubs: "Okay, I'll be there at around six-thirty!"

February 2004

Margaret was very excited today. She chirped "Violet!" and again "Violet!", over and over. It was as if she sensed that today was a special day. Her son Bill with wife and daughter were due to visit. This part of the family lived in Switzerland and Catherine had not met Bill before.

"Margaret, Bill is coming today. Bill, your son? Do you remember?"

Margaret smiled and mumbled, "Bill? Is that the butcher in Laragh? Such a nice man."

"That is a nice man, Margaret, indeed. But this Bill is your son. He's in from Switzerland. And he's bringing his daughter, your granddaughter." Catherine reached for the photo on Margaret's night stand – there were mountains in the background.

"Margaret, look, is that you? Are these Bill and his family?" But Margaret had lost the thread and was quoting a poem from the old days:

"I will arise and go now, and go to Innisfree,
And a small cabin build there, made of clay and wattles;
Nine bean-rows will I have there, a hive for the honey-bee,
And live alone in the bee-loud glade..."

Suddenly Margaret, who usually spoke Queens English with a clipped accent, sounded quite Irish again. And very young.

"That's nice, Margaret. Is that Irish?"

"Yeats, this is Yeats. But you know that, Violet."

March 2005

By eleven everyone had gathered at Murray's office. He disliked the small, musty conference room available to the Local Detective Unit and generally summoned his team to his own office. Of course there wasn't enough space, because Miles Monroe from forensics had turned up, as had the pathologist McManus. Also Desmond "Dessie" Conway, a young colleague who Emma couldn't quite figure out. Aidan leaned against a wall. Modern conference rooms were scarce in Sligo, and the "incident rooms" populated by US cops, if you are to believe the American crime series on TV, with photo walls and all the details relevant to the case, did not exist at the Sligo station.

They had to be thankful that Dublin hadn't shut down their own small forensics department, even if it consisted mostly of Miles and his lab assistants. The closure of his department was threatened every year – for financial reasons. The penny-pinchers in the capital didn't think about what it would cost to centralize the forensics team and then having them drive the three-hour drive from Dublin to Sligo. Bureaucrats. Emma couldn't stand those paper pushers.

"Good morning!" Murray woke her from her gloomy thoughts. "Emma, I would like your report."

Emma explained what she could assume for sure so far, Miles Monroe briefly reported on the half fingerprint that he could not assign. Dr. McManus didn't have much more either, he didn't want to narrow down the possible time of death even now. Even knowing the ambient temperature and body temperature of the body when it was found, he couldn't say anything more precise, so he stuck to his original statement: between half past five and nine in the evening. Otherwise he has nothing, not even skin remnants under the victim's nails and therefore no DNA of the perpetrator. Armstrong was probably strangled from behind and couldn't defend himself.

Then the floor went to Aidan. He reported his call to Mrs. Armstrong's sister in Belfast. "She confirms that Jean was with her in Belfast at the time in question on Thursday evening. She came by train at noon, the two ladies drank tea and then went shopping. Jean bought a skirt and had an appointment at the hairdresser's at four. I called him too; he confirmed that he cut a Jean Armstrong's hair on Thursday."

"Is that all, O'Leary?" Murray didn't look particularly happy, pushing his glasses up onto his bald pate.

"Well, the sister likes to gossip and was only too happy to tell me that Charles wasn't exactly a picture-perfect husband. Apparently he liked the ladies. Jean was heartbroken with the man, who dragged her halfway around the world. She must have been forever homesick for Ireland. Abroad it was either too hot or too cold for her, and besides, she doesn't much like the heathens, says her sister. She also apparently blames Charles for the death of her son Ron. His father never really took him seriously and only ever criticized him."

"What did he die of?" Murray interrupted.

„Cancer, at least that's what Jean's sister says. What mutated cells in Ron's body have to do with paternal criticism, however, is not entirely clear to me."

"Many people believe that stress can trigger cancer. That anger and misfortune weaken the immune system so that people become weak and get cancer," McManus intervened. "Maybe the woman thinks that her husband killed his son indirectly. From a medical point of view, of course, this is nonsense."

"From a legal point of view too. When did the young man die?" Murray wanted to know. Aidan pulled out his notepad and flipped through his notes.

"About four years ago, says the sister."

"Well, if that were the motive, Jean would have attacked her husband four years ago and not just now," Emma said. "Why now at all?"

Murray looked like he'd choked on his bitter coffee:

"Well, to recap: the precious first 24 hours after a murder are almost up and we have nothing. Nothing! No witnesses, the neighbours saw and heard nothing, and no one else spoke up. Also, there's no forensics, aside from a half-fingerprint that goes nowhere and strangulation marks on the victim's neck. There are no remains of skin or DNA under the victim's fingernails, as the perpetrator appears to have been standing behind the armchair and surprised Armstrong. Worst of all, we don't have a motive either." He looked around silently, but everyone present was somehow busy studying their hands, their shoes, or the scratched surface of Murray's desk.

"Well," Emma spoke up again. "One of the neighbours said he saw Armstrong with a blonde at the pub in Mullaghmore. And it didn't look like it was a spiritual counselling session. I'll look into it, maybe we can find the motive in Armstrong's trousers."

Murray looked up irritably. The last thing he needed was a scandal now that the golf season was about to start. "Do that, Emma, but please be discreet. I don't want to read any of your hasty conclusions in the newspapers!'

Emma nodded.

Murray continued, "Well, I've now assigned Conway off to assist Woods and O'Leary."

"Good idea, boss," said Emma. "We need to increase the radius: has anyone seen anything unusual on trains or buses to and from Sligo? What about CCTV, the surveillance cameras at stations and at crossings? Sligo may not be London, but the cameras somewhere must have picked up something. Homicide doesn't just happen. Also, it would be good if Dessie could help us analyse the contents of Armstrong's desk: who did he correspond with? What was in his life that maybe not even his wife knew about? And the telephone connections to and from Armstrong House over the last few weeks must also be evaluated. Okay, busy days ahead."

July 1965

She had been in labour for 18 hours and was so exhausted she couldn't even cry. The baby was apparently stuck, just couldn't get out. Most of the time she was alone, occasionally Sister Magdalena looked after her. The others called her "the butcher" because so many babies didn't survive her midwifery.

"Now that's what you get for not being able to keep your legs together, you little whore," she had told her.

It was summer outside, but it was cool in the delivery room. If you could even call the small, whitewashed chamber that. A jail cell wouldn't have been more forbidding. There was only a bunk and a chair. The hours stretched on endlessly, broken only by waves of pain. "Let yourself fall into the pain", the butcher had said, "that way you will do penance for your sins".

She wanted to die and take her baby with her. Then there would be peace. No more screaming, no more accusatory eyes. No sermons. But she didn't want to let Sister Magdalena win. The child should live. With the next contraction, she gathered the last of her strength and pushed and pushed and pushed. At last the little creature's head pushed out; something tore inside her. The pain was overwhelming. When she regained her senses, a child was whimpering between her legs. A girl. The reddish down on her head covered in blood.

February 2004

Margaret looked cute in her new cardigan, her wrinkled little face excited behind her now oversized-looking glasses. Apparently some part of her holey brain understood that there was a visitor coming today. Catherine had already combed her freshly washed hair and seated her in her favourite armchair in the living room. There she sat and watched Arthur from room number three as he did his rounds. Arthur was suffering from advanced dementia, but was still physically strong, thanks to a long farming life. He spent his old age wandering around the house. It was laid out squarely around an atrium, and old people with a lot of anxiety like Arthur could walk in circles for hours. Many were upset, didn't know where they were, just wanted to go home. That's why all the doors to the outside were secured with a code. Had it been otherwise, the residents would eventually find themselves on the street in the middle of traffic. A few years ago, a clever intern came up with the idea of setting up a kind of bus stop in a quiet corner of the corridor, complete with a sign, a bench and a timetable. Now dementia patients with wanderlust often sat there, as if they were waiting for the bus home. After a while they forgot about the bus again and let the nursing staff take them back to their quarters.

Suddenly Bill Sargent was in the room with his wife and a little blond girl. Catherine knew from experience that many people were shocked when they saw their parents with dementia after a while and secretly stood by to help and distract them. But Bill gave no sign of distress. He sat down next to his mother and took her hand: "Hi mummy, it's Bill."

Catherine joined them:

"Hello, may I introduce myself, I'm Catherine..." Bill had straightened up and was looking into her face. It was then that Catherine's face almost derailed: it was as if she were seeing a male version of herself. Bill didn't have red hair, his was thick and dark brown, but he had the same green-brown eyes as Catherine, the same determined chin and the same strongly curved, sensitive mouth. Bill, however, didn't seem to notice, and Catherine wondered if she was going insane. Such coincidences simply did not exist.

Bill looked questioningly in her face and said:

"Are you alright?"

"Yeah, yeah, I'm just a little dizzy right now!"

Bill looked questioning, but then retreated into the realm of politeness and said:

"Hello, I'm Bill, Margaret's son. May I introduce you to my wife Paula and my daughter Isabelle? We live in Switzerland, in Chur."

Margaret laughed at this and kept saying, "Violet! Violet!"

"Mum, not Violet, this is Paula and Isabelle, my wife and your granddaughter. I sent you photos of us..."

Catherine withdrew discreetly, ostensibly so as not to disturb the family gathering; actually to find her balance again. She took refuge in the staff bathroom and stood in front of the mirror, staring into her face and whispering "Violet!"

March 2005

Emma spent Saturday afternoon working out which duties Dessie Conway should take on: locating CCTV cameras in the area around Armstrong House and reviewing footage between 5.30pm and 9pm on Thursday evening. Go to the train station, talk to bus and train staff – did anyone notice anything that night? Clarify with Aidan which neighbours had already been interviewed, then draw a larger circle and continue asking. Alert the phone company and analyse all connections to and from Armstrong House.

"Look for unusual, infrequently dialled numbers. For connections that don't come up regularly."

Dessie groaned.

"A cop's work is above all hard work, and you can do it," Emma dismissed him for a busy weekend ahead and set about finding Armstrong's boss herself. Not God, of course, but the Archbishop of Armagh, the supreme head of the Church of Ireland and Primate of All Ireland. The last incumbent, Charles' old friend and mentor, a certain Philip Anderson, had died in the meantime, the new one was called Robert Eames. However, she was unable to get the bishop on the phone with either charm or subtle threats; only his assistant, a Reverend Shaw, was willing to speak to her. He had remained monosyllabic, but had finally agreed to meet Emma in Armagh on Sunday at twelve – after the service.

"But I don't know how much I can contribute to solving your case," he had said. "Charles Armstrong's death is of course a great loss to the Church of Ireland. But Charles was also a soldier, and since Bishop Anderson died, his comrades in the army must have known him better than we do here in the diocese."

What did an army chaplain actually do? The internet didn't yield much, except ramblings about the "sword of the Lord". Emma snorted with disgust. She didn't like men of God of all colours, but to her military chaplains were the height of hypocrisy. Go to war in the name of the Lord? Gun at the ready with the blessing of the Church? What actually happened to the commandment "Thou shalt not kill"? In Emma's world a man could either be a soldier or a priest, you couldn't be both at the same time.

Across from her, Aidan was poring over his papers.

"Aidan, who is in charge of military chaplains in the British Army? According to Wikipedia, by the way, they are called padres – and they exist in all denominations. Jews, Presbyterians, Catholics, Methodists. I wonder if they also have Buddhists walking around in yellow uniforms?"

"Are they even wearing uniforms? I'm not sure they have a military rank."

Emma studied her screen: "It says here that they can even become Colonel, Brigadier and Major-General. I find that completely bonkers. On the one hand, the ten commandments and then blessing violence – for me that goes together like sausage and vanilla sauce".

"But why? Soldiers also need pastoral care. Especially when the going gets tough."

Emma brushed Aidan's argument off the table. In her eyes, anyone who wanted to play war had no right to absolution. Especially not when the army supplied it quasi-automatically.

She found another aspect much more exciting: 'But what do you think the IRA would say to something like that? Born in Sligo and Protestant! From the point of view of the Catholic majority, becoming a pastor for the other club is already bad enough. But then also work in the military of the occupiers and run around as a soldier's chaplain in the British army? A mortal sin. I'm almost surprised the Republicans didn't put an end to this a long time ago."

"You're right. Do you think he was afraid of that? Is that why he barricaded his house the way he did?"

"I have no idea, we'll have to talk to Jean about that. Anyway, now I understand why they were always proselytizing and doing missionary work—all a cover so it wouldn't be known that Armstrong was working with the Brits. All a beautiful wall of lies, Your Reverence!"

Who the hell had this Armstrong really been?

CHAPTER 4
Hargadons

When Emma got home, U2 was blaring from Stevie's room on the first floor, Emma's note was still on the kitchen table but the 20 euro had disappeared. She went upstairs, knocked. No answer. "Stevie?"

"Hi Mum," Stevie stuck his head out of a narrow gap between the door and the wall. "I've got a visitor!"

Emma craned her neck and saw dark curls... looked like a girl! She was happy for Stevie. First love, how cute!

"Oh, yeah, uh, I didn't mean to bother you. Didn't expect you to be home either, thought you were with your dad."

Stevie just grinned.

"Me lad, I've got a murder case on my hands, I'm under a lot of pressure this weekend. Can you stay with your father until I am out of the woods again?" Emma bit her lip in guilt, her behaviour not exactly a chapter from the book "Ideal Parenting Techniques".

Stevie nodded, "It's okay."

"Well, I'm going to dinner with Laura tonight. Do you want me to fix something for you in the kitchen?"

"Nope, I'm going to the cinema with Sophie later. I'll make myself a sandwich at Dad's. See you later!"

"I will be at home on Sunday evening. Promise! I could make a roast..."

But Stevie had already disappeared into the noise of his room again. The brat was actually growing up and apparently had impressed a girl enough to become his girlfriend. Did his father talk to him about birth control? Another subject with which Emma needed to deal – as if she didn't already have enough to do.

It was quarter to seven when Emma finally got to Hargadon's. There was a blackboard outside the pub. The daily specials were usually offered on it but today it said "Beer is made from hops. Hops are plants, so they are healthy. Strictly speaking, beer is salad." And after that, in brackets, "(You're welcome!)". This is off to a good start, Emma thought as she pushed the door open into the overheated room.

The noise inside washed over her. Every time she walked in here, she thought of Jim Brady's Pub on Maiden Lane in New York, where she'd first met Paul. That boozer didn't have much to do with a real Irish pub, though. Irish flags everywhere, illustrations of leprechauns and four-leaf clovers. A real Irish pub in Sligo didn't indulge in poor taste like that. Dark wood and a few old jugs were the decoration here. Hargadon's clientèle loved its nooks and crannies, and otherwise the place was about cold beer and hot fries. Unlike most other Irish pubs, which typically only had four criteria for fermented grape juice – white, red, sour and sweet – there was a reasonable range of wine on offer, too. The place was straightforward, just the way Emma liked it.

Laura was already standing at the bar drinking a Guinness. The small woman with the round face and the oversized mouth looked utterly at home in this environment. For years, Emma had wondered if Laura's mouth was so wide because she laughed so much – or if she laughed so much because her physiognomy simply invited it. Which didn't matter in the end, because Emma enjoyed Laura's friendship. The solicitor was quick-witted, gifted with the gift of the gab and the typical Irish sense of humour. She bantered about everything and everyone, but never became mean. She was also quite easy-going for a legal eagle – and wasn't quick to judge others. Or if she did, she kept her opinions to herself.

"Well, how is it? Did you leave your husband in the cloakroom?" Then Emma ordered a small glass of dry red, the bitter Irish stout was not for her. Besides, she was still hung over after last night's whiskey indulgence.

"Michael is on night duty, I won't see him until tomorrow morning," Laura replied. Her husband worked as a surgeon at the General Hospital in Sligo and often had to straighten noses that were damaged during bar fights on Saturday nights. "That means I have the run of the house."

"Well, I don't want to overdo it today, I've got this Armstrong case on my hands. I need a hangover as much as I need a hole in the head. Murray puts enough pressure on as it is. Also, Stevie has a girlfriend now and I have no idea how to talk to him about birth control!"

"Oh, don't worry, they already know everything today anyway. Kids have watched more porn on the internet than we'll ever see. And if not, buy him a Playboy."

"At least it's legal to sell condoms in Ireland now," groaned Emma, not finding the subject amusing at all.

A little later, when the two women sat down to eat at a table, Armstrong came up again.

"I've got a dead man, but no witnesses, no forensics, and most importantly, no motive."

"Are you aware that I knew him?"

Emma looked up from her steak: "Who, Armstrong?"

"The whole family. For many years. Even their parents took legal advice from my father. Actually, I'm not allowed to talk about clients. You know, solicitors have to keep their gobs shut..."

The McDerns were Sligo veterans and Laura had taken over her late father's firm.

"Oh Laura, I've got a case to solve, so if you know anything, tell me."

"What do you know about the Armstrongs?" Laura asked back.

"Not much. Three children, the son already deceased. Mother Jean unhappy but dutiful. The victim himself a pillar of the community – even if he wasn't a good husband."

Laura nodded. "The Armstrongs are from Laragh. They've got a 200-plus-year-old Georgian property and a lot of land to go with it. House is called Linborough House. Beautifully situated on a hill above the sea."

"When we found him, Armstrong had a signet ring on his little finger. Does the family history go back to the Normans?"

"They would like that, but the signet ring is a dud, Linborough hasn't seen nobility in centuries. The Armstrongs achieved their prosperity without blue blood, but with intelligence and diligence. Charles' father in particular, Gerald Scott Armstrong, had a gift for identifying and seizing business opportunities. My father always called him a clever fox. Especially since Gerald Scott bought the big house back in the 1930s. Do you know what Linborough is worth today? A fortune! It was also Gerald Scott who built the meeting house for the Protestant community in the village. Armstrong Hall still stands today. The family has always been bigoted protestant teetotallers and back in the days the clan used to despise the Catholic majority in Ireland, I imagine because they thought they are all drunkards."

"So a real patriarch and a self-righteous arsehole." Emma grimaced in disgust.

"Well, I'm not quite so sure about that. If I'm to believe my father's old stories, it was Maddie, Gerald Scott's wife, who wore the pants in that club. Incidentally, she was also the first woman with a car in the county. She must have hurtled along the country lanes here like a dervish. My father said that she ruled the family with an iron fist. There are also rumours that she forbade her son Henry from marrying the love of his life and that's why he's always remained single."

"Wasn't Protestant enough, the intended bride?"

"No, but probably an illegitimate child, a bastard, as they called it at the time."

"Not good enough for the Armstrongs at Linborough House." Emma raised her glass as if to toast, "Cheers to the good Christian people of Laragh!"

"Oh come on, you with your New York City morals. You still don't get Ireland, even after all this time here. We are different – and that was even more the case in the 1960s," Laura tried to explain.

"I will never understand this country, simply because I don't understand religion. Why is faith the only ticket to paradise? Ultimately, that means that if you are able to switch off your mind and your experiences to accept ideas that your intellect has to dismiss as outright silly, then you will find bliss. I have a problem with this intellectual subservience, it just reminds me too much of what all other ideologies and dictators demand of people. Turn off brain, accept dogma: mission accomplished."

Laura had no desire to get involved in a theological discourse again, as she knew from experience that Emma would not move an inch in her opinion about religion. So she changed the subject: "Do you think the Armstrong murder is somehow aimed at the church? At Protestantism?"

"I have no idea, that's the problem. But tell me what you know about the family. How many kids did Gerald Scott and Maddie have?"

"Well, I know of four. Charles was the eldest, then came two daughters, Margaret and Violet, and then Henry the youngest . At some point all of them visited my father's office for one reason or another."

"But they are your clients no more?"

"Well, that's the thing. Charles Armstrong called after the New Year's to make an appointment to see me."

"And? Do I have to worm every word out of you?" Emma grew impatient.

Laura looked deep into her Guinness. "By law I really shouldn't tell you this, but I'm probably doing the law a little more of a favour by telling you."

"Exactly, and that's what matters in the end!"

"Well then, Armstrong wanted information about the application of the estate law. He wanted to know who could claim the land and the big house. So it was probably about Margaret's children."

"Wait a minute – Margaret's children?" Emma asked.

"Yes, his siblings Henry and Violet remained childless, Charles had three kids – two daughters left after the son's death – and Margaret also has two sons, as far as I know."

"You mean old Armstrong wanted to secure the land for his children and get rid of his nieces and nephews as benefactors?" asks Emma.

"I can't explain it any other way. Charles lived in Germany for a long time and showed me an article from a German newspaper about the change in their estate law. There, illegitimate children now can also inherit with equal rights. That obviously annoyed him terribly."

"Well, it's really scandalous that the children of sin are now allowed to access the accounts of good Christian folks," Emma's voice was dripping with sarcasm.

"Well, not quite. The law has given illegitimate children the same rights as legitimate children in Ireland in 1987 – but this does not mean that they inherit automatically under all circumstances. All the fuss is for nothing!"

"But what did he really want from you?"

"I think he just wanted to know – theoretically – who will inherit what. Do you realize how much money is involved? The big house and the land around it must be worth millions!"

"And Charles wanted to secure that for his own family? And exclude his nephews?"

"I didn't really find Armstrong particularly likeable," Laura had to admit. "He has such big lips that he kept licking like he was perpetually thirsty."

"Had – wrong grammar, the man is no more. Also he was thinking of something completely different if the grapevine has it correctly. Apparently he could not keep it in his trousers... And he obviously found you particularly enticing." Emma had to grin.

That idea made Laura shudder: "The old git! Disgusting! Well, I just explained Irish estate law to him."

"Who actually has the title to the land?"

"Right now Henry owns the property, the youngest son, Charles brother. He is single and has no children. It would be simplest if Henry made a will giving equal consideration to all his nieces and nephews. There would be enough land for all the cousins to get their share. That would also be the fairest. Just not sure if Charles took that advice as I haven't heard from him or Henry since. And, as I said, it could well be that Charles worked his brother Henry to make it all go to his offspring and not to the cousins. So my advice to create a will stating equal distribution among all the descendants would not have been exactly the recommendation Charles wanted."

February 2004

Catherine had signed up for weekend duty at Oak Gardens. She hated Sundays. Those quiet afternoons when the world seemed to rest, always reminded her that she had no family. Couples strolled the streets and parks, fathers played ball with their young sons, mothers rubbed their pregnant bellies... Everywhere Catherine looked, Britain seemed all families and laughing children. In her loneliness she felt like an alien. It would be better to work than to have to fight the self-pity. Today, however, she had another reason to enjoy coming to work. Oak Gardens was always understaffed on the weekends, and Catherine wanted to be left alone and unobserved by her colleagues.

When everyone in Margaret's hall had been washed, dressed and had eaten their breakfast, she returned to Margaret's room. "Violet!" she heard.

Margaret happily said, "Are we going home to Linborough today?"

"We'll do that later, Margaret. Shouldn't we have a look at some photos first?"

Catherine knew Margaret had two boxes at the bottom of her wardrobe. The seniors were only allowed to bring a few personal items with them when they moved into the Oaks. However, photo albums, diaries and a few personal mementos were allowed.

Catherine was curious – why did this Bill fellow look so much like herself? Surely it was just a coincidence. But there were no such coincidences. Or was she going crazy and seeing ghosts because she wanted a family so badly?

She pulled the boxes from Margaret's closet and opened them. On top was an old photo album. With that, Catherine sat down next to the old woman and opened it. At the back of the book were colour photos of Bill and his family, and also photos of another man with his wife and children. Probably the son in Australia, at least the glaring light in which these pictures were taken suggested that. From about 2002 on there were no more new photos, the picture story broke off – Margaret must have gotten too ill to stick in more photos. She tugged at the album with her old fingers. Wanted to take it on her lap. The old lady turned to the first few pages: faded black-and-white photos from the late '50s and early '60s. A woman laughing out of a car window, a young man on a tractor, photos of a Georgian, detached in a meadow.

A Christmas picture – apparently the family: an elderly couple, next to them a young priest in black with a stately wife and three small children. Plus another son in a suit. Next to her was a young Margaret, also with a husband and two small sons.

"Look, is that you? is that your husband ... Oh look, that could be Bill, as a little boy!"

Margaret, however, just smiled and gestured to the young girl who was standing at the edge of the picture, a little off to the side, as if she didn't really belong: "Violet!"

Now Catherine noticed, too, pulled the album towards her and studied the picture more closely. So there really was a Violet! The word was not just a tic in a crumbling brain. The young girl in the picture did indeed have a thick braid, as did Catherine... whether it was ginger, too, was hard to tell from a black and white photo. She actually looked a little like Violet. The shape of the head was right, as were the deep-set eyes. A second coincidence of this kind? Impossible!

"And who is that?" she asked, pointing to the priest and his wife. Margaret said nothing. And then she suddenly said with unusual clarity in her voice:

"Charles, the swine!"

"The man's name is Charles?"

"Charles, the swine." Margaret began to cry and Catherine quickly closed the album. Well, had she not done a great job! Made an old woman cry. Tenderly she took the fragile woman in her arms:

"Margaret, it doesn't matter, that was all so long ago!"

Margaret sobbed, "Oh, Violet!"

Catherine sat down on the floor next to Margaret's boxes and began to rummage around. The second carton contained old diaries. Written in beautiful handwriting. As far as Catherine knew, in a previous life Margaret had been a teacher at expensive private schools. The stencilled writing would go with it. She was about to start reading when the beeper on her waistband went off. Damn! Apparently the management missed her or something had gone wrong somewhere in the house and her help was needed. On impulse, Catherine took some of the oldest journals and pushed the open boxes back into the closet.

"Margaret, I'll be right back! But right now I have to go!"

On the way to the nurses' room, she passed the cloakroom and put the journals in her locker.

March 2005

I should have forgone the last red wine! Again she had at least one drink too many in her blood. Emma struggled out of bed, groaning. And again she had been bothered by nightmares. She had to rescue a small child who was locked in an oven. She could see it through the glass oven door but couldn't hear it – and the door was stuck. Emma pulled and pushed the oven door, but it didn't budge an inch. Then suddenly the child was gone, and Emma decided to destroy this child-eating oven. She took an axe and smashed glass and metal into small pieces. But when she lowered the axe, with a bang the oven stood in front of her, whole again, as if nothing had happened. So Emma decided to burn this monster. But when the fire died out it banged! The oven had risen again. After that she took acid to dissolve the bloody thing. But bang! And everything was as before. Whatever Emma tried, this disgusting black beast of an oven was indestructible. Emma finally woke up in a sweat and staggered to the bathroom to drink water. When she finally fell asleep again, she dreamed that she was suddenly sitting in this oven herself and the door was stuck. She cried and screamed, braced her feet against the door from the inside, but her prison was immovable. It finally got a little lighter around her – someone had found Emma in her cage. The relief of seeing another human being was overwhelming. The man in blue overalls waved at her and pulled thick belts around the oven. Eventually, with the help of these wire ropes the oven—still with Emma inside—was craned onto the back of a pickup truck. The car started and Emma in her oven was driven through a deserted landscape. Through the glass in the oven door she could see dusty roads and drying trees. Finally, the pickup stopped and Emma felt her furnace prison being lifted into the air again. She looked out the window of her metal enclosure and saw a yard with thousands of ovens like the one she was stuck in. From these furnaces, an army of people stared out at her, as imprisoned as she was...

Emma woke with a start, looked around in confusion and found herself in her own bedroom. Just a dream, fortunately just a dream. When the alarm finally rang, she was completely jaded. Having to get up early on Sundays just wasn't fair! But driving the 100 miles to Armagh would take time, and Emma didn't want to be late for her appointment with the Reverend Shaw.

When she finally rolled east on the N16, she felt better. Which of course could also be due to the two painkillers she had downed. With opioids in the blood, the trip almost felt like a proper Sunday outing. The little car seemed as happy to be out of town as Emma was. In the rear-view mirror she saw Sligo's two Bens, Benbulben and Benwiskin. From the West they looked like two boats, keels up. They were two mountains, but the deep valley between them made the massif look, from certain perspectives, as if Benbulben had been simply copied into a second version of itself. A good reminder for a cop, Emma thought. Nothing ever was as it seemed at first glance.

The sun even came out occasionally. The light glittered over the lakes that dotted the north of the country, and the spring air smelled of the coming rebirth of life. When there was light and warmth, there was no more beautiful spot on earth than Ireland. Emma rolled along comfortably in her trusty Peugeot and sipped tea from her thermos – nothing beats a trip to the countryside with really strong tea!

Soon she reached the A46 with its views of Loch Erne, then the border to Northern Ireland, and finally Enniskillen, where an IRA bomb attack in November 1987 killed ten and injured 63. The Past was never really past, at least not in Ireland. Everywhere there were places, smells and sights that whispered of what had been. It was as if the streets still remembered the blood spilled here, the hatred, the betrayals, the roar of guns – just like old tracks of disused railway lines still seemed to remember the weight of the trains they stopped carrying long ago.

At the time, the bomb had gone off at a veterans' monument, the IRA said it was a mistake that civilians were blown up. It had been aimed at British soldiers marching past the monument. Great, thought Emma, the dead can really be happy about the apology. Killed by mistake... At Ballygawley she took the turn for Armagh.

St Patrick's Cathedral stood on a hill that gave the town of Armagh its name: Ard Macha, the Macha Mountain. This in turn was named after a pre-Christian tribal princess – no wonder that the priests had settled here. They liked to occupy the ancient sacred places of the Celts and incorporated them into their own ideology. Not far away, on the nearest hill, stood the other St Patrick's Church – that one of the Catholics. Only half a mile apart, both bearing the same name, yet worlds apart! How ironic, here both denominations were arguing who had more rights to the national saint, old St. Patrick, the first missionary in the country. It is said that he was the first bishop here in Armagh in 444 AD – which gave the town its importance to this day as both the centre of the protestant Church of Ireland and the Roman Catholic Church. What would Patrick have thought of this religious circus in Ireland – and all the bloodshed that the conflict between the two groups had caused and continued to cause?

Emma let her gaze wander over the old protestant stones of Saint Patrick's. The walls, some of which date back to the Middle Ages, still carried the massiveness of Romanesque churches. Heavy and squat, the solid nave had a short square tower above the cross section. It was armoured with broad battlements as if to protect the faithful from attacking Vikings. However, the windows in the stone building were already slightly pointed at the top – a first sign of early Gothic. Emma, who had grown up in New York with much younger churches in faux retro-Romanesque or pseudo-Gothic styles, couldn't help but be impressed by real versions of these architectural styles. Old churches in Ireland were often beautiful, if only their owners wouldn't talk so much nonsense...

Emma quietly entered the church through a heavy, riveted door. The service was not over yet, but the pews were only a quarter full. Even in Ireland the faith waned, so perhaps there was still hope for mankind! Emma sat in the back row and watched as the light streamed through the beautifully stained glass windows to paint brightly coloured spots on the floor. She endured the service.

When the faithful rose and left the church, Emma simply sat in her pew, where a little later a tall man joined her. Reverend Shaw was the ascetic type, everything about him was thin. The skin, the hair, the fingers, the bridge of the nose, the lips and his sense of humour.

"Hello, you must be Garda Woods from Sligo."

"Indeed I am – and you are Reverend Shaw."

"Why don't we sit in the chapter room next to the choir? There is rarely anyone there at this hour and we can talk undisturbed." The side room of the church was laid out with a thick red carpet, a heavy wooden table and high-backed chairs from another century.

"Have a seat!", the vicar made an inviting gesture, and the two sat across the corner at the table.

"What can I do for you?"

"What can you tell me about Reverend Dean Charles Armstrong?"

"Terrible story! Do you know what exactly happened to him?"

"No, we're still investigating and that's exactly why I'm here. I'm looking for the motive. Who had a gripe or grudge, did he tread on anyone's toes, what's the background to his character, what could have provoked someone to take his life... who could have hated the Reverend like that? Who had cause to attack him like that?"

"Why are you asking me? I have no idea." Shaw rubbed the bridge of his knife-sharp nose.

"The newspapers said Armstrong was one of the leading men in the Church of Ireland. Armagh is the headquarters of this church and you are the personal assistant to the Bishop. It's hard for me to believe that you can't tell me about the person, life and work of Charles Armstrong."

"I did indeed have a look at Charles' resume after your call. Coming from a traditional farming family in Laragh, he studied theology at Trinity College Dublin, where he also played rugby. Some say the sport interested him far more than the Bible.., but I digress. After his ordination he was in Drummon parish, County Donegal, for a while. Then he went to the Far East as a missionary, as far as I know he was in China, Singapore, Hong Kong and Malaysia. In 1960 he married his wife Jean here in Ireland. In 1992 he returned to Ireland and became Dean of Sligo, at St John's Cathedral. In 1999 he retired. That means he has served faithfully, the Church, his family, and the state for over 40 years."

"What state? The Irish Republic or the British?'

"Why are you asking that?"

"Because Charles was first and foremost a padre, a military chaplain in the British Army."

"If you already know that, why are you asking?" Shaw regarded Emma silently. His disapproval filled the room like a stench.

"So after 1960 the Church of Ireland sort of lost sight of him because he was one of their own, but worked for the British?" Emma asked.

"Well, I wouldn't quite see it that way, he came back to Ireland regularly to visit. Also to see his old friend, Philip Anderson, the former bishop here, God bless him and rest his soul."

"Armstrong and Anderson were friends?"

"Yes, very tight, until Anderson passed away in 1984. The bishop was a sort of mentor to Charles, a fatherly friend. The friendship of the two goes back many years, they probably already knew each other from the seminary, where Philip worked as a teacher and Charles was his student.

"Is Anderson's wife still alive? Is there anyone I could talk to about his friendship with Armstrong?"

"Not that I know of, Philip is gone and his wife died very young."

"Could you imagine that Armstrong's murder was ultimately directed against the Church?"

Shaw paled. "You know the history of Armagh, don't you?"

"What do you mean?" Emma asked back.

"Armagh, particularly in the south of the county, was long dominated by the IRA's South Armagh Brigade – a particularly aggressive and extremely bloodthirsty bunch. It was so bad that the British army in the region no longer dared to travel on the land. They mainly operated out of watchtowers in this area, and when they had to move, they used helicopters. Driving around in a car would have been lethal. Many people have died in

Armagh since the 1970s in this protracted, but barely declared civil war. The conflict did not exactly make us clergymen any way popular with the catholic folks around here."

"And yet Armstrong always dared to come back here, even as a Padre?"

"He didn't exactly announce that he was in the British army. His family knew, of course, and so did we here in the episcopate. But nobody talked about it, it would have been far too dangerous. Officially, Armstrong was always just a humble missionary, serving abroad."

The two sat in silence. Emma shivered, it was cool in the old walls.

Suddenly Shaw asked, "Are you a practising Christian, Inspector?"

"No, not for a long time."

"So you don't believe in God?"

"I'm a detective, I believe in evidence."

CHAPTER 5

Grassington laughs

July 1965

A girl! Born in pain, now held in love. And the wee thing was healthy. That's all she needed to know. When she woke up again after the seemingly endless labour, the little one lay neatly swaddled next to her in a simple crib. She looked at her daughter in fascination. A face like a Madonna! Only in small. Delicately curved eyebrows, underneath the crescent-shaped closed eyelids, almost transparent in their vulnerability. A semicircle of eyelashes on each cheek. A tiny nose, a bright pink mouth. She had never seen anything more beautiful.

They let her have the baby for a week, then Sister Magdalena came and demanded the child: "This child of sin will now be properly christened. And then she goes to a home where she is brought up to become a true Christian who knows her bible. Let's hope she doesn't become a disgrace like her mother."

"She is mine! She belongs to me! I am keeping her!" She had gone pale with horror.

"Now, you and I both know that you are a sinner and unable to give this child the Christian support it needs."

"I'm a good mother! You can't do that!"

"Oh yes? A good mother? You have no money and no education. If you keep her, you won't even have a home. Your parents won't want your bastard in their house. And the father obviously has no interest in you both. It's not like he's dying to marry you."

She couldn't say much to that, it was true. Just thinking about the stony face of her mother made her realize the sister was right.

"I've already spoken to your brother. He found a place for the child in a Christian charity."

"But I won't give her up, she's mine!"

"Don't make such a fuss and pray that God and your parents will forgive you!"

The next day they took the child from her. It was as if they cut off her leg or arm. As if a living part was being ripped out of her. My baby! My beautiful child! She had cried for days until Sister Magdalena threatened her.

"You stop crying right now, away with you to the laundry or I'll beat you black and blue! Anyone who does not work gets nothing to eat!"

That night she ran away, towards the sea. She wanted to throw herself into the water and wait until the cool darkness enveloped her. But she hadn't even found the courage to do that.

The next morning, this woman was standing on the sand in front of her. She had found her on the beach, shivering from the cold. Hadn't asked many questions, just taken her to her tiny cottage somewhere near Dublin, not far from the water.

There she was now, sitting in the clean, whitewashed kitchen, like a half-drowned rat at a poor table. The woman had lovingly thrown an old blanket over her shoulders and pressed a chipped, thick-walled ceramic mug of tea into her hand. In front of her was a plate of sliced bread heavily smeared with butter. Children everywhere, but there was no sign of the husband.

The woman had poked the fire high. Even in July, a fire felt good after hours in the cold sand.

"You're lucky it's July. In winter you wouldn't have survived the night on the beach!" said the woman.

"That wouldn't have been the worst," she replied and started to cry.

"By the way, my name is Mary," said her hostess, putting a motherly arm around her thin shoulders.

When she heard the whole story, Mary said:

"I don't have much, but it should be enough for the ferry to England. You just have to hitchhike or walk to Dublin and take the boat to Liverpool. Then you make your way to your sister; it can't be that far from Liverpool to Keighley in Yorkshire." Then she had pulled an old biscuit tin off the shelf and handed over £5.

"Unfortunately, that's all I have."

March 2005

"Aidan, is your cousin Ronnie still one of those IRA thugs?"

Monday morning Emma had driven to the office early. Aidan was there already, looking almost more dishevelled than he had on Saturday morning, eye slits narrow as postage stamps, seen from the side. But this time Emma refrained from asking about his adventures.

"IRA? As in Irish Republican Army? What made you think of that now?" came the tired reply.

"I wonder if the provos killed Armstrong."

"Oh come on, since the Good Friday Agreement of 98 the troubles have largely been settled and it would hardly be broken over the likes of Armstrong."

"That's not true! Just three years ago in October, members of the Sinn Féin party were accused of running a spy ring for the IRA in the Northern Irish parliament. The office chief of the Shinners was arrested. After that, the Northern Ireland Assembly was dissolved – so if you ask me, the old conflicts are as virulent as ever."

"But there's no more shooting and bombing!"

"Yeah, and what about the splinter groups like the Real IRA or the Continuity IRA? They are just as insane and violent as the original at its best!"

"And what does my cousin Ronnie have to do with all of that?"

"You know very well that Ronnie is a Republican and would love to drive the Brits into the sea – better today than tomorrow. When you have had one too many, you always let slip odd things about your friends in low places."

Aidan had to laugh himself. "Okay, I'll ask Ronnie if he's heard anything."

There was a knock on the door, Dessie Conway stuck his head in:

"You are laughing? Anything progress?"

"It's just the laughter of desperation," Aidan growled and left the room.

"We were just discussing the question of whether the IRA could be behind the Armstrong murder. The man was employed by the British Army," Emma explained, touched by Dessie's distressed expression.

"Well, the IRA could have killed him long ago. The Troubles started in the late 1960's... Plenty of time to take down a traitor. The civil war in the mid-1980s was really bloody. So why now? The man was retired! And besides, since the Good Friday agreement, things have been largely calm."

"Maybe they learned something about Armstrong that they didn't know before? I don't know, maybe Charles was one of the supergrasses of the 80's and that's only just kind of shone through now."

"So you mean Charles was spying for the Brits in Ireland?" Dessie raised a sceptical eyebrow.

"Well, he was very careful about his protection and made up cover stories, was always telling people he was working abroad as a missionary. Despite this, he returned to Ireland regularly. Maybe just to visit his family, maybe also to question his Catholic neighbours under the cloak of priestly harmlessness. Who knows."

"Well, I have my doubts," said Dessie. "Firstly he was a Prod, I don't think any member of the IRA or Provisional IRA or Irish National Liberation Army, or whatever the splinter groups are called, would have confided anything in him. Secondly, when he visited, he wasn't in Northern Ireland at all, but mostly in the Republic, in Laragh, that's where he's from, isn't it? And thirdly, the IRA is not actually a religious organisation that kills infidels. They are more socialists than Church fanatics. As far as I know, specific attacks on Protestant men of the cloth are the absolute exception. Also, the IRA doesn't kill with ropes around people's necks, and they don't steal radios either. They would have blown up the whole house or kicked in the door and shot Armstrong right away. You know the slogan the IRA party Sinn Féin uses at the annual convention? 'Armalite and ballot box'."

"Yes, yes, I know all that," Emma said. "But Armstrong was also in Northern Ireland, of course. Part of his legend was that he worked for the Bishop of Armagh and converted the heathens to the glories of the Church of Ireland. But that wasn't true. His actual boss was in Deal, in England – his assignment as army chaplain was led from there. And besides, Armstrong must have had a bad conscience – if it was not fear outright: his house is secured like a British barracks in Belfast. But on a completely different note: what did you find out?"

Dessie didn't look very happy. "Feck all, that's it. Northern Ireland has CCTV on public roads and everywhere, but here in Sligo we don't. Plus, the few cameras we have installed don't work most of the time."

Typical Irish sloppiness! But Emma didn't say that out loud.

"Hence, I don't have anything from that source," Dessie continued. "I spent the weekend interviewing Armstrong's neighbours in increasingly wide circles around the crime scene, but most didn't see or hear anything. The same goes for the long-distance bus companies and the staff in the train station. Trains and buses kept arriving from all over the country, of course, but nobody saw anyone who could be connected in any way with Armstrong. I have nothing to show for the whole weekend that I spent on my feet."

"That is not true! You have helped a lot. A lot of policing is about ruling out the unlikely and clearing up grey areas," Emma comforted him. "And that's exactly what you did."

"And what now?"

"Go back to the widow with Aidan. Let her retell her whole weekend in Belfast. Check her out. And forego the politeness, after all we have a murder case to solve. And ask about that place in Laragh, too. What's going on there?

"Why Laragh?"

"Well, you said it yourself, that's where Charles grew up. On a nice country estate, apparently and a little bird whispered in my ear that he was very interested in the question who is going to inherit the place."

Dessie left and Emma leaned back in her chair, exhausted. Mechanically she reached for the painkillers and downed two of them with cold coffee. The sight of her rapidly dwindling supply of pills almost caused her panic. If she had to face her pain alone and the deprivation she suffered without her little friends, she wouldn't be able to work. She urgently needed to see Dr. Egerton.

That Dessie. Why is it so difficult for me to deal with young people? Teaching him how to be an officer was bad enough, but navigating the roller coaster of his feelings as a rookie was taking its toll. Like almost all young officers, he was between the euphoria of being a saviour of mankind from evil and the bitter disappointment that it wasn't like one of those Jo Nesbo thrillers from Norway. Real life policing was so much slower, more systematic, and much more tedious than in the best-selling novels. In reality, it was never half a city decimated by a serial killer as in the American films, but there was one body, maybe two. In everyday life, it wasn't psychopaths who killed as incarnation of evil, but mostly normal people with human weaknesses who somehow lost control. Jealousy, envy, greed, unrequited love, alcoholism – just the usual. Lots of weaknesses Emma, with little imagination, could easily discover in herself, at least on bad days. It was actually a miracle that so few people became murderers or man slayers!

Speaking of conflicts. At least she'd managed not to argue with Stevie last night. Probably because she was home as promised and had served him a decent piece of meat. When he came in and had slammed the front door behind him, the whole house had been filled with the smell of roasting meat.

"Something smells good in here," he had exclaimed. She had listened to his stories about his father and how brilliant it was to play computer games with him. An occupation that Emma avoided whenever possible. But she refrained from commenting and just let her son do the talking. Basically, she was glad that for once he actually talked to her instead of hiding his narrow face behind his overly long bangs and only growling or mumbling as a response.

After dinner they had watched a video together in companionable silence: "Harry Potter and the Prisoner of Azkaban", one of the most successful films of the past year – only that Emma had not made it to the cinema with her son. So now watching a DVD had to make up for another of her broken promises. At age 15, Stevie claimed he was too grown up for these fantasy tales, but when Emma set down a bowl of his favourite crisps – super thin-sliced ones flavoured with sour cream and chives – he was so engrossed in the story that he barely looked up. Suddenly Emma had a lump of her heart in her throat from sheer love.

Emma was startled, feeling like she was being watched. Her boss, Murray, stood in the doorway, staring at her for who knows how long.

"Well, madam, did you find the Armstrong killer in your daydreams?"

"No, but maybe in the IRA." Emma briefly summarized what she learned on her Sunday trip to Armagh and what Aidan and Dessie were up to.

"Do I need to remind you that 98 percent of all homicides are committed by close friends or family members? The IRA? We don't even have a letter of confession. I suspect the truth can be found in Armstrong's home somewhere, not in the depths of Belfast or South Armagh." Clearly Murray had his doubts about the IRA theory.

"I hope you're right, boss. But I still don't understand if this Armstrong was really a reverend? Or rather a soldier? Or maybe even an agent for the British in Ireland? Somehow nothing fits together in this story; on the one hand, I still have no motive. And then again, nobody really liked Armstrong, except maybe the blondie next door."

Murray blinked short-sightedly. Why did he actually wear glasses when he always wore them on his bald forehead instead of looking through them? Emma asked herself this question pretty much every time she dealt with her boss.

'Well, the media likes him, and the Chief Super. I'm under fire from all sides and they want results. The funeral is on Tuesday morning. After that, there will be no more pity ceasefire, we will be grilled mercilessly from all sides. Emma, if you don't come up with something sensible soon, they're going to send the Homicide Squad from Dublin. And surely neither one of us wants that experience, right?"

Rhetorical questions did not require an answer.

Emma left the Pearse Road station and walked down town to the office of Dr. Egerton. On her way, she passed the Courthouse, designed by the same architect who had designed the famous Classiebawn Castle in Mullaghmore, north of Sligo on the coast. The Courthouse almost as lavish, columned and turreted as the castle near the pub where Charles was said to have had his tryst, and both buildings fitted into their surroundings like rhesus monkeys into an oak forest. She had to follow up this tip from the neighbour about Armstrong's alleged affair. If only she could hand over Armstrong's killer right here and now to the court and get rid of the whole messy story!

Finally she stood in front of the medical centre and hesitated. She didn't have an appointment, but the receptionist usually smuggled her in into the treatment room between two other patients. However, the times when the doctor simply renewed her prescription for painkillers were long gone. His rooms were not far from the station – that's why Emma had chosen him, not because she liked Egerton much. The man was always somewhere else with his mind, and Emma often wondered what kind of drug he was on. To each his own. He gave her the usual lecture: Oxycodone, like all other opioids, can lead to physical dependence if taken over a long period of time, blah blah, not a drug for long-term use, blah blah, better try physiotherapy and massages, blah blah. In addition, there is a potential for abuse similar to all other strong opioids, blah blah, the development of psychological dependence is possible. Better to try a pain clinic, blah blah. Emma let his words wash over her. When he was finally done, she snatched the prescription out of his hand: Only 30 pills! Finally, at the very end of his sermon did she hear him:

"Emma, I can't keep prescribing you oxycodone. You've been taking this for far too long. This prescription is the last one, after that we have to think of something else. Please make a proper appointment with reception so that we have time to discuss an alternative."

If the man only knew how long Emma had actually been swallowing the stuff! Every time a doctor told her he wouldn't give her any more prescriptions, she switched practices. Egerton was the fourth or fifth doc she had seen.

It all had started because Paul, drunk, crashed the car into a tree. He had remained unhurt, but Emma had ended up with half the engine block of the old clanger in her lap. Her pelvis was shattered, internal organs were crushed. At the time they had given her the first oxycodone for the pain in the clinic after all the operations – and with it the wonderful emotional anaesthesia that goes with opioids, in which she felt like she could take on the entire world. She was rid of Paul and his fists, but the chronic pain in her lower back, hips, and legs remained, as did the pills. Now she was pretty much through with the doctors surgeries in Sligo. What now? Switch to where? As a cop, she couldn't go on the black market. If she was caught, it would be the end of her career... Besides, who among the dealers would trust a cop?

Emma spent the rest of the morning sipping bitter coffee and using the phone in search of Armstrong's military superiors in

England. His base had been in Deal, Kent, England, somewhere between Dover and Ramsgate. What looked like a dump was the headquarters for the Royal Marines. On top of that, the music school of the British Navy was there – and in 1989 the target of attack by the IRA. Eleven dead, 22 injured. Wherever Emma turned, she found the IRA and the blood it spilled. But the barracks in Deal had been closed in 1996 and turned into ordinary apartments. The army personnel had landed who knows where. Who the hell did know Armstrong – and what exactly had he been up to in the army?

After much back-and-forth and pomposity on the part of the British liaison officers whose job it was to cooperate with other public agencies, Emma was finally given the name of a Colonel Randolph Grassington, based somewhere deep in Hampshire at a property called Amport House. This was a so-called Armed Forces Chaplaincy Centre, a training centre for the British Army, where the Padres were trained. Grassington taught incoming army chaplains how to be soldiers – and apparently he knew Armstrong.

"Grassington here," came a nasal voice from the receiver in the typically polished English upper-class accent, which triggered a lot of Irish people within seconds.

"Woods here from An Garda Síochana in Sligo, Ireland". Emma was tempted to smear her Irish accent on him like he'd spread his Queens English all over her, but she knew from experience that you couldn't provoke educated Britons that way. They guzzled up the arrogance of the imperial power with their mother's milk – and with it a class system that was essentially expressed in their accent. If you are English, let me listen to you for 30 seconds and I'll know if you are a princess or a shop-girl. If she wanted to be taken seriously by an Englishman, Emma needed to speak as clearly and distinctly as she could. So she took a deep breath and described Armstrong's demise as neutrally as possible.

A long silence on the line, then:

"Yes, I've heard it. Terrible thing. Terrible. But I don't understand what exactly you want from me."

"Colonel Grassington, I need help. I have a body, but hardly any forensics, nobody saw or heard anything suspicious. I have no witnesses and, above all, no motive. Also, I still don't understand who Armstrong really was, and I'm pretty sure you can at least help me with that."

"Well, the official version, of course, is that Armstrong served loyally in the army and retired due to his age with distinction and honours."

"And the unofficial version?"

"Why should I tell you that? How would that benefit the army? Armstrong was deployed around the world where our British troops were stationed, has worked hard in Her Majesty's service for decades, has been promoted and, apart from that, has been a family man, raising his children."

"Colonel, Armstrong is dead, murdered by an unknown hand, and if you feel any comradeship for the man – be it as a soldier or as a Reverend – now is the time you put away your swagger stick and high-handed English reserve and perhaps suggest to me where I am supposed to look for a motive."

Surprisingly, Grassington started laughing, and Emma could almost feel how the man on the other end started to drop his guard.

"Okay, lady, that's fine. But the bottom line is that I didn't care much for Armstrong, not at all. And as far as I can tell, hardly anyone else who knew him even a bit liked him either. Not even his own wife. Dear Jean, I think her biggest disappointment was that we didn't send him to the first Kuwait war in 1990. I think she always hoped that a bomb would fall on his head somewhere and that she could finally go back to her beloved Belfast."

Emma was speechless.

"So you think that Jean could be the perpetrator?"

"No, not exactly. She's endured Charles her whole life, and she probably would have had plenty of opportunities to get rid of him. But Jean is not like that. Willing to serve to the bitter end. I wish my soldiers were all like her!"

"Why was Armstrong so unpopular?"

"He was self-righteous and preachy. Always had to have the last word. And he was cold. People in trouble who need a pastor don't want quotes from the Bible, they want an open ear and practical life support. But you didn't get that from Armstrong. Instead, just idle chat. Unctuous – and always doused with his own moral superiority. But the worst was that he was such a hypocrite."

"What do you mean?"

"Well, he preached loyalty, steadfastness and honour, yet he himself was disloyal to the core. On the one hand he dragged Jean and the children along to all posts, on the other hand he was after every skirt."

"Have there been official complaints? Did he mess up somebody?"

"No. After a few female soldiers from the Nursing Corps complained about him, he became more cautious and sought his women among the civilians. If nothing was going on there, he just went to hookers."

"And did everyone know that? Jean too?"

"Barracks are like small villages, everyone knows everyone and everyone knows everything. Jean may not have been in the loop about everything in detail, but she probably knew most of it. But as I said, she had given her wedding vows and was determined to keep them. And with three children..."

"If the man was such a bollocks, how did he charm all these ladies?"

"Well, not with particularly good looks. Really not." Grassington laughed again, and Emma thought of the little fat man with the pursed lips and sausage fingers.

"But he could be charming when he wanted to. He also had that certain Irish sense of humour, you know, gift of the gab, born storyteller and all – and he could sing like a bird. He must have played sports in the past, his movements showed great agility. At first glance the man was a fine fellow, and kept it up as long as he wanted something."

"Where has he been posted?" Emma wanted to know, annoyed by Grassington's clichés about the Irish. Born storyteller! If anyone told stories here, it would be Mr. Super-British himself.

"I remember a nasty story in Singapore, word of it even got around to headquarters in England. On the quiet, of course. He made out with a little Chinese woman. Nice girl, but from a humble background. At some point her father was standing in the barracks, cap in hand. The girl was pregnant and the man poor. He probably wanted at least the money for an abortion... and maybe a little something on top because of the shame and for her silence. Armstrong raged, calling the man a blackmailer and the girl a whore and a liar. It was shockingly undignified. None of his superiors believed Armstrong, they knew him, but back then, as you know... times were different. At that time, such incidents were kept under the carpet and the men involved were simply transferred." And after a pause: "I assume that's still the case in Ireland."

Not at all interested in discussing Irish sexual morals, Emma stuck to the point: "Where did they put him?"

'Well, in such a long career – practically everywhere the British Army went. Bahrain, Malaysia, Oman, Singapore and Malta," came the reply from the phone. "I may have forgotten a station, it's been a long time. From the mid-1970s we had to withdraw almost everywhere. After that he was in Herford, Germany. If you want, I can get you the list of stations and fax it through."

"Fabulous idea. Do that, and please include the dates as well." Emma gave him the police station's fax number.

In the ensuing silence, with Grassington probably taking notes on the other end, she said: "I just wonder why he's been showing up in Armagh so regularly all these years. Could it be that he was spying for you a bit?"

"If that was the case, then that would be highly confidential. Also, that's not in my line. You'd have to talk to MI6 in London directly and there's zero chance of you getting an answer. But personally, I think it's unlikely. Who among the catholic Republicans in Northern Ireland would have confided in a guy who everyone knew was a Protestant vicar and therefore probably on the wrong side of the fence?"

March 2004

It was already late, the apartment was filled with darkness. Only the floor lamp cast a circle of light on Catherine's sofa. There she had settled down after her long service in Oak Gardens to drink tea and eat some biscuits. Sweets were Catherine's passion, which showed in her womanly hips. Now she studied Margaret's journals and admired her wonderful handwriting. When the old teacher had began to lose touch with reality and was diagnosed with Alzheimer's, her sons had taken her to a nursing home and Margaret had obviously taken her old diaries with her. Catherine read, searched around, studied the dates. The earliest entry dates back to the summer of 1965. Nibbling on cookies, she began to read.

"July 16th, 1965. Today I was shocked to the bone. I had just breastfed Thomas and laid him down for a nap when there was a knock at the door. My sister was standing outside, but I almost didn't recognize her. Skinny, deathly pale, hair dishevelled. The last I heard from Mama in Ireland was that she had gone to the Bon Coeur Sisters for a few weeks 'to rest'. What a euphemism for giving birth! Mama was very curt in her letters when it came to Violet, and she never replied to my letters herself. Now she stood there, utterly in distress. Sobbing. I pulled her into the house, hugged her and bombarded her with questions: Where did you come from? How are you doing? Why didn't you ever write to me? Then little Thomas started to cry, the confusion in

the hallway had woken him. I ran and got the little one out of his bed. As I stood there with the child in my arms, my eyes fell on Violet's face: I've never seen such an expression of sheer despair."

Catherine lowered the old diary and tried to sort the facts. Margaret apparently had a sister – Violet. Was that the Violet she was always calling for? The woman with the thick braid in the photos in the album from the 1960s? And Margaret had not only the one son, Bill, whom Catherine had met in Oak Gardens this week, but another too, Thomas. Could this be the one living in Australia? There were photos of grandchildren with koalas or kangaroos on Margaret's night table. But what was Bon Coeur? Somehow the name sounded familiar to her. And then there had been another baby in the family, obviously.

"Violet collapsed in tears. With two people crying around me, my son and my sister, I could not make head or tail fo the story. So, first I calmed Tommie down and put him back in his crib, and then I pulled Violet into the kitchen and made her a cup of tea. We Irish are weird, when the house is on fire we put the kettle on first, to make tea. Hesitantly Violet told me how Charles took her to Bon Coeur and left her there. He must have drilled into her again and again that she must remain silent. Mainly to protect his career. But most of all she talked about the Sisters: 'You can't imagine how evil they can be', she kept saying. Apparently they didn't even give her enough to eat. She had to wash half the county's shirts in the laundry. Then the baby came and nobody helped her. She must have been screaming in pain for hours. Violet keeps talking about a Sister Magdalena, who must be a real devil. She didn't get her

a doctor, said the pain of labour was a punishment for her sins. God can't be that mean. Only people are that mean."

Margaret's words swam before Catherine's eyes. Now she remembered why she knew the name Bon Coeur. The press had been full of it, not just in Ireland but in Britain as well. A "fallen girl" facility run by Protestant sisters. During renovation work, the bodies of babies were found there, apparently thrown away like rubbish. Even the Church of Ireland, in whose name the home had been run, had spoken of "atrocities" and "unpardonable cruelty" in the media. Catherine was so full of memories of Protestant institutions herself she never wanted to think about that her throat tightened. The orphanage, the long dormitories, the sounds of children crying at night, the miserable food.

"They let her have the baby for a week. Then they took it away to raise the little one in a 'Christian' way and to make sure that she didn't become a bad woman, too. My poor, poor sister! And how horrible to turn to me for protection when I've also just had a child. If I imagine my Tom being taken away from me – I wouldn't want to live any more. And now Violet is here, where everything smells like a baby. Her heart must be breaking! She wanted to die, she said so. She ran to the sea somewhere at night, wanted to drown herself. Luckily she didn't dare. The next morning a woman found her on the beach and took her home. She also gave her the money for the ferry. I mustn't forget to send her those savings back, Violet says the house looked poor and was full of children.

And what am I going to do about mum now? At home, they'll be looking for Violet. I have to send a telegram!"

Am I part of this story? Catherine wondered. Am I the baby that was taken from Violet? Her own date of birth roughly matched dates of Violet's drama, July 6th, 1965. Was that why she looked a bit like Bill? Was he her cousin? Did Margaret always call her "Violet!" because the same blood ran through her veins? Had she simply been taken away from her mother? Then she began to cry, tears falling on Margaret's words, the ink blurred. Then the hatred almost took her breath away. All this wasted love! Everything could have been so different! Angry, Catherine ran her forearm across the pages, leaving an ugly smudge.

"July 18th, 1965. Violet stayed and I'm glad. She helps me with the baby, even though I can't stand to see her suffering. She must be missing her baby worse than I can imagine. When I look at my little Tom and think of how she must feel, it brings tears to my eyes. At night in bed Josh would ask me what was going on, but I couldn't really give him an answer. Violet had an illegitimate baby, had to give it away and ran away in Ireland. I'd rather not tell him I sent £5 to that Mary woman in Ireland to pay off Violet's debt. He's already growling: "You Irish with your endless dramas!" He probably would have preferred to take the money to the pub! His salary as a teacher is really not that special either. And now with the baby... I don't know how we're going to get along. I still can't understand why he didn't complete his medical degree. Cambridge! Who gets a chance like this?! And Josh just messes them up. Now he is a teacher at expensive private schools and has to teach the sons of his former classmates. No wonder he acts like life has insulted him. But I digress. I haven't heard from Linborough. Well, that

silence also speaks volumes. Not a word from Charles either! Also, I still don't know who the father of this child actually is. In any case, he can't be a nice man, a man of honour would have married Violet – and quickly, so that the pregnancy wasn't noticed!"

March 2005

Emma hammered her notes about her conversations with Reverend Shaw and Colonel Grassington into her computer. How she hated typing! The paperwork didn't get her anywhere. Why did old Armstrong have to die? – without a motive she would never find the perpetrator.

O'Leary came through the door and looked around. He smelled faintly of cigarette smoke, as always, which Emma didn't mind, oddly enough.

"Em, you still haven't cleaned up. If you keep up the good work, we can start a mushroom farm here soon. You know, mushrooms love dark corners and moisture. You've already accumulated enough crap here and a little extra income would not be bad to top up a garda's salary..."

"O'Leary, you mean old fecker..." Em already had a hardened bun in hand – which she'd actually brought to breakfast last Wednesday and then left on her plate – to throw at Aidan's head. Then Conway appeared behind him in the doorway, and Emma just managed to toss the rock-hard bun into the bin in a high arc. Instead of the bun, O'Leary only had to catch one of her looks and suppressed a laugh.

"So, what is it, you two?" Emma acted practical to distract young Dessie from her near-tantrum. It wouldn't be good if

Conway lost his respect for her after such a short time. It was enough that O'Leary played the clown with impunity! She would have to learn to keep her cool.

"We visited the reverend's wife again and checked her out. Not much came of it," Aidan began to explain. "Her trip to Belfast seems to have played out exactly as she describes it. We have witnesses for that. Between shopping with her sister and going to the hairdresser's she simply wouldn't have had the time to hire a car, drive back to Sligo, kill the old man and then hurtle back to the sister's in Belfast. She just couldn't have done it in time. Apart from the fact that Jean doesn't even have a driver's license and that her sister would have noticed that Madame's hair hasn't been freshly done", Aidan summarized the conversation and grinned. Emma could hear what he was thinking: these women and all their fuss about their hair!

"Being jealous of Sue Morrow next door would also be rather thin as a motive," Emma admitted. I found Armstrong's superior, a Colonel Grassington. He told me that Charles was not only a hypocritical army chaplain whom his soldiers didn't particularly like, but also that the old git was pretty much chasing after every skirt. Jean is said to have known most of it, and there were probably worse misdemeanours than flirting with the neighbour. If she wanted to kill him because he couldn't keep it in his pants, she would have picked up a kitchen knife years ago."

"So we have no motive and a fairly airtight alibi; guess we can probably rule out Jean," summarized Aidan.

"On a different note," Emma frowned. "Dessie, I asked you to find out information about the family. Did anything come of it?"

"So," Dessie began as he leafed through his notebook a little pompously. "Charles Armstrong came from Laragh, where his father Gerald Scott bought a country estate back in the 1930's. The property probably goes back to the so-called Plantation, when the British installed non-catholic settlers in Ireland to secure the rule of the English crown. Jean is terribly proud of this legacy. She couldn't stop talking about it. In plain language, however, it probably means that the original owners went broke at some point, and that's where Gerald Scott saw his chance and simply bought the land for a song."

"Who owns it now?"

„The eldest son, Charles, our victim, went to the Church, the eldest daughter, Margaret, moved to England and married a Cambridge medical student at the time, a Joshua Sargent. The second daughter, Violet, remained unmarried and childless on the farm to look after her elderly parents. She died back in 1986."

"Do you know what this Violet died of?" Emma asked.

Here Dessie had to pass. "No idea. In any case, Henry, the youngest son, now holds the title on the land. He is also unmarried and has no descendants. He recently built himself a new house in the village. That's where he lives now and Charles' daughter Jane is in the process of renovating the big house, planning to move in."

"So it looks like Charles' daughter will inherit the family estate?" Emma asked.

"In that respect, I could not get much out of Jean. Henry has agreed that Jane can live at Linborough House with her family. Whether there is a corresponding will, the good woman cannot or does not want to say. Henry must be an odd fish, by the way. Jean says the only one he trusted was Charles. And he was the only one who understood what Henry was going on about. He might be a few slates short of a roof, this Henry."

Emma was fed up with the office and her futile brooding. She decided to drive to Laragh and see the Armstrongs' gaff. Maybe there was something to Laura McDern's stories and the whole case was about the estate? Also, Henry might be willing to tell her what he planned to do with all that land. Who should inherit it? And was there enough value in it to make it worth killing? But why Charles? If Henry held the title? On the other hand, Charles must have had a lot of influence over his little brother... Maybe Charles was trying to get Henry to do something that a third party was desperate to prevent?

A research trip was also a good opportunity to get her prescription for painkillers somewhere on the tour, so that her pharmacist in Sligo didn't realise how much of the stuff she was actually consuming. On the country road South, the old engine ran like clockwork. Spring finally seemed to be arriving, and Emma rolled down the window to get some fresh air. At Ballysadare she finally turned West onto the N59. Now Knocknarea appeared from the the haze. It is said that Connaught's old Queen Maeve was buried upright on her horse on top of this mountain. Obviously, 3,000 years ago, the Irish still took women seriously. However, that ended with the advent of Christianity. Too bad, actually.

Laragh came into view far too quickly, Emma would have liked to drive a little longer through the countryside. She loved Ireland's green hills, the salty air, the sheep dabbed on the meadows like white woollen flowers, and the ancient stone walls that had been piled up for centuries. Laragh, however, stirred up her resentment like so many corners of contemporary Ireland. She remembered visiting the area as a little girl, when the hamlet was still pretty and had a real heart. By now, however, everything had been subjugated by traffic, and Laragh remained reduced to a handful of houses lining the thoroughfare of the National Road. Gone were the thatched roofs, gone the cobbled paths. On the outskirts of the settlement were new development areas, the real estate boom had hit hard here.

Since 2000, it seemed like every Irishman who would hold a shovel could get a job and be offered cheap credit from the bank. As a result, new houses were springing up on every corner, and yet the prices rose disproportionally. Can anyone understand why my dear compatriots believe that their real estate is becoming more and more valuable just because they keep selling each other houses and inflating prices in the process? The only ones laughing up a storm were the mortgage brokers and the banks. Emma had her doubts as to whether a shack in Laragh that was built quickly and cheaply was really worth the hundreds of thousands of euro that was their price tag. Those boxy gaffs were so ugly! She'd rather buy a draughty, cramped old cottage with character!

At the petrol station near the entrance to the village, she stopped to ask for directions. Emma liked to take every opportunity to talk to people. The petrol station attendant was a picture book Irish cliché. Gnarly, weatherbeaten and monosyllabic, in oil-smeared overalls with a flat cap on his head. A face like a sad wolf, in the mouth the inevitable fag. She had already gone too far, he mumbled out of the corner of his mouth: she had to go back and then up the hill to the right, after the church. She could not miss it.

Emma slowly drove towards the house. There was a driveway behind a little white wall, the rusty metal gate stood open. The two-storey building was situated on a small hill in the middle of meadows, not far from the sea. Old stone walls were covered with ivy, and the windows were trimmed in white. Compared to the small cottages of Catholic farmhands, Linborough House was indeed an impressively stately building. Protestant pride turned to stonework – but why exactly? That they didn't accept the Pope? That the British Crown transplanted them here? Emma had a sense of history, but she would never understand why anyone could be proud of belonging to a particular religion. Or of not belonging to another one.

In front of the house was a massive skip full of debris. Obviously the old house had just been cleared out and at least partially renovated. There were old pipes, rotting floorboards, the remains of a yuck pink bathroom and lots of dusty chunks of mortar in the skip. Today the house was deserted . Emma walked around the property; the signs of decay were unmistakable. The layered old Irish stone walls would have needed repair decades ago, gates were hanging askew on their hinges, behind the house she discovered the body of a rusting old red tractor. Next to it, a ladder rotted in the grass, someone had driven a truck over it. Old plastic bags and containers were scattered everywhere. Who knows what used to be in there! In any case, they didn't come from the most recent construction work, the rubbish had obviously been here for quite a long time. Still, the property had to be worth a fortune. Emma wasn't a real estate expert, and she didn't know how much land came with the house, but at current prices, Linborough House, refurbished and cleared of rubble, would certainly fetch a nice wad of money. Since 1995, the Celtic tiger was developing splendidly, drawing more and more well-educated Irish people back from their exile in America, Australia or Great Britain to found new companies in the green tax haven. Thanks to Dublin's new corporate tax laws! These nouveau riches could certainly be interested in parts of the surrounding farm as building land. Emma made a mental note to ask Aidan or Dessie to find out what this spot overlooking the Atlantic might be worth. People have killed for way less than this place was worth, she thought.

Emma had seen enough and headed back towards the main road, stopping at a pub quaintly named The Fox's Den. It was only three o'clock in the afternoon, but the first drinkers were already sitting in front of their Guinness. They looked like the inmates of a sanatorium. Why was there so much drinking in Ireland? Emma didn't want to know the answer to her own question.

As the door slammed behind her, heads turned, but otherwise the room was silent.

"Hello. How are youse? Henry Armstrong? Where can I find him?" Emma asked into the silence. One man thoughtfully scratched his arse. Then he called out, "Paddy Joe! There is one here looking about someone."

A short, round man with a beard on his melon-sized head looked out of an adjoining room.

"Good day. Henry Armstrong? Where can I find him?" Emma repeated her question.

"Go on into the village, lass. Henry's house is just to the right before the petrol station. Black gate, you cannot miss it."

The three locals at the bar would have known that too. Was there some unwritten law that only the bartender was allowed to give information to strangers in a pub?

Emma parked her car and looked around. Why did Henry live here? While Linborough represented a legacy of good taste in architecture, the new house was simply a grey, faceless gaff just off the road. The yard wasn't a garden, it was paved and full of used cars that had seen better days. Who would want a bungalow like this when you could have a beaut like Linborough House? Admittedly, there was a small waterfall on the other side of the road – but that could hardly make up for the fact that Henry had placed his new house right next to a petrol station. Cosy was something else. She knocked.

The door opened and in front of her stood a tiny goblin straight out of Irish mythology. He was short and stocky, his grey hair still showing traces of ginger, but only the old gentleman's cheeks were really bright red. His eyes were clear and sparkling blue, but they almost sank into the creases that surrounded them. The lips were so thin that the mouth looked as if it had been slashed into his face. The whole figure was clad in a grey suit, the uniform of the older Irish. Many also went to work in the fields in those garments.

"Henry Armstrong?" Emma asked. "Hello, I'm detective Emma Woods, from Sligo. It's about your brother." She shoved her police ID card in his face.

"Terrible story, that. I miss him, dear Charles. Anyway I'm about to get ready. The funeral is tomorrow, isn't it? But it won't be as beautiful as Yeats' grave... You know that one, it's in Drumcliffe? `Cast a cold eye on life. On death. Horseman, pass by´... Ever read anything by Oscar Wilde? `Tread lightly, she is near under the snow, speak gently, she can hear the daisies grow...´"

Emma was beginning to suspect why Jean thought no one but Charles understood Henry. And he was dead. The charming little man in front of her talked a lot and quickly and kept changing the subject like a running hare changed directions. It's hard to imagine that he and cold, slow-moving Jean belonged to the same family. Aloud she said:

"May I come inside? I have a few questions."

"Questions. Yes, I have questions too. I recently asked Betty Watson, 'Have you ever had German measles?' You know, that's what we call rubella. She says: 'Why? I've never been to Germany!'" The old man started to laugh but opened the door wide to let Emma in. Immediately to the left was a modern, but rather untidy and terribly overheated kitchen.

"Sit yourself down! You'll have a cup of tea?"

Faced with the mountains of unwashed dishes, Emma said no. She didn't want to cost the man his last clean cup.

"Questions, what questions?" Henry came back and Emma wondered: was the wee fella just playing the confused one?

"Did your brother have enemies? Can you imagine who would mean him harm?"

"Evil is everywhere. Especially in an old country like this. St. Patrick took away the snakes from us, but left us all the other evils. Charles knew that, oh yes. Charles was a fine man. Now he's gone too. They are all gone, only Margaret is alive. But she's gone in the head."

"Margaret?"

"My sister. But she's out of her mind. She's in a home, in England, in Manchester, she doesn't understand anything any more. Always just calling for Violet. My other sister. She died in 1986 and didn't grow old. Margaret, I once promised Margaret the horse field, so she would take care of our mother. Didn't give her anything in writing, though, ha!" Henry put the index finger of his right hand to his nose and smiled conspiratorially.

"The horse field? Do you mean land around Linborough House?" asks Emma.

"Yes, Linborough House. Everything always revolves around the House. Also with Charles. Everyone wants the land, but I have the title to it. I didn't promise anything to anyone, not to anybody!"

"Do you think the attack on Charles had anything to do with Linborough House ?"

"Bill has already tried to take the land from me. He wanted the crop field, the field towards Ballina. Wanted to build. For himself and this woman from Switzerland. But they won't take anything away from me, they won't. And Tom doesn't get anything either. Not while I'm alive. He lives in sin in Australia. Left his wife. You don't do that! And worse, the new one is a Catholic!"

Who the blazes was Bill? Emma patiently repeated her questions, and patiently Henry repeated his evasive manoeuvres. He mixed up people, times and places. Still, Henry seemed to be one of the few people who cared for Charles. After much deliberation, two things became clear to Emma: Henry didn't like his Swiss-based nephew Bill – Margaret's younger son – with whom he had apparently had a wild argument over part of the property. Margaret's second son, the other nephew, Thomas, lived in Australia with his second wife. Henry didn't like second wives either. For that reason alone Tom should be disinherited, thought Henry. Then it would be better for Charles' children to get the estate, because they were proper Protestants. Or at least pretended to, but Emma didn't say that out loud.

"The land must remain in the family. I say that, and so does Charles. We agree on that," Henry babbled on. "It's not for sale, no way. Because then the Catholics from the IRA all just chip in together and buy up the land. They buy everything they can get their hands on. Every big house of ours, every big farm that comes on the market. Because they want to get rid of us Protestants, you know?"

"Who is going to inherit Linborough House?" Emma asked, finally getting to the heart of the matter.

Henry narrowed his eyes: "If I give it to everyone in equal parts, it will be sold. Neither one of them can pay off the others. Then the land ends up in the hands of the Catholics. They're all in the IRA. All killers! That will not do. But if I officially only give it to one person, there will be a row. Oh, all the noise. Just like with Bill back then! I can't stand all the trouble. Only Charles understands me. And Jane. She lives there now and makes Linborough beautiful again."

On the way back, in the last light of the spring day, Emma took a detour to the bog. She wanted to see Lough Easky again, where her parents used to take her to fish for trout on the rare holidays at home. She drove along the roads used for centuries by the Irish to cut turf from the bogs for their fires. Today the long-trodden paths were tarred, but still so narrow that her little Peugeot could hardly fit through. Hopefully none of those German tourists came towards her in their camper vans!

Emma drove on, the lake was on her right. A lonely fisherman stood by the water. Did he ever catch anything? Emma didn't want to disturb him, if only because that would destroy the living picture – the landscape with him in it suddenly looked like a 17th-century painting. The surface of the water was still, almost like a polished mirror. It looked peaceful and inviting. But Emma knew better. Its dark depths were cold and would kill you with merciless indifference.

It was lonely up here, barren and windy. But the sky was high and wide, the air clear. Mount Nephin kept watch in the distance. There was an old local joke that said, if you can see Nephin, it's going to rain soon. And if you can't see it, it's already raining. Emma grinned to herself. The ruins of old farmhouses lined the road. Hardly anyone lived up here any more. Life was just too hard in the boglands and the winter up here was almost unbearable. The only soul Emma met was a lonely donkey. She got out, took a deep breath, scratched the animal's nose, and presented her latest theory about the Armstrong family and the motive for the homicide. The donkey remained unimpressed.

She was back in Sligo about 20 minutes later, but didn't take her foot off the accelerator, instead continuing north towards Drumcliff and Grange. Whilst she was out she could whiz straight down to Mullaghmore and see the pub where, according to his neighbour, Charles Armstrong was said to have had a romantic tryst last Valentine's Day.

Emma liked Mullaghmore, the old fishing village on the peninsula that pointed like a finger towards Donegal. The view of Classiebawn Castle was breathtaking, Emma had to admit, it was as if the architect had transplanted some fairytale castle onto the bleak rocks. The British castle was oversized and alien here in the world of thatched roofs and red-painted doors, but as a proud demonstration of the triumph of human will over a harsh nature the thing had something.

The village's beach was also impressive, as were the towering waves that broke on it. Surfers from all over the world met here to measure their strength against that of the Atlantic. But wild surf, which made surfers happy, was a problem for sailors. Because of this, a long, high pier jutted out like an arm into the bay. In its lee, a small harbour sheltered the humble boats of the local lobster fishermen, alongside the pretty little sailing yachts of British and Scandinavian tourists who had bought expensive holiday homes in the surrounding fields. Emma stopped the car and got out, staring out to sea and across the bay. Rain or not, she could understand the tourists with their love for Ireland.

Mullaghmore wasn't as harmless as it looked. In August 1979 the IRA blew up Louis Francis Albert Victor Nicholas Mountbatten, 1st Earl Mountbatten of Burma. Louis, as the Earl with the endless name let himself be called here, wanted to take advantage of the good weather and catch his own dinner. It was to be lobster. So he ventured out of his castle, took his boat, the "Shadow V", steered it around the pier onto the open water and out to the lobster grounds. Emma didn't know whether to admire the old soldier's courage in going fishing among the Irish locals just a few miles to the west during the worst of Northern Ireland's Troubles, or despise the stubborn arrogance of the English aristocracy. Louis was, after all, a grandson of Queen Victoria, the uncle of Prince Philip, a retired admiral in the British Navy, and in all these roles, in the eyes of the IRA at least, a symbol of the hated British occupancy.

On that August 27th, 1979, a giant bang rattled the windows as far away as Cliffoney, kilometres down the road. A water fountain shot up, parts of the boat and human bodies flew through the air. At first, many thought the noise was coming from manoeuvrers or target practice at the Finner army camp across the bay.

But this was not the case. Four died that day, Mountbatten, his grandson Nicholas, Lady Brabourne and a man named Paul Maxwell. Three others were seriously injured, but survived as there were many boats out on the warm summer day and local boaters dragged the victims out of the water.

In the days that followed, Emma's colleagues from the Garda painstakingly had fished the matchstick-sized parts of "Shadow V" out of the sea and put them back together in the laboratory to find out what had happened. Divers were out in the water for weeks because the tide had quickly spread everything over the entire bay. In the end, forensics concluded that the bomb must have been hidden in one of the lobster pots where Louis thought to find his dinner. The explosives had been activated remotely by someone who was probably standing high on the cliffs, probably armed with binoculars, when Mountbatten had tried to get to his lobsters.

Incidentally, 18 British soldiers also died on the same day at Warrenpoint, in County Down; the IRA claimed responsibility for both attacks. The 18 dead soldiers were almost forgotten by now, but the murder of Louis, whom many in the village knew as a jovial fellow and nice neighbour, stuck in the collective memory of the area like a bloodstain to the village square that couldn't be washed away, even if the Tourist Office did everything to make people forget the past. Later, two men from Monaghan and Leitrim were convicted for attacking Louis and his "Shadow V".

Emma shivered, pulled her jacket tighter around her and made her way to the pub. It was early evening by now, but on a Monday in March the Pier Head Hotel's Quay Lounge & Bar wasn't very busy. A beautiful wooden floor, comfortable, stylish wooden furniture and a fire in the fireplace awaited guests. Two small windows overlooked the Atlantic ocean, which dominated everything around here. Emma often regretted that in the past the Irish had built so small and low and there were so few windows in the fine old houses. But here it made sense. In a fierce Northerly, there was no use for exposed large windows on this peninsula jutting out into the ocean. They would have blown out and into your face on a regular basis.

The barmaid was obviously bored with the slow early Monday business, she was already awaiting Emma's orders. Her thick, almost black hair fell in long strands over her massive bosom. Her snow-white skin was evidence of a life turning night into day, or perhaps just an indicator of the long Irish winter and lack of sunshine. Bright blue eyes studied Emma. She ordered a cider and just stood at the counter. She was familiar with her

Irish compatriots and knew from experience that most of them loved a chat. It didn't take long before the barmaid asked:

"You touring around?"

'No, not really, I'm from Sligo. I just don't get to go to Mullaghmore that often."

"Sligo. Hm, I go there to shop, but you can only ever find good outfits in Dublin anyway."

The two women smiled at each other knowingly. The whole region wasn't exactly a Mecca for fashion victims. Most people in the area felt sufficiently well dressed by the time they slipped into their wellies.

"I'm Emma."

"My name is Maisie."

"Hello Maisie, pleased to meet you. Sluggish business today."

"It's just fine with me, all hell broke loose over the weekend."

For me too, thought Emma. Aloud she said:

"Do you remember the night of Valentine's Day? Did you work that day?"

"Yes, I was here. Kicked my old man out before Christmas. Was always drunk anyway, good riddance. So no Valentine for me, I could just as easily go to work." And after a pause, with a suspicious look: "Why do you want to know that?"

"Garda. I'm investigating a homicide."

"And what does that have to do with me or Valentine's Day?"

"The victim is said to have been here on Valentine's Day. And not with his wife. I thought I'd ask around to see if anyone here remembered the two."

"How is it to be with the guards as a woman? When I was a young lassie, I wanted to be in the guards. But my father said it can't be done, I'm just a girl and too short..." Maisie was obviously not yet ready to talk about the specific case.

"Yes, this notion has remained with many. But machos are everywhere, not just in the Garda," Emma evaded, knowing full well that when she started talking about Paddy McNulty and the other arseholes who had made life difficult for her throughout her career, she would still standing here at midnight. Maisie just laughed, which made her even more likeable.

"Back to Valentine's Day. Do you remember an older gentleman with a blonde?" Emma asked.

"Oh, you mean the old priest they killed in Sligo?"

"Oops, you're well informed."

"I read that in the newspaper."

"You heard about Charles Armstrong's murder from the media?"

"Yeah, I kind of remembered. I knew him fleetingly, he'd been here from time to time lately."

"Here in the bar?"

"Yep, exactly. And always with a rather washed-out blonde. She looked like she'd seen better days."

"How do you mean that?"

"Well, none of us gets prettier with the years. But some women have such a divorced expression on their faces, ye know what I mean, they look so careworn. Like life washed all the colour right out of them."

Emma knew exactly what Maisie meant. "And the Reverend helped her. Had spiritual counselling sessions with her, so to speak?"

Masie laughed again: "Not exactly. The two always put their heads together, but it looked more like a full-blown affair. The only thing containing spirit around here was the whiskey in the Reverend's glass."

"So they got along well. Or have you ever witnessed a fight between the two of them?"

"You want to know if the woman could have killed the old philanderer?" Maisie grinned. "I don't think so. The blonde isn't particularly tall or heavy, she couldn't have taken on the fat Reverend on her own."

"Do you know the lady's name?"

"Mary something. Mary Jane or something. Or Marion. He always called her Mimi or something like that. In any case, she comes from Drummon. Wait a moment."

Maisie disappeared behind a door that led either to the kitchen or to the neighbouring hotel. Emma sipped at her glass: Drummon was across the bay from Sligo and Mullaghmore was the ideal meeting place in the middle. So that was fine. Had this woman killed the reverend because he didn't want to leave his Jean? According to the motto: If I don't get you, no one else can have you either... Or was the lady married and her cuckholed husband had lost patience? A little later Maisie came back.

"Well, I was at the reception. The reverend has often rented a room here, says the colleague. If you know what I mean …"

"I get it. And does the guest book also state the name of the lady?"

"It says Mary-Anne Armstrong."

"And this Mary-Anne is from Drummon?"

"Exactly."

"How do you know?"

"I don't know, I just heard these two talk about the good old days in Drummon. Somehow I concluded that the lady lives there."

Emma finished her cider. Mission accomplished, now she could finally go home.

"Thank you Maisie, you've been a great help. I hope to be able to come back soon with less baggage than today."

Maisie smiled the barmaid's professional smile and Emma left.

When she got home, her street was wet and dark, the traffic noise muted by the rotting autumn leaves still on the asphalt. The trees were still almost bare in March, their branches casting their shadows on the wet ground in the light of the street lamps. It was late when Emma finally unlocked the front door. There were shoes lying around in the hallway, gym gear, and an empty bag of chips. The kitchen was decorated with the remains of a sandwich making operation. Accidentally, Emma landed her hand in the half-melted butter. Stevie was next door in the living room watching TV. Apparently he couldn't bring himself to say hello to his mother. She just went over to him, despite the pain in her back and legs. It had been a long day.

"Tell me, Stevie, when did you get home?"

"About six."

"And you can't even clean up the kitchen? It's after eight now, I've been working all day and now I'm supposed to have fun with this crap in the kitchen?"

Emma felt the familiar panic rising in her. Luckily she had the pills in her purse.

"Whatevva. Leave it alone if it bothers you so much. Tomorrow is another day..." Stevie's eyes were glued to the screen.

"You're not a child any more, why do I always have tidy up your shit? Can't you..."

"Man, take a chill pill!" Stevie turned off the TV, slammed the remote on the coffee table and disappeared into his room. He had his own little telly – a gift from Paul – from which, of course, the roar from the stadium could be heard immediately. Someone had apparently scored a goal.

Emma poured herself an Irish whiskey and flopped down on the sofa. She let the sharp, peat-tasting liquid circulate in her mouth. The fear of another bout of pain was gripping her, and alcohol seemed to help keeping that at bay. But there it was, the slight dizziness of the pain, the slowly rising nausea. The disgusting taste in the mouth. What was actually worse?, Emma wondered. The pain or the fear of the pain?

CHAPTER 6

Earth to Earth

It is night, the street in front of her stretches endlessly into the black. Emma sits in the dark, she feels Paul at her side. Again and again, lights appear out of the darkness and race towards them. She can't see properly, her eyes won't open, all she knows is that she's deeply uncomfortable. She elbows Paul in the side. She hears his voice, hardly sees him, her eyes are glued shut. He is giving out to her as always.

"You stupid bitch. I'm stuck in Ireland because of you, in that sad wet rag of a country. And you've nailed me down with that brat, too..."

He goes on like this, indefinitely. Paul is drunk, his voice has that slurring, muddy element to it, like it always does when Paul's had a few too many. Emma struggles to open her eyes, through the wreath of her lashes she only sees blurry lights coming towards her. Suddenly her view is clear. Paul is driving the car in the middle of the street, a delivery truck is coming towards them. It's driver honks wildly. Emma screams, a startled Paul pulls the car to the left – then there is a bang! and suddenly everything disappears into a brilliant white light.

"Mum, wake up, you're having another nightmare. Mum!"
Someone shook Emma's shoulder, she struggled to emerge from her dream.
"Mum! Everything is alright. You're at home, in bed." Stevie's voice slowly got through to her. Emma awoke with a deep weariness in her bones, as if some vital fluid had been drained from her body.

"Stevie, sorry. Did I scream again in my dream?"

"Yes, very loudly." Her son was standing in front of Emma's bed in his pyjamas with the horse head prints, which he had outgrown a while ago. Here he was, her wonderful son, drowsy and dishevelled.

"I'm so sorry, go back to bed..."

Stevie gave her a wry grin and made his way back to his room. Emma rubbed her eyes. Again she had dreamed of the accident in which Paul, drunk, had crashed their car into a tree after a visit to the Beach Bar on Aughris Head. He had fallen asleep at the wheel and tried to avoid an oncoming truck at the last possible moment. He had succeeded, but he over steered and had crashed into a tree along that narrow country road. Typical! There were so few trees in Ireland, but Paul found one to make Emma's life miserable. And poor Stevie had to deal with a mother who woke the entire house with the screams from her nightmares.

She slowly relaxed. It was still dark outside, not yet seven o'clock. The hours before dawn, the wasteland of the night. Sleep was out of the question, Emma might as well get up and face the day. Mechanically, she swallowed two painkillers, washing them down with the glass of water that always sat on her bedside table. She quietly got dressed and went out to the river. As always, she was grateful to have found this house in Doorley Park, not far from where the Garavogue river flowed from Lough Gill, winding its way into Sligo Bay before being lost in the open Atlantic. Actually, the rent was almost a little too high for her income, but the opportunity to wander along the waterline to clear her head was worth every euro. She stood there in the twilight, the waves lapping around a moored rowing boat, the birds rustling in the reeds. Life obviously went on, even if she herself often had the feeling of being stuck like a boot in mud.

At a little after seven, freshly showered and fully dressed, she was standing at the kitchen window with a cup of tea, looking out onto the street. Sligo slowly lolled out of the night and greeted the day. Emma was still reeling from her dream, and the painkiller gave her stomach pains. To calm them down, she chewed some stale bread. She pulled her shoulders towards her ears, dropped them again, slowly moved her head from side to side, trying to actively relax and deepen her breathing.

Meanwhile her thoughts were rattling her head. So a Mary-Anne from Drummon had been Armstrong's sweetheart. At least that's how Maisie had described it – and as we all know, an experienced bartender is rarely wrong. But how was she supposed to find a Mary-Anne in Drummon without further details like an address or a telephone number? Even if there were a registration office or residents' registration office in Ireland, just saying "Mary-Anne" and "presumably from Drummon" wouldn't get her very far. She would probably have to drive to this village and ask at the post office or in the pub. After all, in Irish villages everyone knew everybody. And Drummon wasn't exactly a metropolis, actually it consisted of only a few houses, a catholic church and a protestant one. However, there was a possibility that this Mary or Mimi or whatever her name was would appear at Armstrong's funeral today. If the lady dared to face Jean.

Emma loved the trip from Sligo to Strandhill. The narrow country roads led her over green hills, small streams and under fairy bridges – those places where the treetops on either side of the road touched each other and grew together, forming an archway. In between houses, glimpses of the sea kept flashing through the foliage – little vistas of Sligo's coastline and the islands off it. One of them was called Coney Island. The amusement park in New York, which Emma had often visited as a child, was named after that, and she almost had to laugh every time she saw the Irish original: lonely, rough, Nordic – no trace of ice cream, roller coasters and screaming teenagers. Eventually, the road meandered through the ritzier parts of Sligo, whoever lived along those roads had money and influence.

As if thrown there like a rock, St. Anne's sat on a small plain of still wintry grey grass, from which here and there jutted even greyer tombstones. Behind the stone-old church stood the round head of Knocknarea mountain. The Atlantic was so close you could have heard the waves pounding against the peninsula were it not for the roar of the cars on the coast road. The wind had beaten the vegetation for decades, the trees had grown sideways as if they were caught in a perpetual storm and indeed in a way they were. Emma let her gaze wander over the modest church, which was adorned with an undersized bell tower: It looked the same as it did a hundred years ago and a hundred years before that. In her eyes, this little brick church represented everything that was good about Ireland: dignity, resilience, focus on the essential. Bling was about as Irish as Piña Colada. If only the idiots who built these housing estates onto the ancient grounds would understand that!

The late Armstrong almost extracted a little respect from her – after all, he had obviously wished for a grave under that high sky with the screeching seagulls, and not one at the much more pompous St John's The Baptist Cathedral in town. A service had been held for him there – an occasion Emma had spared herself. The mayor would have been there, probably the police commissioner and the other usual suspects. Much more interesting, however, was who stood here at the graveyard in the cold wind from the sea.

People crowded the narrow path meandering between the graves and the damp grass. Emma was astonished to learn that the old vicar was to be buried next to his son Ron. The son on who, according to Jean, he had picked upon constantly. Well, Armstrong was silenced, he would not disturb Ron's rest.

The coffin had already been carried to the open graveside. Most of the bearers Emma didn't know. Everyone gathered around the hole in the ground for the actual burial. Jean was there all dressed in black as was her daughter Jane. The man next to her – one of the pallbearers – was probably the son-in-law. Jean's other daughter, Alice, had apparently not made the journey from Australia in the short time available. Charles' sister Margaret was also absent – "she's in the home, totally gaga," Henry's words from the day before. The little man from Laragh had made it to the funeral; he had also helped to carry the coffin, though actually, he had been a bit too short for the job, the other bearers towered over him; Emma nodded to him. Next to Henry was a much taller, handsome, significantly younger man who appeared to be accompanied by a blond woman and an even blonder little girl. Emma was curious: who was that? Aidan O'Leary had also shown up, irreverently with an unlit cigarette between his lips. He had just finished one, a remnant of cigarette smoke encircled him like a torn chiffon scarf. They placed themselves together in the back row of the mourners. Emma saw lots of black suits with white collars: lots of Church of Ireland bats flying around here, she recognized Reverend Shaw from Armagh, the gentleman next to him probably was the bishop. Some old ladies. In between, a faded blonde with tears in her eyes. Pink sweater under the black coat, lipstick a little too bright for a funeral. Was that Mary-Anne? That would have to be determined after the ceremony. The Morrows were there too, a nod. Emma's friend Laura McDern, the Armstrongs' family lawyer, had also come, but there was no time for a chat now.

When the bishop began his sermon, Emma switched off. Her eyes followed the chasing gulls and the hurrying clouds. She loved that about Ireland: the weather changed every ten minutes. After what felt like an eternity – had they not said enough prayers already in church? – one of the pallbearers, who had previously been standing next to Jean and her daughter, placed himself at the open grave. He introduced himself as Bob Roberts and was in fact Charles Armstrong's son-in-law. Apparently he was to deliver a few last words of farewell: "Charles had a strong sense of community. Wherever he went, he quickly became a part of the local community. He saw no boundaries, only opportunities to connect with others..."

Yes, especially when these others were female. The ceremony was finally over, no one had made a scene, no one behaved suspiciously, and no one had turned up to offend the others in any way. Jean had overlooked the blonde in pink and black. Either she didn't know the woman or she had decided not to know her. Everything had gone like clockwork, a regular funeral after a regular death. When in fact the man had been strangled – but obviously everyone tried to get this fact buried with the body as quickly as possible. Emma and Aidan approached the deeply veiled Jean to offer their condolences and were introduced to both Jane and Bob Roberts, as well as to the young man with the blond family: "This is Bill Sargent, my nephew from Switzerland, his wife Paula and their daughter Isabelle."

After the greeting and the usual condolences – so sorry for your trouble –, Emma asked Bill to drop by the Pearse Road station after the funeral .

As the mourners dispersed, Emma sent O'Leary after the family, "Prick up your ears, you might hear something interesting!"

She attached herself to the heels of the blonde who was walking towards the parking lot. When she was two meters behind her target, she called out, "Mary-Anne!" And sure enough, the woman turned around. Emma saw that she was crying again. At least one who really mourned the old man! thought Emma. The woman just stood under the wide, ash-colored sky and fumbled in her purse for a fresh handkerchief.

"You're Mary-Anne, right?"

"Yes, but please leave me alone. As you can see I'm not in the best of form."

Emma produced her service badge, in the form of a Celtic cross with the initials G.S., for Garda Síochána, and held it up. The inscription means "guardian of the peace" in this deeply troubled Ireland.

"Detective Emma Woods. I need to talk to you."

"About what?"

Emma wasn't used to being asked questions. It was she who asked the questions. So she spared herself and her counterpart the answer and got straight to the point:

"How well did you know Armstrong? And when did you last see him?"

"That was ages ago. We were childhood friends. Many years ago Charles served as Reverend in Drummon, that's when we met. At some point we lost touch."

"Really. Then why were you with him in Mullaghmore on Valentine's Day? Your name in the hotel register reads Mary-Anne Armstrong."

The woman, who had just been standing upright, practically collapsed, a pleading expression in her eyes: "For God's sake, if anyone hears that! Don't be so loud."

Her face had turned a greyish white, a colour like the pebbles on the beach nearby.

"Why are you suddenly so scared?" Emma asked.

"The scandal, the lord bless us, the scandal!", moaned Mary-Anne.

"Well, we don't have to talk here and now, but you will have to talk to me and tell me the truth."

And after a little pause: "What's your last name?"

"Gallagher. My name is Mary-Anne Gallagher."

Emma now had the key to the background of the drama – Gallagher was as catholic a name as names go and Armstrong had been Church of Ireland clergy. An impossible love, how corny. Aloud she said:

"Fine, we can handle this quietly. Just come into Pearse Road Station and we can talk it over.'

"No, not the station! What if someone sees me there!"

"Then I'll come to you."

"That's even worse!"

Now Emma lost patience: "I'm investigating a homicide. That means I work for the dead man and not for the living. Your sensitivities aren't exactly top of my list."

She held her notepad and a pen under Mary-Anne's nose: "Write down your address and telephone number on it and I'll get in touch with you. In civilian clothes and in an unmarked car. That's all I can do for you."

After this conversation, Emma wandered around a bit between the crosses of the churchyard, the Celtic and and not so Celtic ones, to organize her thoughts. Order was out of the question, wild associations shot madly through her head. Among them was an article she had recently read in the newspaper: One day in Ireland, archaeologists might dig up piles of mobile phones next to ancient bones because more and more Irish people allegedly put their cell phones in the coffin of dead relatives and friends. It was a tradition, that for centuries it had been customary to give the dead personal items on their last journey: wedding rings, a soccer ball, a golden lighter, a bottle of whiskey – and now it was cell phones. Not exactly eco-friendly, Emma thought. Then she had to laugh: What if the deceaseds phone suddenly rang at a funeral? Some of her dear fellow Irishmen would surely believe it was an angel on the line, or even the dear Lord...

When she got back to the parking lot, Aidan was standing by her car, smoking. "Be still my beating heart" was about the only quote from Shakespeare that she could really remember from her English classes. How fitting!

"That wasn't really enlightening. We now know that Charles was a pillar of the church. They all act as if he had fallen asleep gently," was Aidan's comment on the funeral.

"Oh, it wasn't that useless," Emma grinned. "I found Armstrong's sweetheart."

"Whatsthatyasay. The blonde you just ran after?"

"Exactly. Her name is Mary Anne Gallagher and she hails from Drummon."

Aidan whistled through his teeth. "A Catholic sweetheart. If that comes out, all hell will break loose."

"Exactly. And that's why she wasn't happy at all that a Garda wanted to grill her."

"Understandable. Speaking of not happy at all. I noticed something earlier," Aidan said. "Did you see Bill Sargent's face when Bob Roberts talked about his father-in-law at the funeral? He looked like he had to drink vinegar."

"It's about the property, I think. Bob and Charles' daughter Jane are in the process of making Linborough House their home. According to Henry, Bill wanted the land – or at least parts of it – and there's been a big row. Now Charles' daughter and her husband are grabbing it all. Bill obviously is less than pleased. So one more open question, apart from the ones around Mary-Anne: I wonder if the motive for the murder is to be found in Linborough House."

Leaning against her sky-blue Peugeot, Emma told Aidan about her trip to the country and her visit to Henry's.

"Could you stop by a real estate agent and find out what the place might be worth?"

"Okay, I'll see you later in the office."

When Emma got there, Jean was already at her office door, accompanied by Superintendent Murray. He was wearing a black suit – apparently he too had attended the memorial service in St. John's, but had avoided the open grave. Quickly thrown in nine more holes of golf? Emma almost laughed at the image of Murray in a black suit, swinging a club, but pulled herself together when she saw Jean's stony face beneath the pulled-back black veil.

"Ah, Woods, it's good that you are here!" Her boss greeted her. "Mrs Armstrong has had another shock today."

The chaos surrounding her desk was embarrassing, still, Emma had no choice but to invite Jean into her office. On the day of her husband's funeral she could hardly put the grieving widow in one of the windowless interrogation rooms where the chairs were bolted to the floor. She really had to clean up here, preferably before Bill Sergeant showed up later. Murray withdrew. Jean was obviously really beside herself, or at least she didn't seem to notice the mess in Emma's half of the office. She sank into the squeaky guest chair and began to rummage around in her purse.

"I found this horrible note in the postbox this morning." Jean leaned forward and handed her an envelope across the desk. Emma put on a pair of the latex gloves she had in all her pockets. That habit came with the job. The envelope was addressed to the "Armstrong Family", the correct address being St. John Street. Stamped in London, on Saturday. With pointed fingers, Emma pulled a blank sheet of paper out of the envelope. It had just one sentence printed out in black and white in huge letters: "Charles was a pig". The person who did this must have had a sense of proportion, since the sentence was placed absolutely in the middle of the page. Aloud Emma said:

"It was sent from London. Who could have done that?"

Emma studied Jean's expression.

She remained motionless: "I have no idea".

"Who has an interest in aggrandising themselves like that or in hurting you?"

Tears suddenly fell from Jean's honey-coloured eyes. She shrugged, shaking her head.

"I have to keep this letter, it's evidence. It's going straight to forensics." Emma was already picking up the phone to call Miles Monroe. Jean sat back in the visitor's chair and wiped away her tears.

"Miles, Emma here, I have an anonymous letter, Armstrong case. I'll send that across – we want the full programme. Fingerprints, DNA from the envelope – maybe the sender was stupid enough to lick the glue. I'd also like to know how it was made... What kind of printer and so on, you know. Can we find out where exactly in London the envelope was stamped? As soon as possible. Please."

"With you, everything always has to be as quickly as possible, as if I was deliberately slowing things down. Can't you invent a new mantra for a change?", came the voice back through the receiver.

"Oh Miles, you see right through me!"

Jean grew restless and the visitor's chair groaned under her weight. The sound seemed to bring the widow back to reality. Disapprovingly, she eyed Emma's messy office.

She got up, nodded and said: "I have to go to the funeral reception, they will surely miss me."

Emma also got up and said: "Perhaps this anonymous letter will help us to find the perpetrator, thank you for bringing it to us immediately.

Emma was still staring ahead deep in her thoughts, when Paddy McNulty poked his head through the door. "Well, still no proper lead?"

His started humming the melody of Molly Malone and his grin showed what he really meant – a satirical version on her abilities she had heard before:

"In Sligo's fair city,
Where the Girls are so ritzy,
I first set my eyes,
On sweet Emma Alone,
As she wheeled her brains in a barrow,
Through the streets broad and narrow,
Crying monster and murder,
Alive alive o!"

Emma could practically see him dance around while singing. She would have loved to kick him in the arse until the heel of her boot would be visible on his forehead. Unfortunately that was against the law.

She decided to keep her cool. "There is a kind of confession letter. Well, at least an anonymous letter. Oh yeah, can you take that to Miles, please? I'm waiting here for the poor man's nephew, who is due to come by for a statement."

"Okay, I'll carry that thing over to forensics for you, but don't think they won't take that case from you because of a scrap of paper. You don't have long before Dublin comes into play!"

As soon as he was out the door, Emma muttered, "Eejit!". She had nothing to show for, and how happy that made Paddy! But of course he didn't say that. The Dublin squad! As if they knew better! Emma suddenly had to think of an old Irish saying: "It is not those who can inflict the most but those who can endure the most who will conquer."

Legend has it that it came from the Lord Mayor of Cork, Terence MacSwiney, a Republican who was arrested after the Irish Easter Rising of 1916. He died in a London prison in 1920 as a result of a hunger strike.

March 2004

Catherine called in sick the next day. And somehow that was not even a lie. After reading Margaret's journal, she had tossed and turned all night, battling with the demons of her past. The bathtub! Every time she fell asleep, she woke up with that horrible feeling of being held under water, unable to breathe, about to be drowned like a rat. One hand on her young belly, one on her face, pushing her under. Again and again, only with short breaks that gave her just enough air to survive. "This will teach you to be nice to me..." She still could hear his voice.

Now she was sitting in her kitchen, rather upset, in her dressing gown, her hands clasped around a mug of tea. But even that warmth couldn't completely thaw away the memory of the cold water and the fear of death. Catherine went back to Margaret's diaries.

"July 25th, 1965. Mother has written to Violet and summoned her back to Linborough to help Henry with the farm. She and

dad can no longer help him much, the work is becoming too difficult at their age. It's obvious that Violet doesn't want to go back to Ireland. She turned white when I read the letter to her. She seems almost afraid of Linborough House and especially Charles. But he's not there at all – he's out and about working for the Church! For the whole week I've been trying to pull out of her what's really going on. She just kept silent, pressed her lips together and wept. Charles must have threatened her if she revealed anything about her pregnancy. Finally last night – little Tom had fallen asleep and Josh was in the pub as usual – she started to talk, on and off, but I couldn't believe what I was hearing...

After a few more sentences, Catherine felt nauseous. She ran to the toilet, where the bitter tea came up again. Everything tasted of bile. She was still gagging when she made a decision. She would finally dare and apply for the original of her birth certificate. Since 1975 it has been possible for adopted children in Great Britain to find out the name of their biological mother and their place of birth. So far, Catherine had not found the courage to do so. She always thought if her mother didn't want her in July 1965, why would she change her mind now? She also thought it better not to poke around in old wounds. Stick a band aid on the pain and that's it, that had been her motto. But Violet's story showed that there were also babies who were loved and wanted but were given away. Mothers who were victims, same as their kids. The fact that Margaret always called her Violet was perhaps a clue. But what if the family resemblance was just a crazy prank of nature? It doesn't matter, she finally had to know for sure!

March 2005

O'Leary was back from the funeral and plopped down in his office chair. "I just drove by Sherry Fitz, the fella there took over his father's real estate agency sometime in the 1980s."

"On Stephen Street?"

"Yep, that's the one. They've been around for a long while and I thought they might have the best idea what a house like Linborough House could be worth."

"And?" Emma straightened up, this it was getting exciting.

"Well, the estate agent,he couldn't say exactly, blah blah. After all, the house hadn't been on the market since the 1930s. Blah blah, you know. Real estate fellas! But of course the old fox knows the property, at least from the outside, even if he hasn't been there for a long time. He thinks the house alone is definitely worth a million. The land as well... but its difficult to estimate without details.. In Laragh, there has been massive construction for a good few years so if the grounds around it also got planning permission, it could easily be a few millions. In Belfast and Dublin they kill for a lot less …"

"For adhering to the wrong religion, for example," Emma said coolly.

"Don't start that again!"

"Yes, I know, the Catholic Church finds it unnatural for two people of the same sex to love each other, but walking on water is totally normal," teased Emma.

"Don't pretend your Protestant priests are any more relaxed…" Aidan made a face.

"Back to the point!" Emma continued. "And that seems to be the IRA. How's your dear cousin Ronnie? Does he still have his firearm collection at the ready?"

"You, if you come at me like that, I'll wander off to get myself some coffee first..." Aidan grinned and presented his dimples, in which Emma would like to put her index fingers. Which she refrained from doing regularly.

"Oh come on, spit it out. What are our veteran radicals saying about old Armstrong?"

"I went to McHughs yesterday where Ronnie and the other bucks like to hang out in the upstairs bar." Emma nodded, knowing the place, one of the most popular hangouts in town with two bars, one downstairs, one upstairs, red lacquered front and golden lettering. The place was always noisy, always full, thick with cigarette smoke, on the telly Gaelic football – a strange and deeply Irish mix of soccer and rugby that Emma's ex Paul loved, but whose rules Em had never really understood.

"Is that the waterhole with that sign outside: 'Pubs - Ireland's Most Effective Sunscreen'?" asked Emma.

"You got it! However, yesterday there was another sign: `Soup of the day: Whiskey!´ It really depends on the mood of the bartender what's outside ."

Aidan began to talk and Emma listened intently. Aidan and Ronnie hadn't really spoken to each other in years. At the typical Catholic family celebrations at which the whole O'Leary clan got together – Christmas, Easter, baptisms, weddings, funerals – they had carefully avoided each other, which normally went unnoticed due to the sheer number of cousins. Since a fight they had never gone back to when they were great friends and drinking buddies. They had indeed fallen out with a gigantic crash.

"What were you guys arguing about?" Emma asked.

"The Good Friday Agreement."

Emma remembered it well. After all, that was one of the most important milestones in finally ending that undeclared war in the North of the country. On April 10, 1998, the governments of Ireland, Great Britain and Northern Ireland signed the Good Friday Agreement. This laid down the repeal of the Republic of Ireland's constitutional claim to British-occupied Northern Ireland. In a referendum, 94 percent of voters in the Republic of Ireland approved a corresponding constitutional amendment. Even in Northern Ireland itself, approval was high at over 70 percent of the vote. It showed that the majority of islanders, whatever their persuasion, had had enough of the IRA, the "Troubles" and the bloodshed.

"Ronnie freaked out at the time," Aidan continued. "He got drunk, threw his Guinness glass against the wall and screamed that he would never swallow this betrayal. And neither would the IRA. Fucking Brits out of Ireland – they should all be driven into the sea! That kind of thing, you know."

"Well, the majority wanted some peace and quiet back then," Emma said.

"Exactly. That's what I said too at the time. When nine out of ten Irish people are okay with it, the fecking IRA must accept it as well. The fact that I stayed calm and argued rationally only seemed to make Ronnie more aggressive, though. And boy, Ronnie disagreed. War on the imperialists forces – forever and to the last drop of blood! Em, you know the rhetoric. Even when the IRA and its splinter groups eventually swallowed the deal, Ronnie couldn't reconcile with me."

"The china between you two had been shattered irretrievably? I didn't know that."

"Ah, well, rather the Guinness glass!" Aidan grinned. "Yeah, no, I felt a bit uneasy last night when I actually saw Ronnie smoking at McHughs at the bar. But it was okay. Ronnie raised his glass in greeting, I pushed my way over to him through the crowd, the pub was surprisingly full for a Monday night. I said: 'Well, how about smashing another a glass?'. Ronnie had to grin too and said: 'Oh come on, don't be such an buck eeejit!' That happened to be a good start.

I said: 'Yes, the Irish blood – it runs hot until it actually flows'.

Then he: 'Forget it. Mate, do you want a beer?'

So I ordered a Smithwicks and we just arsed around for a bit," Aidan said.

Emma could imagine the evening going well, having spent enough time with Irish in pubs to know how things went: the cousins had enjoyed several rounds of drinks, commented at length on the legs and bottoms of a group of young women, the past five years of Gaelic Football and debated the pansy english husband of some cousin or school friend, only to eventually become best friends again as the alcohol level increased.

"Could you get down to business then?" Emma asked.

"Yes, eventually," said Aidan. "Even if that didn't have much to do with an interview. Around eleven I asked him: 'Tell me, did you hear about the Armstrong murder?'

Ronnie goes: 'Yep. Proddie clergyman. One less of those. Never mind.'

Then I said: 'Well, I do mind, because I've got this bloody case on my hands. I wonder if you know something?'

'Me? What would I have to do with that?' – Ronnie, the innocent little lamb... you know."

Emma nodded. "And then?"

"I told Ronnie it was no secret where his loyalties lay and who he's close to. And that I wonder if he's heard anything? Had anything come out about Armstrong that awakened the old animosities?"

Aidan paused, rubbing his apparently sore head, and Emma said: "So you asked him if the IRA or one of their radical arms killed Armstrong?"

"Yes, quite directly even. But Ronnie said that was unlikely. If Armstrong had been a target, he would have been worm food a long time. A decent salvo from a semi-automatic and the issue would have been settled. At least that's what Ronnie says."

"Armstrong was quietly strangled, though. In his own wing-backed chair," Emma interjected.

"Exactly, that surprised Ronnie too: Not paramilitary style, the IRA doesn't strangle. Incendiary bombs, a couple of Armalite AR-18s, yes, but a strangler? Nope. But he promised me that he would ask around."

Emma had listened thoughtfully to the reporting of last night's conversation.

"I'm glad you guys made peace. After all, two Catholic boys have to stick together..."

"Amen!" Aidan replied, and Emma felt once again that she was pissing him off with what he called her "dumb criticism of religion."

"It's good that he wants to ask around," Emma switched back to professional terrain, "Still, I am beginning to see it like Ronnie; I don't really believe in the IRA theory any more. Jean got an anonymous letter from London. A letter of confession from the IRA, however, looks rather different …"

Now it was Emma's turn to tell Aidan and his half-dead office yucca of Jean's visit to the station. Then the phone rang – reception: there was a Bill Sargent down here who wanted to speak to Ms. Woods.

CHAPTER 7

The Horse Meadow

Acting on an impulse that had nothing to do with the clutter in her office, Emma ushered Bill Sargent into an interrogation room instead of into her office. A bile-green room with no windows. There he was, sitting across from her, his hands clasped on the table in front of him and his thumbs twirling nervously. O'Leary had settled himself comfortably in a chair set a little apart, about the same distance from Em and Bill. The two always did this in case the "good cop, bad cop" strategy became necessary, later during an interrogation. It was better if a suspect didn't immediately connect the guard who was supposed to play his confidante afterwards, with the tough, aggressive officer. Most people don't register such small things, but every seasoned detective knew the power of the unconscious.

"We're sorry about the loss of your uncle," Emma opened the conversation.

Bill just nodded, "Thank you. What can I do for you?"

"First of all, and just as a formality, where were you last Friday?"

"Am I one of the suspects?" Bill couldn't manage to suppress a smirk. "I couldn't stand the old bastard, but I didn't kill him. I was at home in Switzerland. There are plenty of witnesses. We celebrated my daughter Isabella's birthday with my mother-in-law and some of her friends. I cut the cake for the kids."

"Thank you, we'll check that out. If you give us some details, phone numbers, it should all be done quickly."

"Anyway, your question intrigues me: Why would I want to kill Charles?"

"Your face when you looked at Jane and Bob Roberts at the funeral spoke volumes. You obviously don't like the fact that they're moving into Linborough. The property is probably worth millions. Your Uncle Henry also told us that you've tried to take possession of parts of the land before. That kinda thing makes a good Garda curious."

Emma smiled.

"But what does that have to do with Charles? Henry holds the title to the land. And that's who I fought with, not with Charles. And Henry is as alive as you and me."

"Right. But Charles was Henry's confidante and apparently the only one Henry really got along with. Charles has no doubt worked him hard to secure the property for his own daughter and to sideline his siblings' children, which is you and your brother. Without Charles's influence, the game would have been wide open again. Don't pretend you don't know that, Bill."

"It's not that easy. My Uncle Henry promised my mother Margaret a field, what we call the estate's horse meadow, many years ago. It's a large paddock right next to the house. After the early death of my Aunty Violet, my mother was summoned back from England, to move to the farm and help Henry care for the elderly parents. Henry is completely disorganized and can hardly boil himself an egg. My mother actually retired early at the time and went back to Ireland for a few years, but didn't get anything in writing from her brother. When her parents finally died, Henry couldn't remember the promise of the horse field."

"And that's why you fought with Henry?"

"Yes, and not only because of that. Part of the land belongs to my mother Margaret and her descendants. So to me and my brother Thomas. And it's true, Charles would like to keep us at arm's length away, so that everything goes to his kids. Henry and Violet both have no offspring."

"Can you imagine why Charles went to the family solicitor and asked about Irish estate law shortly before he died?"

"He saw Laura McDern? I don't know anything about that. I'm pretty sure, though, Charles tried to manipulate Henry into making a will in favour of his own brood. Probably arguing that Jane would then live nearby and take care of Henry."

"Charles' second daughter, your cousin Alice, lives in Australia, right?"

"Yes, in Brisbane. In fact, Jane is the only one from the next-generation living nearby in Ireland."

"You said before that you couldn't stand Charles? Any reasons for this dislike?"

"Charles was a self-righteous, hypocritical arsehole. His image was always more important to him than the well-being of those around him. For example, he treated his poor son Ron like he was a complete idiot."

"Ron has since died of a brain tumour. Is that correct?"

"Yes. That was some years ago. And today Charles speaks of him as if he was his beloved son and God's own gift to mankind. Talked, rather," Bill corrects himself. "He can't talk any more, the damned hypocrite. When Ron was alive, he hardly ever looked at him other than to criticise him."

"Is that it?" Emma asked. "Or are there other reasons why you didn't like your uncle?"

"He talked Henry into building this architectural abomination of a house in the village, right next to the petrol station and moving there, arguing of course that he would be less lonely in the village, closer to people and the supermarket. In fact,

I think Charles did this to clear the way for Jane and her husband. Henry is a difficult man and not the sharpest knife in the drawer, but he doesn't deserve that. He's lived his whole life at Linborough, and now he's sitting in the courtyard of a petrol station. Meanwhile, Jane spreads her big arse around in the house, and we, Margaret's children, can suck on thin air. None of this is fair."

"Do you know what's in Henry's will?"

"I don't think anyone knows for sure, not even Henry himself."

When Bill Sargent was out the door, Emma and Aidan stayed in their seats a little longer.

"We're still not that much wiser," Aidan said.

"No. But it wasn't Bill, my intuition tells me that."

"And now?" Aidan wanted to know.

"Do you know any German? Or French?"

"Nah, why is that?"

"Because you're now calling Switzerland to check Sargent's alibi, and I think they speak German or French over there. As for me. I'll go to Murray and report."

"Everyone can speak a little English these days. What are you going to tell Murray?"

"What we learned today. If I interpret correctly what Henry told me yesterday when I was visiting Laragh, an equal inheritance of Linborough means the sale and loss of the land. Or at least that is Henry's point of view. In a worst case scenario for him it will go to an annoying Catholic dunderhead like you. However, favouring only one person in the will above all others would also mean that Henry would have to deal with the discord in the family for the rest of his life. He would have to defend himself on all sides. Hence, he doesn't do anything. And Charles figured it was up to him to take action and save the property for his daughter Jane. The fact that the desk in Armstrong House was ransacked could indicate that the killer was looking for written evidence who would get the land in the end. So tonight I'm going to put the other Sargent to the test, this Tom fella in Sydney. However, if he did not leave Australia, he also has an alibi and we'll be back to square one."

Aidan picked up the phone and said, "Oui, madame, I'll call Bill's mother-in-law then."

"Oh, and while you're on the phone, call Jean, get her daughter Alice's number down under, and ask her tonight, when it's morning in Australia, where she actually hung out last Friday night. But watch out, the time difference is nine or ten hours, don't ring and chase people out of bed over there."

March 2004

"Violet, Violet!" Catherine heard Margaret calling from afar. She had to hip-open the door to Margaret's room because she was holding the tray with Margaret's tea and some of her beloved biscuits.

"Hello Margaret, how are you? Nice weather today, spring has finally come."

"Violet, Violet!"

"Margaret, I'm not Violet, I'm Catherine. But maybe we can talk a little bit about Violet?"

"Violet!"

"Do you remember home? And Violet?"

"Mum... and Violet."

"Yes, your mother was at home too. And you as well, as a girl and Violet. Who else?"

"Charles." Pause. "Charles was a swine!"

"Who is Charles? Was he there too?"

"Swine, swine, swine."

"Where was that, Margaret? Your records say you were born in Ireland. In County Sligo?" Catherine had to control her impatience. She would have liked to shake the old woman, but her mind had clocked out again and and she declaimed:

"I will arise now and go to Innisfree!"

"Yes Margaret, that's Yeats. He loved Sligo too. Do you remember Ireland?"

"Violet. Mummy. Linborough."

"Linborough? Is that where you come from in Ireland?"

"Charles. Swine." Margaret pressed her lips together.

"Who is Charles, Margaret, who?"

But Margaret was obviously done talking and was now just quietly humming to herself.

March 2005

Emma couldn't get the guys from Dublin out of her head. If they actually sent her colleagues from the capital to "help" with this case, she couldn't imagine keeping her composure. Her back was throbbing, and she longed for that chemical cotton pad between herself and the world that only the painkillers could give her. She stood in her kitchen and put the dinner from the Indian take-away on plates. Hopefully Stevie came home soon! She lost focus and accidentally spooned the Dahl off the plate.

Presented with her status report on the case, Murray hadn't been very helpful. In fact, she suspected that he would be perfectly fine with handing over the tedious Armstrong business to HQ in Dublin. But Emma didn't want to give up. If only she could find the missing piece of the puzzle that would finally turn all her hazy suspicions into a clear picture!

A key turned in the door – there was the boy! She heard the typical noises. A big thud – the school bag hitting the ground – and two smaller thumps – those were his runners. Then he was in the kitchen.

"Indian? Again?"

"Good evening to you too, dear son! Yes, once again I didn't have time to go shopping. I've still got this Armstrong case on my hands and now probably also the colleagues from Dublin breathing down my neck."

"And I got an F in Math."

"Oh shit." Emma placed the plates of rice, Dahl and chicken curry on the kitchen table. "Eat first." She wanted to gain time. Should she give him a piece of her mind about his failure to apply himself at school? Or rather enquire after that girl who had been in his room the other day? What was her name again? Sophie? Telling him he should rather take care of his homework than of the opposite sex? She decided: None of that would help. Aloud she said: "Well then, tell me about your life and about the F in Math."

"Oh, Miller is just a stupid teacher. Nobody understands anything in his class. He can't explain and mumbles and spits when talking. Those in the front row have to take cover if he gets too close."

"Is Sophie okay with him?" Emma was testing the waters. Maybe the girl really was in the same class as Stevie.

"What about Sophie?"

"Wasn't she in your room the other day? She's going to class with you, isn't she?"

"Parallel class. She doesn't have to deal with Miller. But Sophie gets along with everyone, anyway, she's really cool." Her son blushed and Emma chose not to notice.

"Is she good at Math? Maybe she can explain the lessons to you? If you are in the same year, she covers the same subjects, albeit with a different teacher."

"I can ask her."

"She's pretty anyway."

Stevie said nothing to his mother's comment and bent his head over his plate.

Emma switched strategy: "Or do you need tutoring? I can ask your father if he would contribute to the cost?"

Phhh, that went well, Emma thought to herself when Stevie had disappeared into his room. "I have to study," had been his only comment. An evening with a teenager without a fight – what a success! But something had to work out on this dreadful day, after all that crap in the station. Emma put the leftovers from dinner in the fridge, the plates in the dishwasher, and picked up the phone. It was now Wednesday morning in Australia and she wanted to try and call Bill's brother Tom Sargent in Sydney. The number had been easy to find, the man had a software company and the number was listed online.

Dial tone, it rang at the other end of the world. To this day, Emma hadn't really understood how it could work to call someone who was more than 17,000 kilometres away. The Australian accent of Tom's secretary was funny. Her voice rose at the end of each sentence, as if she was asking a question rather than making a statement.

"I 'll connect? The boss is already here? Won't be a minute?"

Then Tom Sargent was on the phone, sounding all English, like his brother. In general, the voices of the two were almost identical. Emma felt like she was talking to Bill Sargent all over again. He had already called to warn his brother, as Tom happily explained to her:

"Hello, Garda Woods. I already know. Bill got in touch. Apparently we're all murder suspects. By the way, I'm an expert in long-distance killing, but unfortunately my skills only work 10,000 kilometres in distance. So I could have caught Charles in Hong Kong or Singapore, but my magical powers don't go all the way to Sligo..."

Jaysus, another joker. It seemed to be a family affliction. Emma took a deep breath and said: "Hello, Tom. So you've been informed and you seem to have an alibi, that was the point of your joke, wasn't it?"

"But you're not laughing."

Emma could almost see the man on the other end smiling, and somehow she liked him, despite the clipped English accent.

"Well, your uncle was murdered, and I find that only marginally amusing. Must be an occupational hazard." Silence on the line.

"I'm sorry. You are absolutely right. No reason for jokes. And yes, I have an alibi, I haven't left Sydney in the past 14 days. We have a software relaunch in the company here, and my head is spinning! You're welcome to ask my secretary and the rest of the corporation as well. I was here in the office, like every day at the moment, around 16 hours a day."

"Can you imagine who would harm your uncle?"

"Charles could be charming, but up close he was just a pompous bloke who used everything and everyone to further his own ends. But kill him for that? I do not think so."

"Which ends?"

"Well, his latest project was to get Henry out of the house and installing his brood in Linborough. But you already know that, at least that's what Bill told me."

"Yes I know that. Could you imagine that the land issue would prompt someone to murder?"

"Apart from Bill and me and maybe cousin Alice in Brisbane – Jane's sister, you know – nobody has anything to lose from Charles shenanigans. And none of us three were anywhere near Charles."

"But someone killed him."

"The only person who really hated Charles was my aunt Violet. I never understood that, because otherwise Aunty Violet was pure love. This dislike for her brother was diametrically opposed to her cheerful and kind nature. We spent every summer in Ireland when we were kids – Violet was like a second mother to me."

"Violet, your mother's unmarried sister?"

"Yes, my mother's sister, and Charles and Henry's."

"Do you know why she was so mad at Charles?"

"No. I was probably too young to ask such questions and Violet died so long ago. Then there was no more chance for such questions..."

CHAPTER 8
Another Letter

March 2004

Nervously, Catherine twisted her paper napkin into a short, thick rope, and then she unfurled it again. She repeated the procedure. Back and forth, back and forth. Across from her sat Sue Ramsey, her old social worker who had looked after her when she was just a girl. Her tired, blue-veined hands lay quietly in her lap. Catherine had phoned her late last night and asked to meet. She choose this cafe as it wasn't far from Oak Gardens and it was delightfully old-fashioned which she loved. A quintessential English tea room: every surface imaginable was decorated with roses – tablecloths, napkins, curtains, wallpaper. Not all the shades of red matched, and the decor was obviously from different decades, with the wallpaper appearing to be the oldest. The flower chaos, which should have been tasteless, managed to look cosy and inviting. However the two women had no thought for the pros and cons of decorative excesses. After the greeting, they first talked about the terrible weather in Manchester and about the Premier League. Sue loved football and especially Man U. But this year, much to Sue's chagrin, Chelsea seemed to come out on top. Catherine found it a tad odd to hear a carefully coiffed, thin, not exactly young lady in a lace collar waxing lyrically about a rising soccer star named Wayne Rooney. Amidst all the talk of sports, however, she did not quite notice how closely the wise old bird was watching her: "Well, dear child, you certainly didn't want to talk about Man U when you asked me for this meeting last night. What's actually going on? And leave that poor napkin alone, it's already a rag, throttled out of existence."

"I'm ready," Catherine said, "I finally want to know," and then continued turning the napkin back and forth.

"What do you want to know?"

"Who my mother is. Where I was born. All of that." Catherine began to cry. Now the crumpled napkin had to serve as a handkerchief.

"But dear, that's no reason to cry. I've been advising you for years to go in search of your roots. I have long believed that the only way to move forward in life is to thoroughly examine and explore the past. No future without a past." Motherly, Sue took Catherine's hand.

"Yes, but I'm so scared. What am I going to find out?"

"It can't get any worse than what you've already been through. Apply for your birth and adoption papers, then we'll see!"

March 2005

Emma stands at the edge of the baseball court in her New York neighbourhood, hands on the fence, and watches as the boys elegantly fight for the ball. On the court the clumsy, pimply guys she knows from school turn into agile leopards. Billy turns to her, teeth shimmering white in his black face. Emma likes Billy and is now trying to climb the fence to get onto the court, too. But her left leg is like it is cast in lead. As she looks down at herself, there is a small child clinging to her jeans, looking up at her pleadingly. Emma can't shake the baby without hurting him.

Then the dream sequences change, wild scenarios revolve around Emma, but she still can't move because this toddler is attached to her like an anchor to a boat.

In the dream, Emma is looking for the source of some loud howling. She walks up the steps to her parents' apartment on the council block in New York's East End, and when she gets there, Paul is lying there, snoring. In the corner lies a baby crying miserably. Emma picks up the infant and tries to comfort the child but the crying continues, because somehow the child can't breathe.

Emma shrieks awake with a racing pulse. Only the annoying noise from her dream didn't stop. The alarm clock! It was just the alarm. Six-thirty Wednesday morning – Emma had set it wanting to get up early and drive to Drummon to talk to Armstrong's sweetheart, Mary-Anne Gallagher, before she left her house to go to work or wherever normal people go in the mornings, people who didn't have a homicide to deal with.

Stevie got the usual note, a crispy blue 20 euro, and Emma, armed with a thermos of tea and her painkillers, headed north.

On the way, Emma was once again amazed at the idiosyncrasies of the rural population in Ireland who had the habit of briefly greeting the driver of oncoming cars with two fingers raised from the steering wheel – even if they didn't know each other at all. Tourists who weren't used to that, often thought they were being mistaken for some rock star because everyone was waving at them. The gesture was probably just leftover from the days when cars were still a rarity in Ireland.

Emma hadn't been to Drummon in ages and on the way she noticed how many old cottages stood empty these days, how many pubs had only blind windows. Tractors stood just rusting away in neglected fields. Rural Ireland evidently benefited little from the Celtic tiger boom that was so much talked about in the Dublin newspapers. There was at best a sick little kitten out here, no sign of a tiger.

By the time Emma found Mary-Anne's house it had started to drizzle. A small house with a door painted bright blue and a few climbing roses next to it fighting heroically against the harsh wind. However, it was already clear who would win. Emma knocked.

Mary-Anne answered the door. She had obviously had a bad night and looked even more tired than she had at the funeral the day before.

"You?" she breathed in greeting.

Emma was unfazed "Good morning to you too.".

A broad-shouldered woman in her forties dressed in blue overalls, with cropped hair and a piercing in her nose appeared in the background. She gazed suspiciously at Emma "Mary-Anne? Is everything alright?"

Emma pulled out her badge and held it up for the lady in the background to see.

"Good morning, my name is garda Emma Woods. There have been a few reported car thefts in the area lately and we're just asking around the neighbourhood if you've noticed anything?"

Mary-Anne just stammered:

"No. We didn't notice anything. Did you, Orla?"

"Nope," replied Orla, the man woman in overalls. "I have to go to work, I am late." With that she pushed herself to the front, gave Mary-Anne a deliberately long kiss and threw Emma a provocative look. The thought behind the gesture was not difficult to guess: Yes, we are lesbians and yes, we are a couple, and don't you dare say anything about that!

Emma just smiled: "Have a nice day, Orla!" Then she stood calmly in the open door and watched her get into her dark blue Astra, turn around and drive away.

Then she looked Mary-Anne in the face and said, "Okay, I get it. You live as a Catholic in a lesbian relationship with a much younger woman. And you were having an affair with a married Protestant vicar. And now you're afraid that all this will blow up in your face."

Instead of an answer, Mary-Anne began to cry. More tears, Emma thought. Lesbian or straight, there are just too many women who start weeping when they can't think of anything better to do.

"You have no idea how jealous Orla is," Mary-Anne sobbed behind her hands.

The same story as among all other couples: jealousy and distrust, relationship trouble was obviously not exclusively a hetero problem.

"If she found out about Charles…" Mary-Anne's tears rolled down her cheeks.

"Yes, I know, the Catholic Church thinks it's perfectly normal for Jesus to walk on water, but they find it strange that two women love each other," Emma offered her standard argument. "Well, I don't give a damn who you sleep with or what the priests say, I just want to know: Did you kill Charles Armstrong?"

Mary-Anne cried: "I couldn't hurt a fly, least of all Charles."

"Mary, it's drizzling. It's wet and cold. Shall we go inside and talk quietly?"

Emma followed Mary-Anne into the kitchen, where her host put on the kettle for the inevitable tea. Emma sat down at the kitchen table.

"Ok, let's start at the beginning. How did you know Armstrong?"

"Charles served in the Church here in Drummon as a very young man, right after his ordination. He was handsome and charming, charmed everyone. Also he was a great man for the rugby. Fit."

"And he connected with you too?"

A smile spread across Mary-Anne's tear-stricken face, and Emma suddenly got a glimpse of how pretty she once must have been.

"Yes, you can say that. We became a couple, but not officially of course. Only secretly. It wasn't possible, he Protestant, I a Catholic."

"When was that?"

"1959. Then he met this protestant girl from Belfast. And promptly married her."

Just be glad you were spared that serial adulterer, Emma thought and said: "And when did you meet again?"

"I bumped into him in Sligo about a year ago. I had gone shopping and he was out for a walk. I recognized him straight away…" Mary-Anne started to cry again.

"And then you met regularly halfway, down in your love nest in Mullaghmore?"

"The way you say it, it sounds so dirty. We just caught up on our youth! And only very rarely. Always only when Orla had to work or was away for training."

"And because he didn't want to part with his Protestant wife to catch up on more youth, you ended up killing him. And don't start sobbing again, that isn't working for me."

"Fuck you! I didn't kill him and I didn't want him to leave his wife. I love Orla, it was just so exciting to be 17 again!"

"Did Orla know about your relationship with Charles?"

"No, she would have gone mad if she found out. Unlike me, Orla has been a lesbian her whole life. If she realized I was with a guy..."

"Mad enough to do away with Charles?", Emma cut her off. "Maybe she did know and fixed the problem in her own way?"

Mary-Anne stared at Emma in disbelief, "Orla would never do such a thing. She seems a bit rough on the outside, but there is a very tender soul behind that front."

Emma said nothing. Silence made most people so uncomfortable that they started talking, accidentally letting out the thoughts they most want to hide. Mary-Anne was indeed becoming insecure.

"When exactly was Charles murdered?"

"Garotted," Emma replied. "He was strangled. Last Friday, between about six and nine o'clock in the evening."

You could almost see the relief in Mary-Anne's eyes. "But we were in Belfast!

We left at noon. We get together with our girlfriends once a month at the Kremlin ."

"The Kremlin? That's in Moscow."

"The Kremlin is a place in Belfast. A gay club on Donegall Street. Orla and I were there last Friday."

Emma looked incredulous. This woman in her early 60s, who looked like an autumn apple in spring, went dancing in a gay club in Belfast on Friday nights? You just couldn't look into anyone's head. But she quickly recovered: "So you both have an alibi. Can anyone confirm?"

Mary-Anne began rattling off names and phone numbers, which Emma dutifully wrote in her notebook.

"We will be checking that of course."

Emma didn't know if she should be relieved that she could let this woman go who was so obviously scarred by life go, or if her heart was so heavy because her investigation was once again at a dead end.

When Emma finally showed up at the office, her room was busy like the butcher's before Christmas, except for the smell. Emma had just told Aidan about her visit to Drummon, had given him the phone numbers to check Mary-Anne's and Orla's alibis and Aidan was about to tell Emma about his calls to Chur and Brisbane when Miles appeared in his white lab coat and announced: "I've spent half the night processing this letter."

And he looked it, Miles was pale, apart from the dark shadows under his eyes. He always grumbled when Em asked him for a speedy analysis, but basically he loved hunting and gathering as much as his peers. So what if that did cost him the whole night.

"And?" Emma could hardly hide her hope for a breakthrough.

"Not much. No fingerprints. Whoever wrote it, must have been wearing gloves. Also no DNA on the envelope or the stamp, the adhesive strips have not been licked."

"Oh shit. So we have nothing."

"The letter is stamped in London, King's Cross Post Office, early Saturday morning."

"Does that help us?"

"Not really. King's Cross is in the middle of the city and between two train stations, St. Pancras and Euston. Half the world travels through there."

"Anything specific about the stationery or the printer used to produce the text?"

"The stationery comes from the British Post Office and is sold in the hundreds of thousands. The printer is from Hewlett Packard, medium price range. Endless numbers of those machines have also been produced. Those things are in every third private household, in every second company and also in an infinite number of Internet cafés. The letter may have been printed anywhere. Unfortunately I can't help you there."

Then Dessie Conway arrived at the door: "Anything new?"

Annoyed, Emma waved her hand. "No, we have an anonymous letter, but still no forensics," says Miles."

Awkward silence.

Dessie plucked up his courage and reported: "I checked Armstrong House's phone lines with Telecom Eireann."

"And?" Emma asked.

"They didn't make a lot of calls themselves. Just the usual. Called relatives in Belfast and Linborough House. A few calls from the daughter in Brisbane. Occasional connection to church headquarters in Armagh. If I find anything else, I'll let you know."

Another thoughtful silence.

Then Murray stuck his head through the door: "What's going on here? Minute of silence? Has anyone else died?"

Murray, his glasses inevitably pushed back on his bald head, squeezed through the door, and now the room was so crowded that no one dared take a deep breath, lest bellies bump against each other.

"Oh boss," said Emma.

"Oh what?" said Murray.

"The anonymous letter from London doesn't give us much to go with," Miles said. "No fingerprints, no DNA, and paper and printers are generic."

"Feck," said Murray.

"Feck, indeed," Emma confirmed. Another awkward silence.

Now the office boy was standing in front of the door with the mail. Try as he might, he and his pushcart would not fit into the room, so he handed Murray, who was standing in front, a stack of documents: "For Woods and O'Leary." Murray absent-mindedly passed the stack to Conway, who put it on top of the mess on Em's desk. Then, indifferently, the office messenger pushed his cart on to the next room.

"Finally there is some good news," Murray said. "Dublin has the flu."

"Ah," said Aidan.

"Ah," Dessie said. And the office palm nodded in the heat created by too many people in too small a space.

"Oh," said Emma, "I don't like the guys from Phoenix Park either, but why is that good news for us when the Dubliners are down?" Do we have pharmaceutical stocks and make money on the flu drugs?"

"Unfortunately not. But half the Dublin Headquarters is on sick leave. That's why they can't help us in the Armstrong case this week. The earliest they can send someone to support us is Monday."

"So no Phoenix from the ashes ... That's a pity ..." Emma had to grin. But Murray couldn't see her face because he was busy trying to free himself from the cramped office and pushing himself through the door.

That's when the phone rang and Emma waved her hand to Dessie and Miles to get them out as well: "Okay, thank you all. Thank you, good job... see you later." She threw the window open, needing fresh air after all the people in the crowded area. It poured in, cold and clear, with a touch of spring.

Aidan had answered the phone and grumbled: "Are you sure?"

Break.

"Okay, and you can count on these guys?"

Break.

"A dead cert?"

Break.

"Okay, thanks very much. I'll see you at McHughs later, I owe you a beer. Or three." Then he hung up.

"Ronnie?" Emma asks.

"Yep."

"And?"

"Not much."

"Damn it, do I have to pull every word out of you? Talk! Or do you need a confessor to get your tongue wagging? Emma was bursting with impatience.

Aidan remained unimpressed: "I'll get myself some coffee now, and when Madam has calmed down and can talk to people normally again, even if they're just poor, quiet Catholics without a confessor, then I'll be back." He took his his coffee cup, smiled his most irresistible dimpled smile and left. Emma used the brief moment alone to throw in two pills. She felt better immediately.

August 1965

Mother hadn't given up. She and father were too old to run the farm and Henry alone wouldn't be able to do it. Violet should come home, do her duty and help. Violet, though, seemed fearful of the thought of returning to Ireland. What exactly caused her anxiousness, however, could not be extracted from her. Finally Margaret had decided to accompany her. She told her husband some story about a summer holiday in Ireland. The air in Sligo was better for little Tom, far from the fumes of the textile mills in Yorkshire. Instead, fresh sea air. Josh had agreed, a little too quickly for Margaret's liking. His son's crying at night probably got on his nerves.

Margaret didn't understand why Violet was even willing to return. If she were her, she would stay in England, find a job somewhere, and start all over again. She was still young. Margaret could only guess at her sister's motives: If she wanted to know how her baby was doing, she would have no choice but to return to Ireland. It's true, that ghastly god-bothering Sister Magdalena in Bon Coeur would never tell her about the child's whereabouts, but Charles had to know. Perhaps he would take pity on his sister and tell her where the little girl had gone?

So now they were back at Linborough House and, on the surface, life was going on as usual. Milk cows, feed chickens, pigs, geese, make hay. The weather suited the mood, as is often the case in August on Ireland's west coast. Even at noon it was often only 16 or 17 degrees with a grey overcast sky. The whole neighbourhood took turns visiting and admiring Margaret's son. Nobody seemed to notice how quiet, thin and sad Violet stood there when everyone cooed at little Tom. She wandered around in the house and yard like a ghost, did as she was told and spoke little. Only when she held her nephew in her arms did life seem to return to her for a few moments.

The West of Ireland, the familiar smells and sounds. Grunting pigs, chuckling hens and barking dogs. The aroma of dung in the air. Behind the hills the sea. For millennia, people here have struggled to survive on the stony soil and in the harsh weather. Why exactly? Margaret kept asking herself. Life further south, on the European mainland, would have been so much easier for their ancestors. And yet – people held on to Sligo, despite the often disastrous weather and famines that plagued it from time to time. Truth be told, many had gone too. In the famine years between 1847 and 1851 alone, over 30,000 people left the county via Sligo's harbour – for England, America, Australia. But all over the county stonework proved that human hands had worked the rock here as early as 7,000 to 5,000 years before Christ. And then, later medieval tombs, monasteries and towers were created in all corners of the county. The tombstones of Carrowtemple – a few miles south and inland of Laragh – showed people as they had seen themselves in the tenth century: upright and pig-headed in the true sense of the word. The biggest thing about these human figures carved in the grey rock was their heads. The second largest: the feet. Stubborn and firmly planted on the earth, as if to say, "I won't leave here unless God calls me."

Today's visitor was Rosa, Margaret's childhood friend. She held little Thomas in her arms and cooed: "Well, little one? Have you come home to Auntie Rosa, to Linborough House, to Ireland… to Sligo?" For the first time in her life, Margaret couldn't tell her the truth. There was another child – but it was missing. This child wouldn't ever be allowed to come home to Auntie Rosa at Linborough House, to Sligo.

Charles didn't appear either. He and Jean were back in Ireland from god knows where for the summer, living in Armagh, along with their son Ron, who had been born the year before. When Margaret asked her mother why Charles didn't come to Linborough House too, her face froze: "Ask your sister!"

Margaret spared her that. Instead, one day she just took the bus and made her way to Armagh. Travelling, she stared out of the window at the Irish symphony of green and grey. Cottages, thatched roofs, picturesque poverty everywhere. But Margaret wasn't really looking, because for the first time in weeks she was on her own and had time to think about her family. She didn't like what was going through her head at all. To her mother, the opinion of the neighbours was more important than the happiness of her own children, the church more important than love, her son's reputation more valuable than the truth. She had her little Tom, and today he was in good hands with his aunty Violet. It would be a long day, but in the evening she would be back with her child.

Charles wasn't exactly thrilled to see his sister.

"What do you want?" he asked when he opened the door to her repeated knocking.

"What do you think, but to see you!" said Margaret, quite startled by his coldness. "May I not come in?"

Reluctantly he invited her into the house.

"Jean and the little one are in Belfast with her sister. I was hoping for some peace and quiet!" As if she were an official guest and not a family member, he led the way into a small study and not into the kitchen as usual. Margaret followed him. Charles sat heavily in his chair, not even offering her to sit, let alone a cup of tea. Hospitality was another thing she could remove from the list of values that counted in her family.

Charles said nothing, so Margaret began: "I did not want to bother you. Basically I am just asking for your help. Violet is suffering terribly!"

"She deserves it! And you ought to be ashamed to have someone like her in the family..."

"Charles!" Margaret exclaimed. "You're talking about your own sister!"

"And what a sister! One that just shames me! And now she torments me almost every day with letters in which she wants to know what happened to her little bastard!"

"Oh, I didn't know she wrote to you."

"Margaret, there is a lot know you don't know."

"I know more than enough, believe you me. Where is the child? What happened to the baby?"

"The child is fine. It is in the care of the good Sisters who watch over its Christian upbringing."

"But Violet loves her child so much!"

"Oh, love! The child is better off in the orphanage. We are looking for a couple who want to take in an adoptive child."

"What excuse does the child's father have for abandoning them like that?"

"The father? Who is that supposed to be?" Charles's voice became cutting.

"Charles, you know very well..."

"Stop it!" Charles thundered. "With your whore of a sister, no one knows who the father is!" Charles began to scream. Suddenly, his round face above his white band of his collar was contorted with hatred: "Violet is a dirty liar and a whore. She accuses men of honour!! And you believe her! What are you stupid women imagining? Have you forgotten where your place is?"

"But Charles, Violet would never..." Margaret felt her stomach turn into a heavy lump.

But her brother kept shouting: "Do you actually realise that you are threatening my career with all your stories? And not just mine!"

"This is about our sister and her baby. They're more important than your career..."

Charles didn't let her finish: "Violet and you, if you don't hold your tongues now, there will be consequences! I'm having the child taken abroad and Violet will never see her again! The Church has long arms and a good memory. There will also be a defamation lawsuit against Violet, that's for sure. And who will they believe? A fallen woman and her hysterical sister – or the representatives of the Church of Ireland? Tell Violet to leave me, the church, and her bastard child alone. Stop these lies! Otherwise there will be a massive fallout! Mother is on my side, she will drive you from the house if any of this ever gets out."

March 2005

Finally Aidan came back. He smelled of cigarette smoke – the flesh was obviously weak again. Emma was still pissed off at having to draw every word out of him and didn't even respond when he placed a cup next to her keyboard.

"Come on, boss, don't be like that!"

Instead of giving in, Emma picked up the stack of letters, papers and documents that the office boy had brought earlier. Ignoring Aidan and her coffee, she began to read.

Aidan, in turn, ignored being ignored and reported: "So I called Chur and Brisbane. Bill Sargent was actually in Switzerland at the time of the crime on Friday and was at his daughter's birthday party. The mother-in-law was there too and confirmed it. There are also ten little girls and their mothers, so Bill's alibi is set in stone. Alice Armstrong says she didn't leave Brisbane, she also has various witnesses who can confirm that she was in Australia the whole time. We could ask the Australian Border Protection Agency to have a look see if her passport movement confirms it but I actually think that's unnecessary."

"Hmm," Emma mumbled, not even looking up.

"It was indeed Ronnie on the phone earlier," Aidan continued undeterred. "He has asked around. Of course, he doesn't want to tell me exactly who he spoke to. But he thinks those bucks know what they're talking about and can be trusted – at least when it comes to about what happened to Armstrong. He says it wasn't the IRA or any of its splinter groups. They have had an eye on Armstrong for a while in the 1980s and would have loved to have kneecapped him. They must have sent him a few threatening letters because they thought he might be spying for the Brits. Armstrong then disappeared back to China or somewhere else on a mission and went out of their sights. Then he retired and no one wanted anything from him any more ..." Finally, Aidan was losing his nerve. "Em, are you even listening to me?"

Finally Emma looked up.

"I have an anonymous letter here. Addressed to Sligo Garda Homicide Squad this time, which means us. Postmarked in Manchester."

"Oh, I see. OK. And what does it say?" Aidan came around the desk to look over Emma's shoulder. While walking he put on latex gloves. Emma stared at an old black and white photo of a pretty young girl, maybe 19 or 20 years old. Not much older anyway. She smiled happily for the camera, a thick braid resting on her shoulder. Emma, who had now also slipped on gloves, carefully turned the photo over. On the back was just a year, written in black ink: "1963".

Emma put the picture in an evidence bag. Also the envelope, stamped Monday at Manchester Piccadilly.

The letter was short: "Charles was a swine."

It also went into a bag and got clearly labelled: who, where, when, what.

"Well, we already knew from letter one that Charles was a delightful fella," Aidan said dryly, but Em was already on the phone:

"Miles, I'm afraid you have to get back to the treadmill. We have another a letter."

Break.

"Yes, the same procedure again. Fingerprints, DNA... the whole programme. This time we also have a photo; can you find out where it was developed?" Emma put the phone down.

"Ok, forget about the IRA," Emma said, now turning to Aidan. "Ronnie's right. Terrorists don't send 40-year-old photos from Manchester to the guards."

"So you *were* listening to me..." Aidan smiled.

When their eyes met, the two had to laugh. At the same time, Emma was annoyed because her heart beat faster when she and Aidan were having fun together. The guy is your colleague and a few years younger than you, pull yourself together, Emma! Before blushing at her own thoughts, she became all business:

"I'll photocopy the letter and the photo and drive to Jean's. Someone here knows more than we do. Especially since this whole affair seems to go back to the 1960s!"

"Looks like an old love affair!" said Aidan.

"Please bring the originals of the letter and photo to Miles and urge him to hurry. I want to know what's actually going on. If the Armstrongs don't tell me the truth and soon, I'll have the whole clan in custody – even if it gives Murray and the Bishop in Armagh a heart attack!"

When Emma came back from the photo copier, Paul was standing in the room. Aidan gently took the evidence bags from her and discreetly left the room.

"What do you want?", Emma greeted her ex.

"I want to talk to you about Stevie and your so-called parenting methods!"

"Aha. And you come to the station for that? Couldn't we have discussed this on the phone or over a cuppa in a café?"

"This is urgent, and you're never home anyway."

"Oh don't give me that shit again, I don't have a nine-to-five job, but I'm a good mum." Emma felt the familiar guilt of the working mother. Don't freak out now!

"No, you're not," Paul continued in a scathing voice. "The boy has a girlfriend! At 15! And you can't think of anything better to do than to drive him into her arms!"

"How did I do that? Because I'm such a dreadful woman, he seeks his salvation with other beings of the female sex, is it that what your are thinking?" Laughing, Emma brushed her long hair back from her face.

"You think you're funny! He got an F in Math! That's bad enough, and more importantly, it means you're not looking after him well enough. And when would you, you're never home! And on top of it you suggest that he lets the little bitch help him!"

"How do you know she's a little bitch?"

"A boyfriend! At 15! We are in Ireland! In rural Ireland! There are different standards here than at home in New York!"

"Wait a minute, I'm as Irish as you! And you appreciated the fact that my standards weren't particularly steadfast back in New York..."

"Don't give me that now..."

Emma interrupted him: "You started it! But while we are at it, as far as I know Sophie is a very nice, polite girl with good grades. She's better at Maths than Stevie. Why shouldn't she help him with his homework?"

"Because then the two of them will be sitting unattended in Stevie's room and you'll be out chasing some car thieves! The neighbours will talk, and I'll have to hear them natter on about the boy doing stupid things. And in the end, the little slut will tie him down with a baby and ruin his entire life..."

Like I did yours back then. Aloud she said: "First of all, I'm not chasing car thieves, I'm investigating a homicide. And secondly, it's not my fault you're paying so much attention to the neighbours' gossip. Stevie is a good boy and Sophie is a nice girl. The two like each other, but that doesn't mean they're fooling around! This obsession with morals is a pathological disorder with you." Inside, however, she had a guilty conscience: she really had to talk to Stevie about contraception. A teenage pregnancy was the last thing she needed.

"I've had enough of your excuses. I'm going to seek full custody of Stevie!"

Paul turned on his heel and slammed the office door shut.

Shit, what a disaster! As if she did not have enough on her plate already.

Two more of her precious pills found their way into Emma's stomach. Then, with shaking hands, she dialled Laura McDern's number. Her secretary put her through immediately.

"Hello darling, how are you?" Laura's cheerful voice.

"Hi, couldn't chat with you at the Armstrong funeral, was there on business."

"Yep, that's what I thought. What else? Ready for a drink at Hargadons again?"

"That too. But most importantly, I'll soon be ready for the madhouse. Paul was just here. He wants to seek sole custody of Stevie."

"What? Why?"

"As I told you in the pub the other day: the boy has a girlfriend. And a F in Maths."

"You are kidding me!"

"No, he really got an F."

"Not that, but that Paul wants custody because of that."

"I am serious. I don't care well enough for my son and throw him into the arms of some young vixen who will ruin his life. Just like me back 16 years ago. Also he worries about what the neighbours say when the girl comes and goes."

To her surprise, Emma found that she had tears in her eyes.

"Well, your ex isn't exactly a legal expert. Custody isn't that simple. In most cases, the mother gets it, and in the event of a dispute, the children are also heard if they are old enough to make their own decisions. So if Stevie doesn't actively want to live exclusively with his father, Paul doesn't stand a chance..."

Emma had to get out. She tossed the copies of the second anonymous letter into her bag, grabbed her black leather jacket and was through the door. She walked to get some air and to calm down. The town was busy this Wednesday lunchtime. She headed north on Teeling Street and turned left on Castle Street. In fact, all she had to do now was walk straight ahead to get to Armstrong House on John Street. But Emma turned right onto Water Lane, heading first towards the Garavogue. She stopped and stared at the river's peat-brown water. Gathering her thoughts she continued walking down Rockwood Parade. The view of the colourful shops and pubs across the quay was comforting: there was a reality beyond murder, crazed ex-spouses, the threat of Dublin's interference and custody trials. In fact, the world was reassuringly normal that spring day. The trees were showing their first leaves, early tourists stood on the footbridge over the water and took pictures, the sparrows did what sparrows do on the sidewalk, and the housewives were out to buy bacon and cabbage for dinner, as they had done for decades.

Suddenly she was standing in front of the practice of Dr. Kennedy. She hadn't been here for a long time. The receptionist remembered her, or at least pretended to when she fished Emma's old index card out of the filing cabinet.

"There you are, Emma. You haven't been here for a long time!"

"I am way too busy to be ill." Emma smiled broadly. "Do you think I could quickly stick my head in Dr. Kennedy's room?"

Ten minutes later she sat opposite the old doctor and reeled off her monologue: pain in the back, in the legs, all the sitting in the office. The accident, sleepless nights from pain... Stress at work, single mother, no time for a stay in the spa...

Kennedy rummaged through Emma's papers and started scribbling away – "That's why you last saw me, three years ago!"

"Yes, I got better at times. Everything was alright, for a while. But now I'm so stressed at work, my son has problems at school and I am in way over my head. All that has done my back in, and my neck, the old injury, you know. I think I need another recipe to get me through the coming few weeks."

"Oxycodone?"

"The stuff you gave me back then. Is that what it was called?" Emma lied to his face.

"Mrs. Woods, it's not my habit to just write out a prescription without a thorough investigation. But apparently this is an emergency and I'm making an exception. But please do come back soon for a thorough check-up, Carolyn at reception will make an appointment for you."

30 new tablets. Not bad, Dr Kennedy.

Back on the street, Emma took a deep breath – somehow the world would go on. It always went on somehow. Finally, she turned left and took O'Connell Street. There, she revelled in the pretty white, green, or pink-washed gables and dormers of the two-story houses, trying to ignore the chain stores at street level below. Cheap clothes from Penny's, phones from O2 and mortgages from those fancy banks that sold home loans like sweets. The boom years of the Celtic Tiger shamelessly ate away at the human reason. Emma thought of the TV advertisement from the Bank of Ireland, one of the largest commercial banks in the country. They acted like it was okay to lie to the bank when asking for a loan. In one spot, for example, a young woman asked to get "ching-ching" to get braces for her teeth... But the subtitles made it abundantly clear that she wanted the money to buy shoes on credit. This will all end in tears – at least that was Emma's prediction.

Finally John Street came on the right and then, after a few meters, Armstrong House on the left. Its entrance was set back from the street behind pillars and looked just as forbidding as ever. Emma threw one more look at the dark looming church that stood behind the house, rang the bell and finally stood in front of Jane Roberts, née Armstrong.

"Yes?" she said, as if a tramp had not knocked on the servants' entrance, but had used the driveway reserved for the masters.

"Detective Emma Woods. We met briefly yesterday at your father's funeral. I would like to speak to you and your mother."

"Come in." Emma was ushered into the kitchen where she had been sitting with the housekeeper Mrs. Higgins a few days ago.

"Would you like some tea?"

"Sure." Jane, a short, stocky woman with short legs, put the kettle on and left the room, presumably to fetch her mother. The ladies appeared a little later, and Emma admired the family resemblance. Less so in appearance, more in attitude and facial expression. Emma thought of two female nutcrackers. Well coiffed and with pearl earrings, but with jaws from steel.

"Jane, how are you getting on with the renovation of Linborough?", opened Emma the game of chess.

"Good, thank you for asking. But I am not quite sure why my masonry work is of interest to the guards?"

"We're looking for your father's murderer."

"Oh, and you suppose you will find him among my bricklayers? It's scandalous that the case is still unresolved but I'm beginning to see why. We've already made representations to Dublin Headquarters. Apparently Sligo is not up to the challenge."

"They've got the flu in Dublin, you will have to make do with us village cops for a few more days," Emma replied calmly. She paused a little: "Did you sign a lease with your uncle?"

"With Henry? No, why?"

Jane got up to put cups on the table and brew the tea. Her short legs made her behind look rather plump, Emma noted with satisfaction. She said: 'Because Henry holds the title at Linborough, but you will be living there with your family. As far as I know, you make a rental contract for something like that."

"Henry has built a house in the village for himself and has allowed my husband and I to restore Linborough House. It stays in the family, we don't need any contracts."

Jane touched her hair briefly to tidy it up. A gesture of insecurity, of reassurance, like a cop sometimes instinctively reached into his jacket to see if his service weapon was actually still in its shoulder holster.

"So you invest without any security?"

"What do you mean?" Jean wanted to know.

"Henry holds the title on the land, as far as I know he has not made a will. If so, all cousins have equal rights to Linborough. Bill and Tom, same as you and your sister Alice in Brisbane. But surely you are aware of that?"

"My dad spoke to Henry and took him to our solicitor as well. I thought that was all settled."

Jane looked shaken, at least more affected than at her father's funeral.

"As far as we know, nothing is settled," Emma replied, "and the Sargent brothers aren't thrilled with what's going on at Linborough."

"But what does that have to do with my husband's death?" Jean intervened.

"That's what I'm asking you. You and your daughter! You're hiding a lot from me, aren't you?"

"Like what?" Jean's expression was even more closed than before, and Em would have bet a lot that this woman couldn't have looked more dismissive if she had tried.

"Why, for example, did Charles ask the lawyer Laura McDern about the inheritance rights of illegitimate children?"

"I don't know anything about that."

"What exactly don't you know? That your husband saw the lawyer? Or anything about Irish estate law? Or don't you know why he asked about illegitimate children?"

"All of this is completely new to me. I have no idea what you're talking about."

"And who is this?" Emma placed the photo copy of the young woman from the anonymous letter on the kitchen table. But she didn't look at the picture, but at the faces of the women. Jean's eyes widened for a split second, she had recognized the woman. Jean picked up the copy: "Where did you get that?"

"This is a copy of a photograph sent to Sligo Gardai. Arrived this morning. And the reason for my visit."

"This is Violet, many, many years ago. That's what she looked like before Charles and I got married," Jean said. "It must have been taken in the early 1960s."

"Violet? Your husband's sister who died so young?"

"Exactly."

"And why is this photo being sent to Homicide in the Armstrong case, ladies, if I may ask?"

Jean looked up from the picture and met Emma's eyes. "I have no idea."

"What was going on at the time this photo was taken?"

"Charles was then a young pastor in Drummon and was courting me. His sister Margaret had already gone to England and was teaching at a expensive private school called Malthus or something like that. I hardly knew Violet and Henry at the time. I had only been to Linborough once or twice to meet Charles' parents."

"So you have no idea what happened back then and why anyone would send us this picture?"

"No." Stony expressions on both women.

"You get surprisingly little, I must say."

"What are you implying?" Jean demanded to know.

"Nothing at all. Except that you seem to notice only facts that suit you."

"This is outrageous." Jean's voice had grown low and menacing. Her contempt hung in the air like fog. "I'm going to complain about your impertinence. Not only are you still poking around in the dark about my husband's death, now you're attacking his grieving family! You are a disgrace to the Garda. Get out of my house." She rose to see Emma out.

"Don't bother. I'll find my way out."

What a shitty day. What a shitty job. If only I had become a midwife, I would at least occasionally meet nice people. On impulse, Emma left Armstrong House to her left and walked towards the gloomy church set back from the road in the meadow behind Jean's fortress. With battlements like a castle, the building crouched there on a slight rise in the terrain and looked down wearily at the first bluebells of the year.

No wonder you're exhausted, you've been watching people and their nonsense for twelve hundred years and then some! Emma nodded a greeting to the church tower, pushed open the door of the old building and immediately felt the soothing coolness of the old stones. How many tears had been shed here? The raw walls were saturated not only with candle smoke but also with the prayers, hopes, deep sighs and cheers of generations. Emma walked the red rug of the aisle toward the altar, smelling the familiar smells of old churches— dust, fear, hope, candle wax, withered bouquets, sweat, and unwashed choirboys. Above her, the ceiling arched upwards. She sat down on a bench and studied the two glass windows to the right and left of the aisle. One of them was dedicated to W.B. Yeats' grandparents. If there was one good thing about churches in Ireland, it was that they were the living memory of the country. Everything that ever happened here was noted and recorded by the churches. Everything was observed and written down – and by no means only in glass windows.

On the way home, Emma bought rolls, tomatoes, a cucumber and mince from the supermarket. She was going to serve Stevie hamburgers tonight, onions and ketchup were still in the fridge. In addition, a delicious beer for mother and apple juice for the little Maths genius. Equipped in this way, she could probably have the difficult conversation that was due. The thought that her son might actually prefer to live with his father made Emma very anxious.

As she pushed through the door, U2 boomed out at her. "How to Dismantle an Atomic Bomb". Em loved Bono and the lads almost as much as her son. She kicked the boots off her feet and danced into the kitchen. As an exception, the little sod had cleaned it up today. What was she supposed to do if this fecker of an ex took him away from her? She would like to strangle Paul... and slowly. She had started preparing the mince, singing along to "Love and Peace or Else", oblivious to Stevie coming out of his room.

"You don't have to bribe me with burgers," he said, wrapping his arms around his mum's waist from behind, much like he did when he was a little boy. Em had a lump in her throat. Today was obviously crybaby day. She turned and took the skinny guy in her arms.

"So, and now we have to talk about contraception."

"Mum, don't be ridiculous!" Stevie tried to act cool but was blushing.

"Teenage pregnancy is not at all ridiculous and you know the laws in Ireland. Abortion is and will remain forbidden, and I have absolutely no desire to change anyone's diapers. At least not yet."

"Yes, but you don't have to explain to me how sex works, I already know that."

Emma grinned, "Well, birds do it, bees do it, even little fleas do it..." Stevie squirmed.

"We'd better get you condoms. I'm not saying you should use them. You can just put them in the drawer, no harm done. But you should have some, it's safer. I'll go to the pharmacy and buy you some. Now let's eat!"

When Stevie had disappeared back into his room and the mess in the kitchen had been cleaned up, Emma picked up the phone. Again the Australian accent and a intonation that turned everything into a question.

"It won't be a minute? I'll connect you?"

Then Tom Sargent again, this time slightly annoyed: "Yes. Hello. What do you want?"

"I know you're busy. But last time you mentioned your aunt Violet, who died young...your second mother in Ireland. Do you remember?"

"Yes, Violet, the great love of my childhood."

"At Sligo station we just received an anonymous letter with a black and white photo from 1963. It shows a young woman with a thick braid; Jean Armstrong today identified her as her sister-in-law Violet."

"Why is someone sending the Garda in Sligo a photo of Violet from 1963? My aunt has been dead for many years…" Tom sounded incredulous.

"That's exactly what I'm asking you. Can you remember anything that might connect Violet and the death of Charles Armstrong?"

"No, just that Violet really didn't like her brother and avoided him whenever she could."

"Well then, I don't want to keep you any longer. Thank you very much…" Em was about to hang up when the voice on the other end of the phone said: "Detective, one second…"

"Yeah?"

"I don't know if that matters, but I just thought of something. When I was a little lad, eight or nine years old, and at Linborough House as always on summer holidays. Violet took me to the village… She had this little old scooter she used to zip around on. You can't imagine what she carried on that thing. At some point she had a sheep on the back of this tiny Honda. The animal had gotten lost and Violet didn't know what else to do. That was some sight, my tiny aunt on the Honda and behind her a bleating, utterly filthy sheep …"

"Yes, and?"

"Well, we were in the village, it was a hot summer day. On the way back we were so thirsty that we stopped at the pub. The Foxes Den. There we were at the counter, drinking lemonade when another customer, a well-known drunk, pointed his finger at my aunt and kept saying, 'Violet Armstrong, I know what you did. Violet Armstrong, I know what you did…'"

"How did your aunt react?"

"She turned white as the wall. I thought she was about to fall over. That is why I remember it, in the first place, she was so shocked. But then the landlord, Paddy Joe, grabbed the guy by the collar and hissed, 'Shut up, you ould wanker, one more word and you'll be barred.' Then he kicked him out."

"Paddy Joe? I think he is still around today," Emma wondered. "He didn't look that old."

"No, that's the son. Another Paddy Joe. You know Ireland. Generations of Paddy Joes."

"Did you ever find out what the man was referring to and why it upset your aunt so much?"

"No. I was just a little boy. I tried to comfort my aunt, but we never really talked about it. Today that might be possible, but Violet died when I was still so young that we just never had enough time for adult conversations."

"Why did she die so young?"

"As far as I can remember, she had pulmonary emphysema. The Irish call it farmers' lungs – the hard work and then the perpetual dust of rotting hay inhaled while feeding the livestock."

"The poor woman."

"Yes, she worked herself to death but my mother always said about her sister that she died of a broken heart. However, I never quite managed to get out of her what she meant by that."

CHAPTER 9
Kindergarten

Thursday morning it poured with rain, straight down lashing stuff. And when a soaked Em finally got to sit in her car, it wouldn't start. Damned piece of shit! She probably hadn't taken care of it well enough and now oil was missing, coolant or something else vital for a car. Angry at herself and her incompetence, Emma pounded the steering wheel with both fists. She just couldn't bring herself to deal with engines. Bad enough that you had to keep feeding them fuel. Paul used to take care of the family car, but that was long gone. Em rummaged around in her purse. Apparently she had forgotten her cell phone, too, it was probably still on the charger in the kitchen. Cursing loudly she ran back to her house to call the mechanic and then a taxi.

What felt like hours later she finally arrived at the office with pounding pain in her lower back and hip. Aidan made a long face.

"You are due to see the boss. Immediately."

"Good Lord, what does he want?"

"I don't know, but he's pissed. What have you done?"

"Nah, nothing much. I basically told Jean Armstrong that she was a lying, selfish cow."

"Oh great. Sounds good. Exactly this choice of words?"

"Not quite, but pretty much."

"Have fun with the boss then."

Two oxycodones and a few minutes later she knocked on Murray's door.

"Come in!" he growled.

"Good morning, boss." Emma was ignored. Murray was reading some papers. Finally he looked up. "It's great that you're showing up in the office after all. Do you actually know what time it is?"

"I'm so sorry, my car..."

"Yes, yes, the dog ate the homework! I really don't want your excuses, Woods." Emma felt queasy when Murray called her by her last name, experience had shown that it meant the start of a new Ice Age.

"I'm not at all happy with your work," Murray continued without even offering Emma a chair. She had to stand and listen to his tirade. Jean Armstrong had complained to his superior in Dublin and he in turn had complained to him. Charles Armstrong was a pillar of the community, a well-known man blah blah, disrespectful behaviour by officers blah blah, lack of the most basic courtesy blah blah, respect for the family blah blah, police image in jeopardy, especially with the Church of Ireland, blah blah. And blah.

"And then he asked me if we now have an idea of the motive and the perpetrator, Garda Woods. I had to tell him that that's not the case. No motive, no forensics, no suspects!" Murray continued.

Emma said nothing.

"What do you have to say for yourself?"

"It is not true that we have no forensics at all, there is half a fingerprint, which cannot be assigned, and two anonymous letters, one from London, one from Manchester. Miles Munroe is still working on the analysis of the second one."

Murray's phone rang. He picked it up, listened, and then barked:

"Send him up!"

He slammed down the phone and hissed at Emma:

"Now we are in trouble! Dublin has arrived."

Emma turned to go.

"Stay there! You have to deal with this!"

A knock, and without waiting for an answer, a tall man entered the room. Everything about him was square. The chin, the shoulders, the heavy hands.

"Morning all, I'm Eamonn Kelly, Dublin Homicide, here to support the local team."

Murray rose heavily from his chair and stretched his hand across the desk in greeting.

"Good morning and welcome, I'm Liam Murray, the senior officer. This is Detective Emma Woods, who is currently leading the investigation into the Armstrong case. She will put you in the loop."

Emma just stood there and said nothing, her face impassive.

Kelly didn't care. "From now on I will lead the investigation, instruction from the top".

His whole attitude seemed to express: You don't get far with collegiality.

"I need an office, a big cup of coffee and all the relevant documents and reports concerning the investigation. Once I have read up on it, I want a conference with everyone involved, including forensics and pathology. Shall we say twelve? Where is the conference room?"

Murray nodded.

Kelly nodded. "Unfortunately I couldn't bring my partner with me, he has the flu. Could I get a colleague assigned, please? Preferably someone who hasn't been involved with the case before and is willing to look at the facts with an open mind?" Kelly looked Emma in the eye and smiled. The resemblance with a crocodile was uncanny.

"Patrick McNulty is a good man, I'll let him know in a moment," Murray hastened to say while already picking up the phone obligingly to organize for a desk and a partner for Kelly. Exactly what I needed, Emma thought, two narcissistic idiots to deal with on top of the case.

At twelve everyone gathered in the small conference room of the Serious Crime Unit: lab rat Miles, Dr. McManus, Emma, Aidan and Dessie. Plus Eamon Kelly and Patrick McNulty, who couldn't help but smile. Word had spread like wildfire that Dublin and Murray had taken the Armstrong investigation off Emma. Emma could almost hear McNulty's thoughts:

"Finally this smartarsed, divorced, feminist, proddie bitch gets the comeuppance she deserves!"

Kelly cracked the joints in his fingers, a sound that always gave Emma the creeps.

"Woods, would you summarize the status of the investigation to date?"

That guy had the guts to take over the leadership from Murray in his own conference room. Murray had obviously rolled over to present his throat.

Emma began her report in a matter-of-fact manner. After that, it was Dr. McManus' and then Miles Munroe's turn.

"Are there any new insights into the second letter and the photo?" Emma asked.

"As with the first letter, the sender was very careful. No DNA. Printers and stationery are generic. We are still working on the question of where the photo was developed. Probably somewhere here in Sligo," Miles replied, carefully avoiding looking at Kelly. Then followed a lengthy discussion of a possible motive and why someone had sent these letters; first to the widow and then, of all people, to the police.

Emma put on an interested face and let her associations run free. Why couldn't Violet stand Charles? What had he done to his sister? Who is actually avenging what here? And why now? After all, Violet had been dead for many years. Said to have died of a broken heart... Whatever that meant. But what had finally led to the attack? And what the hell had been in Charles's desk – what was the killer looking for? And why did the anonymous letters come from England? Suddenly Aidan elbowed her hard.

"Woods?" she heard Kelly's voice at the same time.

"What?" Her gaze fell on McNulty, who was sitting next to Kelly, smirking.

"It would be nice if you could give us your valued attention," came Kelly's vitriol. "I asked you how you want to proceed now?"

"Eamonn, you are the boss of this case now. Tell me how you want to proceed," Emma smiled. It was the first time Kelly had ever spoken to her directly. Kelly stared at her for a few seconds like he didn't know what to do with what was in front of him. Finally Murray coughed. Then Kelly turned and began distributing tasks. As expected, he wanted to do everything all over again. Every interview, every phone call. Eventually it became too much for Emma and she cut Kelly off:

"I would like to go to Manchester."

Now it was Kelly's turn to say "What?" in surprise.

"I would like to fly to Manchester. We've talked to everyone involved, but so far that hasn't helped us much. We haven't spoken to Margaret Sargent, née Armstrong, though. Personally, I believe the roots of this case go back further than we realize. This theory is supported by a photo from 1963. Someone sent it to us to point a finger into the past. Margaret, the surviving sister who we have not yet spoken to, lives in Manchester. That's where the second letter came from. That can not be a coincidence. I think we should talk to her."

"Good idea, get in touch with colleagues in Manchester, explain the case and ask someone to go and see the old lady."

"No, I want to fly to Manchester myself and talk to Margaret."

Kelly was apparently not used to contradiction and raised his eyebrows.

"I think we owe it to the Armstrong family not to delegate that task, but to take action ourselves," Emma added.

"I wish you had thought of that early on, Emma. So far you've only managed to antagonize pretty much all of the bereaved." Kelly sounded almost menacing.

"Homicide investigations aren't a Sunday picnic in the sunshine, no one knows that better than you, Eamonn, right?" Emma smiled sweetly. "After such a violent crime, the affected families mourn and are particularly sensitive, so the emotions sometimes run high. And after all, the Armstrongs are well-known folks around here, hence the special sensitivity. That's why I suggest we do our part and talk to Margaret Sargent ourselves. Quite informally, I would suggest. 'Cause I'm not sure the Armstrongs would be happy if we hounded the old lady with the local police in uniform..."

Emma didn't recognize herself, diplomatic contortions weren't usually her style. But if it served the case, that should be fine with her. She ignored Aidan's questioning look. He knew that Margaret had dementia, but he was loyal enough not to announce that in this group.

Kelly turned to Murray, "Is there a budget for this?"

Emma's heart sank, there were all sorts of things in Sligo, but certainly no budget.

But Murray said to her astonishment: "A flight to Manchester should be feasible."

Apparently he didn't want to expose himself to Kelly with a lack of finances after allowing himself to be robbed of the leadership of the conference in his own station. Embarrassingly enough, he had yet to come up with a solution to the Armstrong case for Dublin and his superiors. Emma also suspected that Murray wanted to avoid any further conflict that would interfere with his ability to go home early. After all, it was spring and the golf course beckoned. And his mutts wanted to be walked. All the better, then, if his rebellious investigator was away for two days and didn't mess with Kelly, the Armstrongs and HQ in Dublin. For all of the above he got a beaming "Thank you, boss!" from Emma. An expression that should also make it clear to Kelly who, from Emma's point of view, really had something to say here.

When she left, McNulty hisses at her: "Nice brown-nosing, Em. Shopping in Manchester, huh? Well, have fun!"

But before Emma could take a deep breath to shoot back, Murray's voice came from behind, "Emma, please stay here for a moment."

At least he's using my first name again, Em thought, turning around.

"Well played."

That was Murray's comment when everyone else was gone. He leaned back in his chair, placed both hands flat on the table and scrutinized his detective.

"Steady on, I really think that..."

"It's okay," Murray interrupted, "Get a cheap flight and an even cheaper hotel. I'll find the money for it somewhere. I don't want that Dublin braggart taking the butter off our bread either."

"Aye, aye, sir." Emma grinned and was about to leave when Murray stopped her.

"Most importantly, ring our colleagues in Manchester and let them know you're coming for an informal briefing."

"Does it have to be that way?"

"Yep."

When she finally stood in the hallway and had pulled Murray's door closed behind her, Emma took an audible deep breath. Done! There was something about controlling your temper and being strategic for once, she had to admit. She slowly walked down the hall to her own little hole of an office. Aidan waited there with two cups of steaming coffee.

"What's the delay? Your coffee is getting cold." Aidan smiled his infamous dimpled smile and Emma melted inside. She grinned back and slumped into her chair.

"By the way, I called Belfast this morning and spoke to some of the dykes with whom Mary-Anne Gallagher and her Orla say they spent Friday night with."

"Oh I understand. If women are interested in you, then it's girls, ladies or sweethearts. If they don't, and prefer to hang out with other women in a lesbian bar, then it's dykes?"

Aidan made a face. "Oh, don't be like that, you of all people should know that I adore the female sex in all its forms." A wink at that.

"Oh Aidan, maybe we shouldn't have this kind of conversations? They don't exactly bring out our best qualities."

"I don't have a 'best quality.' I have at most 'least bad qualities'. The least bad trait has to serve as the best in my case."

Emma had to laugh. "You may be a goddamn macho, but at least you're entertaining. But right back to work. What did the 'dykes' from Belfast tell you?'

"Well, Mary-Anne and Orla, both were actually in Belfast Friday night. In the Kremlin. drinking and dancing. They stayed with a couple of friends. A certain Collette O'Dea and a Bernie Murphy. Appropriately, the two live in South Belfast on My Ladys Road... I spoke to O'Dea and she confirms the alibi."

"Anyone else?"

Aidan rummaged through his notes.

"Yes and then another, a Mary Brady, a former girlfriend of Orla's. She was also at the Kemlin that night and saw the two of them. Spit venom and bile that Orla is now with 'such an auld one' – her words, not mine! But I guess that confirms the alibi for the two."

Emma frowned. "That brings us back to square one in this messed up case. Somehow I already suspected that."

"You and your assumptions. Is that why you want to go to Manchester? Another wild guess?"

"Maybe."

"You sailed real close to the wind today. I thought Murray was about to rip your head off, and instead you talked him into giving you a ticket to Manchester. Did you mention at all to him Margaret Sargent has dementia?"

"Honesty is overrated as a virtue."

"Not when honesty is the only virtue one has!"

Emma grinned tiredly.

"Oh my Prince Charming! But seriously, the old lady Sargent can't be any worse than Henry." Suddenly, Emma felt exhausted and gratefully drank her coffee.

"Oh come on, stop kidding me." And then with a rather serious tone: "What do you really want in Manchester, Emma?"

"I actually want to talk to Margaret, Aidan. I hope that there is still something left in her long-term memory from the past. I especially want to see her reaction to Violet's photo. I just hope I finally stumble upon a motive for Armstrong's murder. It's all deeply rooted in the past, somewhere in Linborough House, methinks."

Then she finally got around to telling Aidan about her phone call to Tom Sargent in Sydney the night before.

"'...I know what you did...'" Aidan repeated thoughtfully. "Well then, you better book that flight."

August 1965

Tyres squealed, mud spattered. There was a white Austin Morris 1100 in the yard. Margaret was doing the dishes in the kitchen and ran outside to see who had come up the driveway in such a fancy vehicle. Charles stepped out, as always clad in a grey suit with the white vicar's collar. So he had come to see his family after all.

"Hello Charles, where are Jean and the baby?" she greeted her brother.

He did not spend much time on greetings. "I'm not here for fun. This isn't going to be a family celebration. I just came because I need to talk to Violet!"

She had obviously heard the car too and had came running across the yard. When she recognized her brother, expressions that reminded Margaret of disgust and hope passed alternately like clouds over her little sister's face.

"Charles!" Violet said breathlessly. "Do you have news of my daughter? Where's my baby?"

However, he just grabbed his sister's arm and said: "Don't be so loud. We're going for a walk now!"

He dragged the reluctant Violet across the sheep pasture in front of the house towards the orchard, where the living balls of yarn fled away in terror. Even the sheep found the angry man in black scary. Margaret stayed at the front door and watched them both. Finally, out of earshot, Charles stopped and gestured at his sister. Gestures like punches. Violet kept getting smaller, backing away. Finally she turned around and ran back to the house. Margaret saw that she was crying. She wanted to stop Violet in the door and hug her, but she just pushed her aside and ran into the hallway, up the stairs to her room.

Eventually Charles came back too, mouth pressed so tight it looked like a lipless gash in his face.

"Charles. Do come in, mother will be so happy to see you", Margaret tried to create something similar to normality.

But Charles already had grabbed the handle of the car door. Leaning against his vehicle, he said: "Tell your sister to forget about that child. It's better for everyone involved. If she sends another letter to Armagh or anywhere else that has to do with the baby, she will regret it bitterly. The Church has a long arm."

The Austin Morris with the Northern Irish number plate sped away, followed by Margaret's gaze for a long time.

March 2005

Emma wearily listened to the soporific hum of the engines. She'd gotten up early, driven to Knock Airport in neighbouring County Mayo while listening to the death notices on the radio. Another Irish speciality she couldn't understand. Her countrymen were obsessed with death. Back home in New York, for Emma's mother there was no more important news from the old country than who had died. "Ah, old O'Grady. No wonder, he was a great man for the drink …" or "Patrick Dunne – he always had a bit of a bad chest!", were her comments when she read about the latest dramas in her sister's letters. Emma had thought it a morbid quirk of her mum's, but moving to Sligo had made her realise that the obsessive study of obituaries was part of the Irish national character. While the list of those who had recently died was being read out on the radio, Emma had taken it upon herself to count how often each phrase was repeated as she drove and listened. Today she had three "sadly missed", two "peacefully at home" and two "unexpectedly". Whatever, it whiled away the time at the wheel. When she finally arrived, the existence of this funny "international" airport amused her once again . Abandoned looking, the place sat in the deserted, lonely hills around Knock. In 1897, after a series of famines, two housewives in the small village of Knock, on their way home on a rainy August afternoon, had seen the Virgin Mary and a few other Catholic saints – Emma could not remember exactly which ones. In any case, the holy troupe had reportedly been surrounded by angels. A lamb and a cross were also there. Small wonder, in Ireland lambs were everywhere.

Afterwards, other villagers remembered a bright light they claimed to have seen. In the bitterly poor area, everyone was probably slightly mad from lack of food, at least 'hunger delusions' was Emma's interpretation of the visions. The Church, of course, saw things differently, and in 1936 the Vatican recognized the famished delirium as a miracle. But the real miracle was that in 1986 an international airport was built in the impoverished area after a long campaign by the priest Aidan Horan – mocking tongues, though, said the runway was only built to lure the pope to Ireland. Amen!

Finally, when she checked in to her low-cost Rynair flight, Emma was annoyed, as always, about the additional cost of her luggage, and when she took off – as always – she was anxiously clutching the armrests. Hunting murderers was not a problem, but a latent fear of flying was.

Now the Irish Sea passed beneath her. Maeve Binchy's "Island of Stars" lay on Emma's lap – unread. Emma couldn't concentrate on the text, instead she thought about Stevie, who was still in bed when she had left the house this morning. He would spend the next two days with his father, who suddenly wanted to have his son all to himself. Oh Stevie, if you only knew, thought Emma, who remembered Paul's anger when she confessed her pregnancy to him at the time. And he was right, they were both so young, Emma was only 20.

After graduating from high school, she had had no idea what to do with her life, and since her Irish parents had never quite succeeded in the planned economic restart in New York that had caused their move to the US in the first place and could not or did not want to support their daughter financially, Emma aimlessly trailed through a few jobs. Eventually, following an impulse, she applied to work as a waitress at Joe Brady's Irish Pub on Maiden Lane in South Manhattan. A dark, beer-stinking place full of highly polished yellow brass and the inevitable shamrocks and harps behind the counter. At the on-site interview, the publican hadn't believed that Emma was actually Irish, as a child of the seedy Lower East Side she sounded as Yank as any American brat.

"You can't work here. You're pretty enough to lure the Wall Street bankers from around the corner, alright, but you also have to sound Irish, and you don't," he had said after a thorough examination – sounding quintessentially American himself.

"But I really am Irish!"

"Don't lie to me, you must have run away somewhere. Kansas? Illinois?", came the reply in a thick Brooklyn accent.

"I grew up here in Manhattan, on St Aidan Street, around the corner from the Police Headquarters. But I was born in Sligo, on the West coast of Ireland..."

Then a good-looking giant with laughing eyes, who had previously been silently polishing glasses behind the counter, joined the conversation: "Sligo. Really? Where exactly?"

His Irish accent was unmistakable, the guy in front of her spoke just as broadly as her parents.

"Ballymote. But I rarely went there as a kid, only on vacations... I went to school here in New York City."

"Okay, what's the most important thing about Ballymote?" he asked in his Irish brogue.

"From my point of view: my grandmother. She had a house there, not far from an ancient, overgrown cairn or ring fort. She always told me: 'On that grave, at night, the little people, the Shee or fairies, they dance'. I sat on the windowsill all night to see the fairy princess...' Emma grinned at the young Irishman.

"But from your point of view, the most important thing about Ballymote is probably the old 13th-century castle. Some Norman Earl of Ulster or some fecker like that built it. As a child, however, the old stones didn't interest me much."

The giant grinned back, turned to his boss and said:

„She's alright and, by the way, really from Ireland. We'll get the accent thing fixed. I'll teach her to talk in a proper Irish lilt in no time!"

That was exactly what Emma had always wanted to avoid: sounding like her parents, so foreign, so rural, so homesick. She was proud to have a cheeky New York mouth on her. But back then she had swallowed a flippant answer – not necessarily because she wanted to work for this stupid American in the fake Irish pub, but because something about that tall stranger had magically attracted her. It turned out that the alibi Irishman who was supposed to give Joe Brady's pub an air of authenticity was Paul Woods, a Protestant like Emma, and from the town of Sligo, which gave her home county its name. In the end, he taught her a lot more than her parents' accent. However, her pregnancy horrified him almost as much as her father, who had never fully trusted Emma since. Emma couldn't even think about what would have happened if Paul had turned out to be an Irish Catholic... Her father would probably have beaten her half to death and then cast her out.

In the end, they married without further ado and without their families in the Manhattan City Hall and soon after went back to Sligo. Firstly because they barely made enough money to pay a New York City rent, and secondly, that way the Irish community on either side of the Atlantic didn't know that she was a "fallen girl" and had been pregnant before marriage. Paul's charm, which had previously bubbled like Irish cider on tap in Joe Brady's Pub, now only foamed like chamomile tea. A wife and a child... This was not how he had imagined his return to Ireland. He had dreamed about driving home on a fancy Harley Davidson, being a successful hotelier... and he certainly didn't want to take over his father's feed and seed business. Faced with this fate, he had fled to New York in the first place, like countless immigrants before him.

But that's how it was in the end, the small family moved into the little flat above the shop and the marital unhappiness took its course. Whenever Paul felt like it, Emma felt his fists, mostly for no reason, simply because he was frustrated and had been drinking too much. Sometimes, however, Emma provoked him too, suddenly finding her tall, handsome giant only dull and banal.

After all, he largely ignored the little one, which was fine with Emma. She was so lonely in the foreign country that Stevie quickly became the sunshine of her otherwise dark days. Steve and her practical, loving, hands-on mother-in-law, Anne. God bless her! Emma had always wondered how this kind-hearted person could have raised such an immature son. But now, as a mother of a teenager herself, she had to recognise that parental influence on the offspring was relatively small, and saw Anne's parenting efforts in a milder light. After all, Anne was the one who looked after Stevie so that Em could go to the Garda training college and turn her life around.

Of course, Paul saw this as a betrayal by his mother and wife, since he wanted Em to work in his shop and take over the household goods division he was building in addition to the seed and fodder business. However, Emma always suspected that in the end he was a little afraid of his wife becoming too independent. Rightly so, for as soon as she had landed a steady job in the guards she grabbed her boy and moved out. She paid dearly for this independence – with Paul's hatred, the distrust of her Garda colleagues and the pain of her son, for whom she had shattered the more or less intact world of the core family. Especially since he had lost his beloved grandmother Anne, too, who had died of cancer, at about the same time... But from Emma's point of view, pretty much anything was better than Paul's aggression and his fists.

Suddenly she was snapped out of her thoughts by the flight attendant's voice: We are on approach to Manchester, sit down, buckle up, fold up the table. For once, Emma obediently did what she was told.

The taxi drove through endless grey suburbs. One terraced house leaned against the next, and many of them showed that their residents fought tooth and nail against poverty in the battle for their respectability. Many had already given up, paint was peeling from doors and windows, plaster crumbling off the walls. Fences were crooked, garden gates hung at an angle. Manchester was Nordic, grey, dreary. The rain didn't make it any easier for Emma to discover anything beautiful about the old industrial metropolis, where Charles Stewart Rolls once met Sir Frederick Henry Royce and founded a car factory.

Margaret's sons had both fled from here, one to Switzerland, the other to Australia, and Emma could understand that as they drove through ashen, overcast Manchester. Meanwhile the cab went over canals and through old brick industrial plants. Many of the abandoned 19th-century factories had small turrets and almost late-Gothic tapered windows. Funny, the factories here all looked like churches – and the churches look like factories, Emma thought as her taxi drove past an ugly 1970s house of God. It finally got greener and then Oak Gardens came into view. Individual houses stood scattered under trees in a park-like garden. For once, a field name like Oak Gardens was not deceptive; usually street names only expressed what had been destroyed to make room for development. If a street was called "Ash Grove" or "Birch Lane" or, as here, "Oak Garden", the names only expressed that the ashes, birches or oaks had not survived some development.

The Sargent boys hadn't been stingy when it came to choosing their mother's nursing home, even if they did not nurse her themselves, Emma thought with satisfaction. She hadn't bothered to call Manchester Police Headquarters. She could always inform her colleagues later on if an arrest or something else official became necessary. She had pocketed her handcuffs, though, just to be safe. I'm here incognito; Emma almost laughed at the thought before realizing she had better come up with an excuse for the receptionist at Oak Gardens, since she couldn't show her Irish police badge there. Somehow she had to justify why she wanted to visit Margaret Sargent. She would just put on her thickest Sligo accent and mumble something about being a distant cousin.

In fact, there was no reception at all, and Emma was suddenly standing in the middle of a kind of living room in which old people were dozing in heavy armchairs or wheelchairs. It smelled of disinfectant and toast. Apparently breakfast was just over. A very old man shuffled past her. He was fully clothed at the top, but from the hips down his bare skin shimmered frighteningly white, only under his toenails did the flesh appear bluish. A petite young Indian-looking nurse ran after him while waving something made of cloth and kept shouting, "Thomas, please come back! You still have to put on your pants!"

Getting old wasn't fun. Especially not if you were supposed to wear scratchy tweed. Thomas apparently preferred cold legs to his warm trousers and just kept walking. Emma believed that by the age of 80 everyone should be allowed to do what they liked, including going commando.

Eventually, she spotted the ward nurse, a plump woman in her 50s in pink nurse's scrubs and the white sandals typical of the medical industry.

"Hello, I'm Emma, over from Ireland. I would like to visit Margaret Sargent."

"Oh, that's nice. A visit from the old homeland! I'm sister Patty. Margaret is down in her room. Along the corridor to the left, number five."

Emma thanked her and was on her way. As she turned into the hallway, she thought she had misheard: "Violet! Violet!" And then again: "Violet!" It sounded muffled through the walls. That sound was clearly coming from room number five. Emma knocked and opened the door.

Two faces looked up at her. That of a tiny, very old lady with a tousled grey fringe of hair and glasses that seemed almost oversized on her small face. She said "Violet!" again, this time questioning. Next to her was a plump woman in her 40s who was busy cleaning up the leftovers from the old lady's breakfast. She straightened up and looked at Emma: "Hello, can I help you?"

But Emma just stood there and stared. It was as if the photo in her purse had come to life and aged 20 years – only to be wrapped in a purple scrubs. Everything was as pictured, even the thick braid that fell over the caregivers shoulder, the woman looked almost exactly like the one in the photo of the late Violet with the inscription "1963".

The two women stared at each other and Emma saw how an understanding played like a film behind the other woman's forehead. Then she composed herself and said:

"Hello, I am Emma from Sligo, Ireland, here to visit Margaret ."

When Margaret heard "Sligo" and "Ireland" her wrinkled little face broke into a smile. "Linborough," she said then. And "Mummy," and finally "I will raise and go now, and go to Innisfree..."

Emma smiled back and said: "Yes, Linborough. I was there this week. And I spoke to Henry as well. And to Jean."

However, she did not take her eyes off the nurse, who continued to sweep up toast crumbs with her hand.

"And who are you, if I may ask?" Emma said, deliberately addressing the nurse this time. "Is your name Violet?"

"No, my name is Catherine. I work here. Margaret has dementia and her brain provides words from long-term memory, but that doesn't mean anything, most of it is incoherent."

"Margaret's sister's name was Violet, did you know that?"

"No," came the dismissive reply. Catherine grabbed the tray and left the room with a curt "I have to go!", followed by Margaret's now anxious-sounding "Violet! Violet!".

Now what? Emma wondered, glancing at Margaret's photo collection on a side table. She recognized Bill Sargent and an old view of Linborough House. The silver-framed little blond boys with a kangaroo would have to be the Australian grandsons, Tom Sargent's children.

But Emma wasn't quite with it, though her brain was working feverishly: What exactly have I just experienced here? An identical twin of the late Violet? Was that why Charles Armstrong asked Laura McDern about the rights of inheritance of illegitimate children? But why should that have cost him his life?

Finally she sat down next to Margaret and smiled at the old lady: "Well, are you homesick for Ireland?"

But Margaret had long since withdrawn into her own world. Emma dug out the photocopy of Violet's photo from her purse and asked: "Do you remember your sister? Violet?"

"Violet," Margaret murmured.

"And Charles?"

Silence.

"What happened then? 1963, what happened?"

Silence.

"Did you send me this letter with the photo of Violet? Look, it's stamped in Manchester." Emma pulled the photocopy of the second letter's envelop from her purse and placed it with the photo.

Silence.

When Margaret finally fell asleep in her chair, Emma put the photo and envelope back in her purse and decided to take a stroll around the grounds to clear her mind. It was still raining outside, so she sat on a bench under the nursing home's eaves and looked out into the garden. She pulled out her phone and called Laura McDern.

"Hello darling, are you alright?" Laura's cheerful voice came over the airwaves.

"I am okay. I'm sitting in a retirement home in Manchester and don't know what to do."

"I actually thought you were ageing quite well. Isn't it a bit premature that you're about to book yourself into a retirement home?"

"Very funny!"

"Seriously, what are you doing there?"

"I'm visiting Margaret Sargent, née Armstrong, you know, my case. Well, whilst with her I bumped into a woman who looks exactly like Margaret's long-deceased sister, Violet Armstrong. It can't be a coincidence, but my brain is blocked. What am I seeing here?"

"And you're calling me? I'm sitting in my office in Ballisodare, staring at the latest issue of a family law journal. I have no idea what you encountered there!"

"Yes, but you told me something in the pub the other day. Old Armstrong's visit to your office. Something to do with the estate and illegitimate children. I didn't register it properly at the time. What exactly did you say at the time?"

"I don't know what exactly I said. Armstrong came to see me because he wanted some information about estate law. He wanted to know who could lay claim to the land and house. I assumed at the time that it was about Margaret's sons."

"You mean the old man wanted to secure the land for his children and get rid of his sister's kids as heirs?" Emma asked.

"I couldn't explain it any other way."

"Laura, you are a darling. Thanks very much. I'll let you know when I'm back in town."

There was, of course, another explanation. But how was she supposed to drag that out into the light of day?

It had stopped raining and Em was wandering around in the wet gardens, lost in thought. 'Violet Armstrong, I know what you've done, Violet Armstrong, I know what you've done...'

CHAPTER 10

Manchester

Emma had stopped under a tree to get her bearings when her phone rang. Her "Woods" sounded almost like a hiss.

"O'Leary," it growled back. Instantly, Emma's features softened.

"What's up, mate?"

"You better come back quickly, strange things are happening here. Kelly from Dublin is kind of hooked on an IRA theory and is digging around in the scene because he thinks the Republicans murdered Armstrong."

"And stole a radio? That's ridiculous. In addition, there is no letter of responsibility."

"Tell me something I don't know. But Kelly apparently believes the latest generation of republicans has changed strategy and is now operating covertly. He thinks they're putting up a facade so that IRA murders don't appear as such."

"But that's crazy."

"It gets a lot crazier. He suspects Paul."

"Paul? Paul who?"

"Your ex, you eejit," Aidan sounded suddenly exhausted. "Kelly is giving the whole brotherhood of IRA sympathizers a hard time here in Sligo. In the process, he somehow started fixating on Paul Woods."

"It's like a lousy cop movie."

"Ha, there you said it! My entire life is like a lousy cop movie!" Aidan laughed, not sounding amused at all.

"But why Paul? He sells dog food, shovels and saucepans..."

"Kelly says he had to flee to the US in the late 80s because Sligo gardai suspected he was involved in some robbery schemes to fund the Provos. Dublin must have had him on the radar for a long time."

"Absolute bollocks!"

"Paul may not have said anything to you, but Kelly is convinced that he has his fingers in the Republican pie."

"That's completely bonkers, Paul is a Protestant!"

"So was Charles Stewart Parnell. And he invented Irish nationalism, so to speak. At least he gave it a voice. There are quite a few Protestants in the IRA who care more about the Irish Republic, including all of Ulster, than their religious affiliation."

"Parnell. Isn't that the one with the statue on O'Connell Street in Dublin?"

"Exactly him, he fought for land reform and against the British landlords in the 19th century. The supreme nationalist, so to speak – and an Anglican by birth."

"Well, Paul is a Republican and he hates the Brits. That's correct. But that's pretty much all he ever let me know about his politics."

Emma had become thoughtful.

'Kelly seems to know more than you do, he thinks your ex is one of the heads of the IRA in Sligo and has gotten stuck on the idea that Armstrong is on his conscience. I wouldn't be surprised if he arrested your old man first."

"My ex old man, if you don't mind. And why should Paul concern himself with Armstrong now? The man was retired!"

"Em, this is Ireland. Once married, always married. Divorce may be in your head, but not in Eamonn Kelly's Catholic skull.

As for your other point, Kelly suggests that even after his retirement, Armstrong may have had active links with the Brits and supposedly Paul figured it out."

"The most important thing is to keep Stevie out of this. Because he's with his dad right now..."

"Call him and tell him he can stay with me; or send him to a friend's place until you get back and come back soon. Clan liability may be somewhat medieval, but if they pin something on Paul, it won't exactly be great for your career either. It would be better if you were here to convince the gentlemen personally of your qualities."

"All right, I'll call Stevie and get him to go to you at the station. I would be very grateful if he could stay at your place until tomorrow, then I'll be back. In the meantime I'll call Laura McDern, Paul will need legal representation..."

"Okay. That's how we'll play it. And what's going on with you in Manchester? Have you learned anything from your meeting with Margaret? The easiest way to help Paul would be to find the real killer quickly."

"Margaret? I'll tell you what's going on here tomorrow at noon when I'm back." And after a pause: "Aidan, you don't know how grateful I ..." But O'Leary had hung up already.

Emma phoned her son, who promptly complained: he was still at school and wasn't really allowed to use his mobile phone here. She made it clear that it was an emergency: "Your dad seems to be having trouble with a colleague of mine, an Eamonn Kelly from HQ in Dublin. Please don't go to your father's house after school, but to the station. You can stay with Aidan tonight."

Stevie liked the idea. He didn't mind hanging out with his mother's sidekick. When asked what his dad was up to, Emma had no real answer: "Nothing. My colleague is off his trolley. But I don't want you to be there when the police is visiting your father."

"But Aidan is a cop, too."

"Yes, but a cop with a brain. That's different." Both had to laugh.

"But who takes care of Dad? I can't just abandon him like that when the going gets tough!"

"Dad will be taken care of by Laura McDern. I'll call her next. She's a solicitor and can do a lot more for Paul than we can, believe you me."

"When are you coming home?"

"I'll be back when you get home from school tomorrow. Promise."

"Okay." Stevie was now audibly relieved.

"Everything will be fine, don't worry."

Emma hung up. If Paul was in trouble with the law, he could hardly start a custody suit. Suddenly Emma felt almost grateful to the guys from Dub.

Emma picked up her cell phone again and rang Laura.

"Sorry to disturb you again. I think I have a little emergency."

'Oh, do they want to keep you in the old people's home in Manchester? Or have you messed up something?"

"Well, not me, but maybe Paul..."

After Emma had briefed Laura, asked for help on Paul's behalf, and absorbed Laura's reassuring words like a sponge, she returned to the Oak Gardens home. She still had a homicide to solve and needed to focus, after all. Hopefully Margaret had woken up by now.

Emma wasn't quite through the door of the retirement home when Catherine stood in front of her.

"Who are you really?" she challenged. "I just got off the phone with Bill Sargent in Switzerland and he doesn't recall any relative with the name Emma. All he knows is that there is a police woman in Sligo by the name of Emma Woods who is investigating his uncle's murder!'

"I didn't say I was related to Margaret Sargent, I just introduced myself as Emma from Sligo."

"How dare you go after the old lady? She is vulnerable, sick and should not be bothered. Especially not by police. What do you want from her anyway?"

"Someone killed her brother and I wanted to see that the old lady was okay and that she wasn't in any danger either. Besides, I have no need to explain myself to you."

"Oh yes, you have, because when people have dementia, the family has to agree to visits from non-relatives. And if you don't stop bothering Margaret, I'm going to call the police!" Catherine's face had turned white, with frantic red spots on her neck. Small beads of sweat stood out on her upper lip, and single strands hung from her thick, red braid, as if she had torn her hair.

"Calm down," Emma said reassuringly, "I'm the police and I'm already here. Besides, I just wanted to say goodbye anyway. Margaret is clearly in the best of hands here. Make sure it stays that way."

Half an hour later Emma was lying on her bed in the Copthorne Hotel by the old shipping canal at Salford Quays. When she arrived, she hadn't seen how that part of the city was trying to transform its industrial past into a chic urban landscape of restaurants and shopping malls, nor had she really noticed that Old Trafford – the home grounds of Manchester United – was just a few meters away on the other side of the water. Had it been Saturday and a match day, Emma could have heard the roar of the fans all the way up in her room. But it wasn't and hence she lay flat on her back in deep silence, staring at the ceiling and brooding.

Paul an active IRA man? That would have been one reason why this man, who was so attached to his homeland, had turned up in New York one day. After all, quite a lot of Irish people who were part of the troubles in Ireland fled to America when the ground at home got too hot under their feet. Especially to Boston and New York. There were large Irish exile communities in both cities. In her days as a pub waitress, out of the corner of her eye she often had spotted boys with Irish accents hitting on bar patrons for "donations" for "Ireland's liberation." Freedom fighters, my arse! Did the drinkers in New York with Irish ancestors realise that they were supporting illegal arms trade, kidnappings and bombings in their fathers' homeland?

At that time, Emma, newly in love, had asked Paul about the reason for his stay in the US, but he had only murmured something about wanting to travel to see a bit of the world and then changed the subject. There had never been any mention of the IRA, and in any case they had never discussed politics at the time. But, God knows, he had made no secret of the fact that he detested the British and wanted a united Ireland under the leadership of Dublin. On the other hand, this rhetoric was considered good manners by many Irish people. Until now she had regarded his latent violence as a weakness of character, but perhaps the roots of his aggressiveness lay a lot deeper.

Aidan O'Leary was of a different calibre. Rather the quiet type, but when push came to shove, reliable as a rock. Oh dear, don't think about Aidan right now... She didn't need butterflies in her stomach at the moment. But Emma's thoughts were already with the Sligo guards. She could easily imagine what it would mean for her career with the Gardai if Paul was really dirty. She would be caught in the mess and hung out to dry. After all, she had married the man. In Catholic Ireland, hardly anyone took it seriously that she had left him but few would believe that she was ignorant of his terrorist activities. She of all people, a successful detective, shouldn't she have noticed an IRA conspiracy in her own house? They would think she was either thick as two wet planks or a liar. In many ways she remained the outsider, the independent woman who, after 15 years in Ireland, was still being treated like something the cat had dragged in. Emma could see the mocking faces of McNulty, Kelly and the likes and knew that apart from O'Leary and maybe Murray few would stand by her.

Paul pulling strings in the local IRA? Was he smart enough for that? Or indeed stupid enough? Instinctively, Emma felt that all violent people were stupid per se; even if her job had shown her often enough that this view had nothing to do with reality. There were plenty of intelligent thugs, and not just in Ireland. Not only among the crooks, but also among the cops. But Paul as the brains behind a strategy shift in the IRA? He was supposed to have dreamed up a murder cover-up instead of a confession letter? Her colleagues would probably even insinuate that Paul had studied the methods of conventional criminals with his ex from the guards in order to imitate them as well as possible ... Really? Was Paul that smooth? Did she even know her ex? At the end of the day you couldn't look into anyone's head. Least of all into that of your own partner. And that was her conclusion on this matter.

Yet today she had almost gotten a glimpse into the mind of another person. This Catherine not only happened to look like Violet, she obviously had something to hide. A nurse did not develop a hectic cold sweat and red spots on the skin to protect one of her patients from the coppers. Especially when it was abundantly clear that this protégé was far too old, weak, and confused to do anything beyond spilling cocoa in terms of criminal energy.

Emma sat up, picked up the phone, and let the operator put her through to Oak Gardens administration.

"Hello, Emma Woods here. I was visiting one of your patients in Oak Gardens today and forgot my jacket. Could I speak to the nurse who looked after Margaret Sargent today, please? I must have left my jacket in Margaret's room and would like to know if the staff found anything. The sister's name was Kate or Cathy or Catherine or something like that."

Break.

"Yes, I'll be happy to wait." Muzak played on the line – and Emma hated it. Why couldn't anyone stand silence any more? All the time there was noise pollution coming from somewhere. Acoustic junk. Then the voice was back:

"Are you still there? We don't have a Kate, but we do have a Cathy Flack and a Catherine Payman, both working on the ward where Margaret Sargent lives. Which one would you like to speak to?"

"Oh, you know what, it's not that important. I'll put on a warm sweater and just drop by Oak Gardens again tomorrow and get my jacket," Emma stuttered. "If I really lost it there. Maybe I left it in the taxi…" Emma tried to appear as bedraggled as possible, didn't wait for an answer and just hung up.

Catherine Payman. How many Catherine Paymans could there be in Manchester?

Emma took the lift down to the hotel reception and asked for the local phone book. She stopped right at the hotel concierge's reception desk, flipped open the book, and ran her finger down the row of "P's." There were only two C. Paymans in Manchester, one in Sale and one in Chorlton-cum-Hardy. She turned to the young hotel clerk behind the desk, who didn't have much to do in the middle of the afternoon and was already looking curious.

"Where in Manchester are Sale and Chorlton?"

"Sale is further south, the A 46 out, quite a noble area, expensive houses, it is beautiful out there. Chorlton is not far from here, you can almost walk. Past Old Trafford, through Firswood and you're more or less there."

Em wrote down both the C. Paymans' addresses and phone numbers, thanked the receptionist, and went back to her room. Whilst there, she zapped herself absent-mindedly through the TV programs and got stuck on a "Dirty Harry" film with Clint Eastwood.

The age-old flick had only just begun. A bunch of nasty little thugs wanted to rob Harry's favourite coffee shop, but he was having none of it . At the end, only one of the baddies still stands upright, gun in hand, and Harry with his battered visage, magnum at the ready, asking the thug to please pull the trigger so that he can kill him and rid the city of this plague... "Go ahead. Make my day." Simply wonderful. Emma's favourite quote. Mainly because it had absolutely nothing to do with the reality of the police service. If Emma were to just shoot down a handful of small-time crooks in a coffee shop, she would be suspended immediately, there would be endless internal investigations and a lengthy process. Not so with Harry, he just killed all the crooks, got barked at by his boss for it, and then the world was right as rain again. Hollywood made it possible.

Emma also amused herself at the recklessness with which Harry took on the mafia and provoked one of the mob bosses at his daughter's wedding to the point of giving him a heart attack and making him fall face down into the food. If she were to single-handedly take on the IRA like that, or the drug mafia in Belfast or Dublin – which was exactly the same thing, at least in parts – she wouldn't have long to live. Nobody in the Garda would ever behave like Dirty Harry and ignore personal risks so consistently, but in a hotel bed in a foreign city, Emma had great fun thinking about being so uncompromising. Not even the scenes that were slow and boring by contemporary standards bothered her, because it all fit the 1970s. She couldn't get enough of the perms, moustaches, oversized lapels and ties of the era.

After Harry had finished cleaning up San Francisco, Emma decided to take a nap and try her luck later. Catherine couldn't be on duty at Oak Gardens twenty-four hours a day.

CHAPTER 11
Family ties

When Emma woke up, it was nearly five o'clock, and her phone, which had been left on mute, was blinking. There were missed calls from Paul, which Emma studiously ignored. After all, they probably hadn't arrested him yet, because then his colleagues would have taken his mobile. No message from Aidan. "When the phone didn't ring, I knew it was you," thought Emma. The wonderful Dorothy Parker and her satirical rhymes, which were supposed to help hide deep wounds... But Emma had other things to do now than wonder about poetry.

The back pain was excruciating, but she slowly got into her boots and took the leather jacket from the back of the chair. Then she inspected the contents of her bag. The handcuffs were where they belonged. Two more painkillers and she was ready.

At reception she asked for a map and set off. The air was cold but clear after all the rain. Emma took a deep breath and walked quickly into the beginnings of dusk. The exercise would do her aching bones some good, hopefully. In early spring, Manchester was not much warmer or brighter than the west coast of Ireland. The neighbourhood she wandered through certainly wouldn't be featured in the "Manchester Evening News" under "Family & Kids" as an area to spend a nice Sunday with the little ones.

By the time Emma got to the corner of Newport and Oswold Road in Chorlton, it was almost dark. The corner house she was looking for was small, two-storey and plain, the garden neglected. An unkempt shack – a geriatric nurse would not be able to afford much more on her salary. Emma was glad she hadn't started her search in the much more noble part of town, because she was almost certain that she was on the right track here. Opposite was a school, according to the map, Oswold Primary. Somehow Emma vaguely remembered a radio feature about the Bee Gees, which said that as children the future stars went to a school by that name in Manchester. Apparently they had started out small and poor too.

The school was deserted and dark, but Catherine's house had a light on. Emma quietly opened the rusty gate to the front yard and walked towards the door. The green paint was peeling. She knocked, her left foot ready to be shoved in the door in case Catherine was about to slam it in her face. Blessed is she who wears sturdy boots.

When the door opened, Emma was briefly blinded by the backlight, all she could see was the silhouette of a small, slightly plump woman. Thick red hair framed her head. Catherine's voice sounded slightly stressed:

"What do you want?"

"To talk with you."

"Talk to me? About what?"

"About the sorry end of Charles Armstrong, Margaret's brother."

"What do you want from me? I don't know anything about that. And get your foot out my door or I'll call the police." Obviously, Catherine was a better observer than Emma had expected. Reluctantly, she withdrew her foot a few inches.

"Why do you keep wanting to call the police? I am the police, Irish Garda to be precise. And I just want to talk to you. What do you have to lose?"

Silence. Then Catherine said, "Why are you here? What do you want from me?"

"To find out why someone from Manchester is sending me a photo of Margaret's sister Violet Armstrong from 1963 and why you look exactly like that particular Violet."

Catherine said nothing.

"But most of all I want to know why you're so sad." Emma was probing.

Catherine let her shoulders sag, and it was only now that Emma realised that the woman had had pulled them up so tightly. She opened the door a little wider and Emma pushed it open all the way, taking a step forward, now standing in a brightly lit hallway.

"All right, I'll make us some tea."

Catherine led the way into the kitchen and Emma thought about why she always ended up in people's kitchens in this case. Anyway, at least it was warmer there than in the hallway.

Catherine asked Emma to sit down, filled the kettle, placed two earthenware mugs on the table, and got milk from the fridge while Emma sat down at the short end of an L-shaped bench at the table, put her bag beside her, and settled into looking around. From the outside the cottage might look unkempt, but inside the little house was clean and almost cosy, with herb pots on the windowsill and the old kitchen clock over the door. Catherine returned with a steaming, heavy ceramic teapot, placed it on the table and flopped into the chair next to Emma's place.

"My feet hurt after a full shift. Care for the elderly is no picnic."

"You're comfortable here though, I like your kitchen."

"Thanks, but compliments won't get you anywhere with me. Why should I even talk to you?"

"Because you're an Armstrong. And because your uncle was murdered."

"Armstrong? My uncle? What on earth gave you that idea?"

"Your roots are in Ireland, in County Sligo. Just like mine."

"Emma, you are boring me."

"Bored? I don't believe you. Well then, I'll tell you a story."

Catherine said nothing and traced the grain of her wooden table with her right index finger. Emma saw strong hands, long fingers, manicured nails, no nail polish and began:

"In the 1960s in Ireland's North West, County Sligo, Violet Armstrong became pregnant and gave the baby away. Probably under pressure from her brother, Charles Armstrong, a clergyman in the Church of Ireland. Forty years later, Violet's child, a girl, by crazy coincidence comes into contact with her aunt, Margaret Sargent. As fate would have it, this girl works in the nursing home where her cousins put their mother, her aunt. The old lady is confused and unable to express herself, but keeps sending signals from the depths of her damaged brain by repeatedly calling this girl – now a grown woman – Violet. After all, this woman is the spitting image of how the nurse's mother Violet – Margaret's sister – looked back in the day."

Catherine poured Emma a cup of tea without comment.

"Milk?"

"Yes, please."

Emma wrapped her hands around the mug, took a sip and continued. "Maybe this woman in the nursing home looked at Margaret's family photos and realised that she might be dealing with long-lost relatives?"

Catherine studied the backs of her hands.

Emma had gotten too warm in the well-heated kitchen. She stood up half way and leaned forward to remove her beloved black leather jacket. Catherine moved as well, as if to politely help Emma out of her garments. But before Emma understood what was happening, Catherine had jumped up with surprising agility and pulled Emma's half-open leather jacket down to her elbows. Now the thing was like a straitjacket around her upper body and tied her arms to her torso. At the same time, she shoved the heavy kitchen table forward and into Emma's midriff. There it hit old wounds and Emma almost fainted from the pain. While Emma flopped back onto the bench, wedged between the table and the corner seat, gasping in pain and struggling to free her arms, Catherine grabbed Emma's handbag and took a few steps back from the table. While Em was squirming to free herself from her jacket like a caterpillar from its old skin, Catherine had taken a long and sharp looking knife from her kitchen counter.

"Remain seated!" she yelled, pointing the knife at Emma.

But Emma didn't even think about it. By now she had freed her hands, pushed the table away, grabbed the heavy teapot and threw it at Catherine. Unfortunately, the weighty earthenware pot was so hot she barely had time to aim properly. Catherine, agile as a rabbit despite her chubbiness, ducked and the pot smashed against the wall above the sink. Hot tea spilled over the counter tops, the floor – but Catherine just stood there, smiling triumphantly.

Shit, shit, shit, she was behaving like a complete beginner, that's what happened when you were arrogant enough not to take a fat little geriatric nurse seriously. Emma was panting, stuck helplessly and only half upright behind the table. Tea dripped into the silence.

Catherine pointed the long knife at Emma with her right hand and said calmly:

„Slowly now. I don't have much to lose, so I'll stick this into your liver if you don't sit down immediately." Her left hand rummaged in Emma's bag. There she found what she was looking for and finally tossed Emma her own handcuffs.

"Put these around your wrists and shut them – and I want to hear the locks click. Don't underestimate me again!"

Emma sat down. Everything inside her screamed for her pills. What an idiot I am! And all this without a safety net or reinforcements! Nobody knows where I am, nobody knows who I suspect, nobody in the Armstrong case has ever heard of Catherine Payman. And the Manchester Police have no idea I'm out here either.

Aloud she said, "So the story is getting more and more interesting. Boredom? I knew I had your attention!"

"The handcuffs, and pronto!"

Emma reluctantly put the handcuff on her left wrist and used her right hand to squeeze the locking mechanism shut. Click. Then the left put the second steel ring around her right wrist and squeezed again. Click. If Catherine didn't get close enough for Emma to smack her in the chin, stomach, or face with her bound hands, Emma was screwed. But for the time being she was quite defenceless, especially since Catherine had pushed the table back tightly in front of her stomach. Catherine pulled her chair back a meter, out of Emma's reach and sat down.

"So you're a storyteller," Catherine resumed the conversation as if nothing had happened. "How Irish. Aren't you lot just notorious for the gift of the gab? And you're not particularly clever either, or at least the English like to joke about the stupid Irish. Do you know that one? Paddy and Johnny go hunting. Paddy accidentally shoots Johnny. There he lies in his blood and Paddy calls the ambulance on his mobile phone.

`Oh god, I've accidentally shot my friend whilst out hunting. He's lying here and isn't moving. I think he may be dead!´.

The woman from the emergency services on the other end asks: `Ok, now, stay calm, but can you make sure he's really dead?´

`One moment´, Paddy replies and puts down the phone.

The woman from the emergency services hears a loud bang that sounds like a gunshot, then Paddy's voice comes down the receiver again: 'Okay, now he's 100 per cent dead, alright. Now what?'"

"Oh come on, Catherine, you're Irish yourself and not at all stupid. Why are you telling me ghastly jokes instead of your own story?"

Catherine said nothing. After a long pause, she looked Emma in the eye.

"All right, I'll tell you a story about a little Irish girl with thick red hair. This girl's earliest memory is of the Eagle Lodge orphanage in Newcastle-upon-Tyne. She was maybe three and, like all the other girls in this place, wore a short blue dress with a white collar, summer and winter. In addition, white socks and black shoes. If the white collar or socks got stained, the sisters would give them terrible beatings. Sister Geraldine, in particular, liked to hit, preferably with a rod. Sometimes she gave a little girl that was to be punished secateurs and sent her out to the willow trees in the garden. Then the child had to cut a sally rod, bring it back to Sister Geraldine, who promptly used it to punish her."

Now it was Emma's turn to stay quiet.

"And keeping collars and socks white and clean wasn't easy at all. Our little Irish girl, who didn't even know she was Irish, had to clean. Fill a large bucket with water, dissolve soft soap in it, and then drag the bucket with a brush to wherever it was wanted for cleaning. In the kitchen, in a lavatory or – worst of all – in one of the bedrooms on the first or second floor. It was almost impossible for a little girl to hoist the heavy bucket up the steps without the sudsy water sloshing into her shoes and wetting her socks. The slightly older girls tried to help, but when one of them was caught they both got spanked – the little one and the bigger one as well. The girls should pray while cleaning because they were bad girls, the sisters said. Born out of sin, and that's why no one in the world wanted them. Not their mothers, not their fathers, and nobody else either. Some girls were adopted, but many stayed at Eagle Lodge until they were adults. There they would be on their knees for years, scrubbing the floors until their hands bled. Others worked in the laundry, and everybody in the Eagle Lodge area who could afford it brought their dirty laundry to the orphanage.

Nice story, isn't it?" Catherine was silent and stared straight ahead. Then she caught Emma's eyes.

"What was the name of our little girl?" Emma wanted to know.

"Oh, that doesn't matter."

Apparently, Catherine's will to survive meant she had to tell her story on the one hand and blame it on a non-entity on the other: mental hygiene without any admission of guilt. Actually clever.

"Why didn't the little girl run away?" Emma asked.

"There was no point in running away, everyone far and wide knew and recognized the little blue dresses. Besides, none of the girls even had enough money for a bus fare out of Newcastle-upon-Tyne. And where would they have gone? Nobody wanted them, at least that wasn't a lie. Those who tried were picked up by the local people like apples fallen from a tree and brought back to Sister Geraldine and the others. The penalties were terrible. Eagle Lodge was a kind of concentration camp for children." Catherine's gaze seemed to be drawn inward.

"What did the sisters do to the runaways?"

"Usually the girls showered upstairs in the washroom next to the dormitories. But there was another bathroom downstairs in the basement. All in pink tiles, only the tub was white. There was always cold water in it, already prepared, so to speak, always as a silent threat in the background. Or in the underground, to be precise. In winter it was often so cold that there was a thin layer of ice on the water. Whoever had really screwed up had to go down to the basement with Geraldine, take off their clothes, lay them neatly folded on a wooden chair by the tub, get in the tub and dive under. It washes away the sins, was Sister Geraldine opinion. Those who did not dive voluntarily were knocked over and pushed under water. With the bigger girls, two or three sisters often had to help keep them submerged. Backwards into the ice-cold water. Often again and again."

Catherine had tears in her eyes and Emma felt a surge of pity.

"It's almost like water boarding," she said, "and that's officially considered torture."

But Catherine didn't hear her at all, she just kept talking:

"It wasn't easy for her to warm up after such a bathing procedure. Because Eagle Lodge was cold, freezing cold. Especially in winter. The girls were all very thin, for there was little given to eat for the fruits of deadly sin, as Geraldine called them. Meat or fish were particularly rare – protein in general. Instead, morning and evening, thin oatmeal that hardly deserved the name porridge; that's not much for child slaves who do hard physical labour. Instead of food there were prayers; the main thing is that the soul is well fed, said Sister Geraldine.

But she was lucky. Because someone loved her. A Vicar of the Anglican Church. Let's call him Samuel Bell. He was responsible for the salvation of the girls at Eagle Lodge and regularly appeared for Bible studies and services. He stroked that little girl's head, sometimes brought her a biscuit and praised her when she read aloud from the Bible. He often took her to the front. There he sat behind the desk, the girl clamped between his legs and the desk, the Bible in front of her. She had to read aloud while he massaged her buttocks. The fact that the vicar began to breathe so strangely didn't bother her, she was so hungry for affection and tenderness that she ignored it. She also felt privileged to the other girls in the class, a feeling she didn't often experience.

Once he grabbed her between the legs and she started crying in the middle of the Bible study. The result was another visit of the bathtub in the basement; she hadn't been nice enough to the vicar, Sister Geraldine explained. Had embarrassed him in front of all the others with her 'groundless howling', when a good girl 'should be happy when she reads the Word of God!'

When she was about eleven, the vicar took the girl to the orphanage director's office, Sister Geraldine was there too. She said to her: 'You must pray and thank the Lord for your happiness. Vicar Bell and his wife Martha will take you home. You will be adopted. You always have to be very grateful to them, because nobody else wants a sinner like you.'

A little later, the girl found herself with the Bells in a northern English terraced house. Kitchen, toilet, dining and living room downstairs, two bedrooms and a bathroom upstairs. Martha was a tall, thin, angular woman who had no children of her own. She didn't talk much and did the housework mechanically. At least she could cook, and the child finally got proper food and regular meals. In addition, she was given a few items of clothing that were not itchy institutional smocks and a room of her own. It had a floral patterned wallpaper instead of the painted bile green walls of the home. The house was warm too but even so, she found it hard to fall asleep under the flowers for a long time, her being so used to the sounds of a dormitory where some child was always coughing, moaning about a nightmare, or just crying in despair.

Her bedroom was always silent. Until the door opened at night and the vicar crept in to her, whispering encouragement, stroking her hair and then laying down on her. It hurt terribly at first, and he always held her mouth tight so that no noise came from the room. In the morning the sheets were covered in blood. But Martha didn't say anything, just made the bed up again. However, she never hugged the girl either. In fact, she never really looked at the child. Instead, she went to church twice a day to pray.

She believed it had to be like this, that all fathers do that. That's why she never said anything. Once she wanted to apologize to Martha for the dirty sheets. But she just said, 'Silence. For God's sake, shut up!', and gave the girl another piece of cake.

All the good food made the child finally grow and the she became rounder. When she was 14 and developing breasts, he lost interest.

She tried to kill herself then, because no one loved her any more. At the hospital they diagnosed depression and gave her pills."

Suddenly, a ringing sound broke the silence in Catherine's kitchen. Without taking her eyes off Emma, Catherine fished around in the black leather pouch, looked at the cell phone display and said:

"It's the 'pain in the butt'. Who is this?"

"My colleague, Garda Aidan O'Leary."

Relief swept over Em. If I don't answer, he'll get nervous and will call the hotel, and if I don't answer there either... she thought. But too soon. Catherine had simply waited for the ringing to stop. Now she started typing into the device: "I'll text Aidan that you're too tired to talk and already are in bed. Then he will probably leave us alone."

Shortly thereafter, the ringtone came, signalling that an SMS had arrived on Emma's phone. Catherine looked at the display:

"The pain in the butt wishes sweet dreams and asks for a call in the morning!"

"Did the girl ever find out where she came from?" Emma picked up the thread. She desperately needed to continue the conversation with Catherine. Occupy her until she had an idea how to get out of the mess she had gotten herself into, thanks to her own blasted arrogance. She had simply underestimated Catherine. At the same time, she wanted to learn her story and understand her motive.

"No. Apparently she was brought to Eagle Lodge as a baby like a damaged egg that had fallen out of its nest and no one ever bothered to explain anything to her."

"What happened after the hospital? Was the girl brought back to the Bells?"

"He had lost interest in her, probably dying to get her out of the house so he could fill the nursery with new and younger flesh. And Martha just tried to take in as little as possible of the life around her. The Bells were happy to be rid of their ward."

"It can't have been easy for the young girl."

"In the end it was the best thing that could have happened to her. Someone in the hospital realized that something had gone terribly wrong in the girl's life and sent a social worker to the hospital bed. Sue Ramsey. That lady was the first who ever actually spoke to her. Like pulling twisted, used nails out of an old board, she pulled out of the girl what had happened to her, piece by piece. Maybe not the whole truth, because the girl was ashamed of her experiences, but enough for Sue to understand what was going on."

"Did Sue call the cops?"

"The police?" Catherine laughed bitterly. "When have you guys ever stood by a little girl or a little boy against the church? Don't make me laugh. It was at the end of the 1970s and you all kept your mouth shut when it came to child abuse. Most people still think that the little vixens had only themselves to blame for seducing old men with their cuteness."

Emma wanted to defend herself and her colleagues, but the words caught in her throat, knowing that Catherine was dead right in many cases .

"Sue didn't call the police, but she took the girl to Manchester and found her a place in a residential community for underprivileged and neglected young people," Catherine continued. "There she finally found peace. Meanwhile the Bells acted as if they had been insulted to the core by her suicide attempt. 'You do everything for a child like that and that's the response!' Martha must have said something like that to the doctors when they asked her what the girl's motive might have been."

"And this Sue?"

"Sue Ramsey was about to be transferred to Manchester herself at the time and stayed at the girl's side, so to speak. The kid could finally go to a non-denominational school and learn something other than memorizing the Bible forwards and backwards."

"And then she trained as a nurse."

"Yes, exactly, she wanted to help others."

"And today she looks after elderly people with dementia."

"Maybe."

Tears ran down Emma's cheeks. "Can I get a tissue from my purse, please?"

Catherine just sat there. "First I want to know why you're crying."

"I cry for the little girl in your story and for the childhood she wasn't allowed to have and for the mother she never met."

Catherine said nothing.

Emma wept.

"And I cry for the little girl I used to be. A young girl who ended up with the wrong guy, got pregnant too early and then got beaten regularly for it. I weep for all these young women whose wings someone clipped long before they learned to fly."

Emma had thought up this crying fit as a ruse to get Catherine close to her, but now she realised in amazement that she really meant what she was saying. Apparently the emotion showed on her face, because Catherine rummaged in Emma's bag, found a packet of tissues and got up to take them to the weeping policewoman. The knife dangled loosely and as if forgotten from her right hand.

Emma knew she had only one chance. When Catherine got close enough, she jumped up. The table skidded away as Emma threw up her bound arms and aimed under Catherine's chin. The nurse hadn't expected the aggressiveness of a crying woman. Her head snapped back, she staggered. Em followed, turned sideways and hit her a second time in a twisting motion, this time thumping her opponent in the side of the stomach. The knife flew away in a high arc, smacking the tiles in front of the stove. Catherine sank to the ground. Before she could move again, Emma had grabbed the knife. It was now aimed at Catherine for a change.

"Just lie still and you'll be fine," Emma said. Her hip hurt like hell. And her wrists bled. She must have hit Catherine pretty hard if it had split the skin under her handcuffs.

Emma sat down in Catherine's chair and bent down for her leather pouch. On the keychain she found the keys to her handcuffs. It was quite a fumble, but in the end Emma managed to free herself.

"Turn around!" she bellowed at Catherine. "Turn onto your stomach."

But Catherine only groaned in a daze. Her mouth was bloody, she must have bitten her tongue or lip when she was hit under the chin. However, the blow to the kidneys had knocked her out. She would pee blood for at least a week. Emma approached her cautiously, remembering Catherine's agility all too well. She snapped the one metal ring of the handcuffs around Catherine's right hand, lifted her right arm and dragged the entire woman across the floor to the stove. Then she snapped the second ring around the oven handle. For now, Catherine could only attack with a heavy gas range in tow, Emma thought with satisfaction. Then she grabbed the injured woman's shoulders and sat her up, resting her back against the oven. Catherine tried to grab Emma's long hair with her left hand in an uncoordinated manner, but in the end she had no strength left to seriously engage in a physical altercation.

Emma dropped to the floor a safe distance away, leaned against a cupboard, and sobbed. Meeting Catherine had tearfully dissolved an oxycodone-cemented knot in her that Emma didn't even knew existed. How did this happen to a person who liked 'wailing women' as much as snails in a salad. But sometimes you just had to cry!

Tearfully, she pulled her bag towards her, pressed a tissue into Catherine's free hand, and blew her own nose in a second one. The adrenaline that had been pumping through her body ever since she'd stood on Catherine's doormat was draining away, and Emma felt the exhaustion. She kind of liked that ginger firebrand. Catherine had courage, you had to give her that. She moaned softly. Apparently she had regained consciousness.

"Rather shitty, the way we are here. We're supposed to be beating up the abusers of this world, not each other," Emma said.

Catherine looked over at her in surprise and then spat a mouthful of blood onto the kitchen floor.

"I'm sorry, I didn't mean to hurt you," Emma said. "But I can't let you commit another murder."

Now Catherine was crying too.

"I'm almost forty years old and I'm trying to smile," she said. "Every time I look into a mirror I see an empty shell. A pointless being, only waiting to die. I have never learned how to trust somebody or how to love somebody, I have no partner, no children, no family. Only Sue Ramsey and the old folks in Oak Gardens. Apart from Sue, no one knows my story I'm clean and dressed normally, braiding my hair. I smile... I learned to hide my feelings from a very young age. Since then I have become an expert, everything can be hidden behind a smile."

"I know."

The two women said nothing. It wasn't a hostile silence.

"How does the girl's story end?"

"In the nursing home where she works, she meets an old lady who always calls her Violet. She looks at the lady's old photo albums and realises that she herself looks exactly like that Violet in the family photos ."

"Is that old lady's name Margaret?"

Catherine nodded.

"And then one day when Margaret's son comes to visit, the nurse seems to be the only one apart from Margaret who notices the family resemblance. But Margaret is already too ill to tell the nurse what's happened," Catherine said.

"And that's all?" Emma asked.

"When the old lady, Margaret, started to lose touch with reality, she was taken to a nursing home by her sons. With her came some personal items: old photo albums and diaries from her younger years. She took those, searched around, studied the data. The oldest of the diaries dates back to the summer of 1965. So she started reading."

"What happened then?"

"Margaret's brother Charles was about to become a priest. His mentor, Philip Anderson, supported him in this."

"Wait a minute, the Philip Anderson who later became Bishop of the Church of Ireland in Armagh?"

"That's him, but he wasn't a bishop at the time. But a friend of the Armstrong family who regularly appeared in Linborough in Laragh for tea. But not because the Armstrongs' pickle sandwiches were so delicious. No, Anderson had a much bigger appetite for Charles' little sister Violet. One day he simply raped her in the barn. Violet became pregnant and the family was horrified. No one believed the girl that Anderson was involved, on the contrary, they all pretended that Violet was the criminal. The family honour was more important to the mother than her daughters well-being. Her brother Charles in particular kept threatening her to make her shut up and not jeopardize his career in the church."

"Is that really all in the diaries of the old lady in the nursing home?"

"Yes, Violet had told her sister the sad truth at the time, and Margaret wrote it down."

"So it all started with Charles' role in the Church of Ireland?"

"Yes. And Violet's bigoted mother was so proud of her golden boy. But instead of going after his buddy Philip, he put his pregnant sister in a home for unmarried mothers, where the girl was born in July 1965. A week after the birth, the sisters there took the child from Violet. After that, the young woman ran away, actually wanted to kill herself, but ended up with her sister Margaret in England. She gradually told her sis the whole story, who in turn put it all in her diary. Margaret then travelled back to Linborough with Violet a few weeks later to find out what had become of the baby.

But the two women hit a wall of silence. Violet's child was gone, Charles just kept repeating his threats; and otherwise it was about protecting the family honour and Charles' church career at all cost."

"And she read all that in Margaret's diaries?"

Catherine nodded.

"When was that?"

"Pretty much a year ago, March 2004."

"And then?"

"Then she spoke to her old friend, social worker Sue Ramsey, and she helped her find her adoption papers, or at least the little bit of data that the UK welfare system had in its archives. Then everything fell into place like a solved jigsaw puzzle: The girl was born on July 6th, 1965 in a Bon Coeur Protestant institution for 'fallen girls' in Ireland to a Violet Armstrong, taken to a Church of England children's home in the UK and then put up for adoption."

"So she finally had it in black and white: She was Violet's daughter, Margaret's niece, and she had had a mother who loved her and wanted to keep her," Emma said thoughtfully. "A mother who wanted to kill herself after her baby was taken from her by force. She had had a family, even if some of the relatives didn't want her," Emma concluded.

"Exactly. The orphanage and the vicar – she would have been spared all that if these ghastly people had just allowed the baby to be with her mother!"

Catherine sat motionless.

Emma said nothing. What could she say? Any word of comfort would amount to an insult. There was no comfort for an abandoned, abused child.

"Then on New Year's Eve, the girl decided to gather all her courage and find her family. It was not difficult to clarify the whereabouts of her biological father. Anderson had meanwhile become a bishop and a well-known man, but, as she quickly found out, was long dead. The search for Violet was more difficult. She had disappeared without a trace as if swallowed up by the earth. At the Armstrongs' family home, Linborough, no one ever answered the phone," Catherine continued.

"Small wonder," said Emma, "Violet never really recovered from the trauma, died young and Linborough was a practical ruin, nobody has lived there for a long time."

"Eventually, she found Charles Armstrong, a retired priest, in Sligo, not far from Linborough House. So the assumption was obvious that this was the Charles Armstrong mentioned in the diaries. She then wrote him a letter, explaining her concerns and asking to be allowed to meet him and her mother."

"And? What was the reaction?

"Nothing. Only silence. She was about to go to Ireland unannounced when finally a letter from Charles Armstrong arrived at the end of February, inviting her to Armstrong House in Sligo. She should be there at six in the evening."

"How did she get to Sligo?"

"By plane to Dublin, then on by rental car. However, she could not find a parking space on St. John Street. At first she was upset that she had to park a few streets away, but that turned out to be a blessing in the end."

"Nice and far away from the crime scene. In fact, Gardai never found out about this rental car," Emma confirmed. "We didn't know what to look for either. Bus? Rail? Ferry? Rental car? And to look for whom? A needle in a haystack."

"She stood in front of the house for a long time. It looked so big and scary. Finally she rang the door bell. Charles stood in the doorway. Was very friendly at first and offered wine. The two sat across from each other in his office in these heavy leather chairs and drank red wine."

"But something went wrong."

Catherine looked up and for the first time Emma saw a light in her eyes that she didn't quite know how to read.

"She asked about her mother first," she continued. "Charles interrupted her and wanted to know exactly why she thought she was Violet's daughter. Hence she told him about her encounter with Margaret in the old people's home in Manchester, about the photos, the diaries.

'Is that all you have?' Charles asked back. He sounded incredulous.

She remained undeterred and asked again about her mother.

'She's been dead for 20 years,' came the reply. 'You are too late. And there is nothing to inherit.'

'To inherit? I'm not here for any inheritance, I came to meet my mother, to meet my family. To find out who I am and why I wasn't allowed to stay with you.'

'Oh, don't give me your lies', Charles replied, 'you didn't turn up after all these years to meet some old people. You want the land, you want Linborough. But you won't get the house.'

'This is a colossal misunderstanding!' She had started to stutter, to defend herself and then realised that all those justifications somehow sound like self-accusations.

But Charles wasn't done yet.

'You must have read that under Irish law illegitimate children can now claim their inheritance as if their parents had been married. Our country is getting more immoral and dishonourable every year. Even divorces are now allowed! Then people like you sniff an opportunity! But believe you me, I will fight this to the grave! Just because your mother couldn't keep her legs together doesn't mean a bastard can become the lady of Linborough House!'

She couldn't believe her ears.

'Couldn't keep your legs together? Bastard? What does that mean? Your friend and mentor, Phillip Anderson raped Violet! At Linborough, in the barn. And then sat down calmly for tea with your mother. With Maddie, my grandmother.'

'Don't call my mother your grandmother! It's all lies!' Charles thundered. 'If Philip had his hands on Violet, which I highly doubt – Philip was a man of honour – it was only because the little witch seduced him.'

'Charles, why are you still clinging to those lies? It's been 40 years now, my mother and Anderson are both dead. Why don't you believe your own flesh and blood? Margaret has always tried to tell you the truth …'

'I'm not lying! If anyone is untrue here, it's you lying women! First whore around and then shift the responsibility onto the men. And now you're here, you bitch, and want the money!'"

Catherine faltered. "He was so angry that I thought he was about to have a heart attack."

Emma sensed that they had reached the core of the story. But Catherine – or "she" – didn't want to divulge the truth that easily.

"And that's when she lost her cool?" Emma asked.

"No, it wasn't like that. Actually, she had only jumped up to run out of the house. But Charles had also stood up and was blocking her way. He said 'Come on, admit that you're just a little cheat. You met my sister Margaret at your job, read her old diaries and gathered from the photos that the family is not exactly impoverished. You quickly came up with some idea because you think that a curate like me, who has turned grey in the service of the church, becomes sentimental in old age. But you were sorely mistaken!'

She wouldn't believe what she was hearing and kept insisting that non of this was true.

`I could call the Garda now and charge you with fraud and extortion. But if you're a little nice to the old man, then I'll let you go...' The old face twisted into a sly grin. And then he roughly grabbed her breast and tried to pull her towards him." Catherine groaned at the memory.

"So she just resisted?" Emma asked.

"First she pushed him in the chest to make him let her go. She was already at the door to the hall to leave when he hissed:

'You disgusting little bitch, you're going to regret that!' Then he attacked her, wine bottle in hand, suddenly no longer lustful, just angry and aggressive.

'I'll show you! I'll show you!' he yelled and went at his niece with the bottle. There was a scramble, she managed to shake off the old man. But he still didn't have enough, pursued her and wanted to prevent her from leaving the house. This man had ruined her entire life and that of her mother, accusing her of lying, proposed incestuous sex, threatening and physically assaulting her. And now *she* was the bitch? Armstrong, Anderson, all those bastards lived the good life, and she walked through the world like an empty shell."

Emma held her breath. Just don't say anything, don't move. Don't do anything that might break the flow of the story.

"When the old man attacked for the second time, she grabbed the next best thing at hand to fight back, that happened to be a small transistor radio that was on a side table next to his armchair, she took its cable, threw it around the old man's neck and pulled it tight. He flailed his arms a little, dropping the bottle, his fingers grabbing air. They had turned white as a result, like veal sausages. In the end she pulled him back into his chair with the cable around his neck. It was over surprisingly quickly."

Emma was breathing very shallowly. She was relieved, he was finally dead. He really had it coming. But she shouldn't feel like that, she was a guard. Her job was to get the perpetrators. But who was the perpetrator here and who the victim? A good barrister would turn the story into self-defence and an acquittal anyway. Rightly so. Why should she be the one to put Catherine through the wringer again?

"I would have killed that stinking piece of shit too," Emma heard herself saying.

And then she felt a wave of pity roll over her, pity not for Catherine aka "she", or Charles, but for all of humanity. The stealing, murdering, raping, warring, avenging humanity that couldn't shed its skin and ended up being and remaining predatory. And people like Emma had to take the rap and bring order to the chaos.

Only that there was no order.

Catherine just stared at her.

"And then you wiped everything and searched the desk. At least I would have done that." Emma had long since given up the pretence of Catherine's alter ego. But Catherine herself clung to it adamantly.

"When the old man was dead, she first stood and listened in the hallway. Everything was silent. Apparently no one else was home in the enormous house," Catherine continued with her story.

"Charles' wife Jean was in Belfast that Thursday night," explained Emma, "at her sister's, shopping. Then you rocked up, confronted him with the lies he had lived with his entire life and that made him vicious."

"He was vicious before."

"Charles must have deliberately invited you on a night when he was home alone. After all, he wanted to keep the family secret – apparently even from his own wife."

"So she was lucky." Catherine smiled weakly. "For the first time in her life, to be honest. So she went into Charles's kitchen, took a cloth and carefully wiped everything down. All the door handles, the glasses, the socket."

Emma bit her lower lip, not telling Catherine about the half-fingerprint next to the socket she had missed.

"She picked up the wine bottle again – luckily he had corked it properly after pouring it, otherwise the mess would have been too annoying. Then she put on her winter gloves, it was still cold outside," Catherine continued, "opened the desk and looked for her letter to Charles. There was nothing else that would connect her with the Armstrongs. She put the letter in her pocket, along with the kitchen towel, the radio and the cable that went with it. Otherwise she left everything as it was. Out the door, in the rental car, back to Dublin. Leave the car in the airport car park as agreed with the rental company, and off by taxi. She stayed overnight in a cheap hotel, paid in cash. She skipped the return flight and instead took an early morning ferry across the Channel and continued on to London."

"To London? Why not towards Manchester? That's a huge detour."

"To cover her tracks. She didn't know exactly who had seen her and where."

"Nobody saw you. Nobody knows anything. But what did you do with the radio and the other things?"

"Broke them up into pieces and threw them into the sea off the ferry on the way back to England. Where it is deep."

The two women stared at each other.

"Why did you write the letters?" Emma finally wanted to know.

"Charles was a swine. The world should know that. My mother wasn't a whore. My mother and I were slaughtered by this family on the altar of Protestant honour. As simple as that."

"But why the letter to the Guards? Do you want to be punished?"

"No. I want to stay with Margaret. She's the only thing I have left. I sent the letter to the Irish police because they should realise who was the actual victim. Not Charles, but my mother."

"I understand that," said Emma. And after a pause: "Have you ever been violent before?"

"No. If I were violent, I would have blown up Eagle Lodge a long time ago. And I would be dead by now." A bitter laugh.

"And now?"

It was getting late. Catherine suddenly looked very old, much older than 40, as she sat there, her mouth smeared with blood, her right hand tied to her own stove.

Emma made up her mind.

"I'll go now, sleep in at my hotel and fly back to Ireland tomorrow morning as planned. I will tell the colleagues that Margaret is demented and could not help me. That's it."

Catherine looked incredulous.

"Why?"

"You said it. Charles was a swine."

With that, Emma took the keys to the handcuffs from her waistband, tossed them to Catherine, and left the house on Oswold Road.

CHAPTER 12

Dead End

The next day, after an uneventful early flight to Knock and a wet drive to Sligo, Emma stood a long time outside the Cathedral of St Mary the Virgin and St John the Baptist on St John Street, staring at the ancient stones. Unlike Catherine a few days before, Emma had easily found a parking space. The sky opened up, the sun was shining, shreds of cloud were reflected in the puddles. The old tombstones around the church looked downright picturesque. Emma's hands hurt, she had bruises around her wrists and a few lacerations but nothing that her pills couldn't fix.

She could easily pin Catherine down now, she had the motive and half a fingerprint Catherine didn't know about. Finding the Dublin car hire company that Catherine had used to go to Sligo would also be a walk in the park. Ditto for the ferry back. Security cameras were everywhere in England. If you knew what you were looking for, you could nail Catherine down every step of the way. Right down to the letter addressed to the guards. Once her colleagues had picked up a scent, they hunted down game, no problem.

And yet. St. Mary the Virgin and St. John the Baptist – the virgin and the baptist. In this church Anderson had been Bishop and Armstrong Archdeacon. Violet and Catherine's torturers. Two women tormented by the church. Not for the first time, the great anger at Ireland and its religious hypocrisy came upon Emma. Catherine must have felt exactly the same anguish. Her mother was oppressed and raped, she was terrorized and abused, and then the women were stigmatized as "bad" while the men happily went on with their lives.

Thine is the kingdom and the power and the glory... All in the name of religion. In the end, Charles, a representative of this church, in the end he demanded sex from his niece and threatened to report her as a blackmailer. When he then physically attacked her with a bottle in his hand, she finally started to fight back. And about time. The Virgin and the Baptist, if it wasn't so tragic, it would be laughable.

Emma got into her sky-blue Peugeot, drove to the station and parked in the car park behind the building. She took two pills, got out of the car and braced herself for the upcoming fight. Murray would not be thrilled with his officer.

And he wasn't. Emma stood in front of his desk in his office, he was leaning back in his chair, the glasses pushed back on his bald head.

"So you didn't achieve anything? Two days in Manchester and nothing, absolutely nothing came of it?" Murray sounded almost incredulous.

"I wouldn't say it like that. We made sure Charles' sister is safe and in good hands. Nothing bad will happen to her in Manchester."

"What, Woods, do I tell the super now? What do I say to our colleague from Dublin? What to the widow Armstrong? What to the press? Goodness gracious, this whole case is a nightmare!"

Emma said nothing.

"By the way, Kelly has now taken your ex into custody. He suspects he has something to do with the Armstrong case."

"That is bullshit and Kelly is an idiot!"

"Damn it, Emma! Eamonn Kelly wants to triumph over us culchie cops! Will you give him that satisfaction?"

"Kelly isn't going to get very far with his theory on the IRA's change of strategy in the Armstrong case; quite simply because it is nonsense. Then the case will remain open. It is not the first and not the last unexplained death in the books."

Murray's face turned red, he got up, leaned forward, put his hands on the table and started screaming, "What's with this attitude, Woods? An open case and my investigating officer just shrugs? Unbelievable!" Murray became formal, as he always did when he was really upset.

"Chief, it was you who first allowed Dublin to interfere in our investigation. You pushed the case up the ladder and now *you* accuse *me* of indifference?" Inside, Emma had remained completely calm.

"Detective Woods, you are off the case and assigned to desk duty until further notice."

"You took the case out of my hands a long time ago, boss," Emma replied. But Murray just yelled: "Out! Get out of my office! Now!"

Emma paused in the hallway and stared out the window at Pearse Road. Apparently school was over for today, children and young people in school uniforms were running through the town everywhere. Emma picked up the cell phone and pressed the speed dial for her son's mobile phone.

"Hi darling, I'm back."

"Hi Mum, how was it?"

"It's okay. I'll come home early today and I'll cook us something nice."

"Have you heard from Dad?"

"He's here at the station and is being questioned."

"Is that bad?" Stevie asked anxiously.

"If he didn't do anything, it doesn't matter. And at least he won't be up to any mischief around here." Emma laughed, realising how artificial that sounded. "So you can't see him today, but maybe in a few days." And after a pause: "He wants you to live exclusively with him in the future anyway."

"So you've heard it already," Stevie replied.

Emma said nothing.

Her son tried to comfort her: "You know Dad. Dogs that bark do not bite!"

If only you knew! Emma thought back to many a bruise she got from Paul's temper tantrums. Aloud she said:

"Oh you darling, what would I do without you!" She noticed that her voice was shaking with emotion.

"Mum, don't worry so much. I don't even want to go living with dad. If it wasn't for me, you'd just be working all the time, or sitting at Hargadons' pub, drinking too much wine with Laura." Like any sane teenager, he was embarrassed by open displays of parental emotions.

"Don't be cheeky or I'll change my mind!" Emma couldn't tell him how relieved she was due to the lump in her throat.

Then her son asked what they should about Paul now, so that he would calm down again soon. "Because of Maths and grades and stuff," her son added.

"How about we poison him?"

"Hehe, very funny. Police officer as a poisoner. Insanely original."

"Seriously, I have no idea how we're gonna get this sorted. It's best if you keep on going to him regularly in the afternoon, as soon as he is out. And do your homework carefully. It would also be advisable that you no longer produce Fs in Maths."

"And what about Sophie? Should I hide her from him?"

"Lies are rarely a good idea. Especially in a small town like Sligo. Your father knows everybody and their mother around here and he doesn't have to be a detective himself to quickly discover that you two hang out. But you don't have to keep waxing lyrically about your conquest either..."

"Okay." And suddenly he sounded like a little boy again: "When are you coming home?"

Everything was as per usual. Aidan was sitting in the tidy corner of their shared office, meditating over his half-dead palm tree, when Emma pushed open the door.

"That thing used to be in better shape," Emma said in greeting and nodded her head in direction of the plant in the flower pot.

"Hello, I missed you too!" said Aidan and his film star smile.

Emma dropped into her chair

"Have you cleaned up?" On her side, the dirty coffee cups and half-eaten sandwiches were gone. Emma smiled gratefully. Luckily there were men like Aidan too.

"Pure self-protection," Aidan grinned. "If the health and safety inspector shuts down shop here because our office poses a health risk, I'll lose my job. I cannot afford that."

If only you knew, Emma thought, I really think I've lost my job. And my mind. Oddly enough, she didn't find that thought particularly frightening. She would just do desk work, shuffle a few stacks of files back and forth, go home at five and take care of her son.

Aloud she said, "And how did you get on with Stevie?"

"I played chess with him last night. Not stupid, that boy, I wonder where he got it from. This morning he went to school. I think he's looking forward to his mother to give him a break, she's not nearly as intellectually challenging as his new chess partner."

"Intellectually? Challenging? My precious, you don't even know how to spell that," Emma grinned back.

"It's okay, you are welcome!"

"And Paul? Murray says Eamonn booked him this morning."

"Detention," Aidan replied. "To make him think whether he has something to tell us about his participation in the IRA. About a new strategy. You know."

"Paul will enjoy a few days of rest. But he won't say anything. You can forget that." Emma was sure. Paul was stubborn, she knew that from experience.

"Why are you saying that?" Aidan acted indignant. "I have nothing to do with it. I personally doubt that Paul can count to three. Let alone be a strategic thinker for the provos. That's a joke."

"How did you come to this realisation?"

"Paul let you go. The man must be an eejit."

To her chagrin, Emma found herself blushing with delight.

Meanwhile, Aidan stared at her hands on the table and then glanced at the potted plant: "'That thing used to be in better shape' – one could say the same about you."

Emma looked questioningly.

"Your wrists. What happened to you in Manchester? Has a beer carriage been driven over your paws?"

"Something along those lines. It's not that bad." Emma involuntarily pulled the sleeves of her blouse over the blue welts.

"Em, where are your handcuffs?" Like any old cop, Paul knew this kind of injury from experience.

"I must have left them somewhere."

Aidan got up and walked around the two desks and approached Emma. He stopped short of her and grabbed her handbag from the table. Why did everybody suddenly dig around in her handbag? All and sundry seemed to think they could just rummage through her stuff!

Meanwhile, Aidan had fished Em's bunch of keys out of the leather pouch. Dangling, he held it up: "Emma, where are the keys to your handcuffs?"

"Lost. That's what I'm saying."

"Stop kidding me. You lost the handcuffs and the keys? Are you serious?"

"Yep."

Aidan stood silently in front of her, just shaking his head.

"Well, if I were you, I would wear shirts with very long sleeves and cuffs for a while because no one will believe that story."

"Hmm."

Emma turned away to turn on her computer.

"What happened in Manchester?" Aidan asked, "apart from the wild sex games at the hotel where you lost your handcuffs."

Emma had to laugh out loud.

"Good idea! Next time I'm stuck in a cheap hotel in a seedy shithole of a town, I will let a total stranger tie me up and spank me silly. Brilliant idea. That will sure lift my spirits!"

"Seriously, did you dig out anything with regard to the Armstrong case?"

Emma swallowed hard. Then she looked Aidan in the eyes and said:

"No. Margaret is indeed totally demented. The trip to Manchester was a dead end."